The Veiled Captain.

THE VEILED CAPTAIN,

THE HERO OF EAGLE CRAIG.

CHAPTER I.

THE WORD OF WARNING—A CRUEL BAND—BLACKMAIL OR DEATH—A FALL OF TWO THOUSAND FEET.

"THE Red Robins are out!"

As the cry was heard, a dozen men, engaged in digging for gold in the soft sandy soil of Sweet Water Plain, laid down their tools and stared at the speaker, a young fellow about eighteen, tall and straight as a pine tree, and attired in the blue shirt and trousers of the digger.

"Who's seen 'em?" asked one of the men.

"I have," replied the young fellow, "half-an-hour ago, as they rode down from the mountain."

"Well! we'll have to pay blackmail as usual," said another of the men.

The young fellow's eyes flashed.

"Have you really British blood in your veins?" he asked, "enduring, as you do, the horrible tyranny of these scoundrels!"

"We are peaceful people, Harry Foster," said a man near him, "and we think that a handful of gold dust is not quite so valuable as our lives. Besides, there's no getting at the Red Robins. They are a cunning lot."

"If you showed fight," said Harry Foster, "they would not come near you. You know that, Farley."

"Of course not," Farley replied, "but they would single out somebody and make an example of him, and they would have him when he least expected it, some time in the day or night. We can't always be at war."

"We came here to dig for gold," said another.

Harry Foster impatiently shrugged his shoulders.

"Pay your tribute then," he said; "we have decided not to do so any more."

"For Heaven's sake don't be a fool!" cried Farley.

Harry Foster did not answer him, but, turning on his heel, strode quickly away.

B 👑 M

"There goes as good a bit of manly stuff as ever came out of the dear old country," said Farley, "but he will never go back to it. If he keeps his word, he will sign his death-warrant to-day."

"Poor fellow!" said the others.

The diggings on Sweet Water Plain were as yet carried on on a limited scale. At the outside there were not more than fifty men engaged in it. Some half-dozen were married and had children, the rest were single.

The field was a rich one, and it was being worked in secret, lest there should be a rush upon it; but the secrecy which ensured their being saved from a rush of diggers was against their personal safety.

They were working at the foot of a huge rugged mountain known as the "Great Cone," which, by some extraordinary convulsion of nature, had been cleft from the summit almost to the base.

At one end, nearest the diggers, the division was very narrow—in some places only a few feet wide, and the opening thus strangely made had never been penetrated or fathomed.

The west side of the mountain bore the name of the "Eagle's Craig," while the other part was called the "Robin's Rest."

The latter part obtained its title from a band of men who had located themselves there under the leadership of a gigantic ruffian named Larry Turrell.

They did not dig nor toil in any way, but levied black-mail on the almost helpless diggers at odd intervals.

Sometimes they came for gold, at other times for food or drink, and, as there were no law-officers of any description, they got what they wanted.

It was not that the gold-seekers individually lacked courage, but, as Farley said, they thought it more prudent to pay a percentage than to refuse and put their lives in peril.

This brief description of the men and place will serve for the present, and now we will follow Harry Foster, who, with a rifle poised in his hand, strode away to one of the huts nearest the Great Cone Mountain.

As he approached it, a fair-haired boy of fifteen came to the door, and hailed him with a wave of the hand. He answered with a similar salute.

They were brothers, but bore no resemblance to each other Harry was dark, tall, and strong, while Dick—generally called "Little Dick"—was slight and fair.

"Where's father?" asked Harry.

"Gone to get the mare home," the boy replied; "she's broke her rope and made for the mountain."

"I wish he had remained at home," said Harry, looking uneasily about him. "Those accursed Robins are out again, and he said he would make a stand against them."

"Then he will do it," said Dick, with an air of conviction.

"He can't do it alone," returned Harry, "but here he comes. He's got the mare."

"And there are the Robins riding towards him," cried Dick.

The boy pointed to eight or nine men on horseback galloping towards a solitary rider, Adam Foster, the father of the boys, who was coming leisurely along.

Apparently he did not see the advancing Red Robins until they were within a quarter of a mile of him. Then he reined up.

"Why did he do that?" asked Harry, impatiently. "Father, come here!"

Of course Adam Foster could not hear his son, for he was quite half a mile away, but Harry observed that he cast a quick glance towards the hut, then drew out a pair of revolvers and waited for the foe.

It was all pantomime to the boys, but they understood too well what followed.

The Red Robins drew up and parleyed for a few moments with Adam Foster. He answered them with defiant gestures.

"Rash! mad!" said Harry, although he had resolved, if he met the Red Robins away from home, to defy them himself.

Then followed a brief but terrible scene. The Red Robins unslung their rifles and brought them to the level. Adam Foster emptied two barrels and brought one man down, then urged his horse on and came galloping towards his home.

Half a dozen rifles belched forth their fire. Adam Foster reeled in the saddle, and fell heavily to the earth.

It was all over in a moment. Harry uttered a wild cry of rage, and little Dick put his hands before his eyes.

No help could be given to Adam Foster.

The Red Robins galloped up to the fallen man, and

deliberately poured half a dozen shots into him as he lay helpless on the ground.

Then with yells that reached the ears of the two brothers, they turned their horses' heads and galloped back up the path that led to their hiding-place on the mountain.

They were not the only witnesses of the scene. A score of diggers had beheld it from afar, and as the Red Robins vanished in the distance they came running forward.

"Go in, Dick," said Harry, "this is no scene for you. Wait for me; I shall not be long."

The boy, with his head bowed, groped his way into the hut and closed the door.

Farley was at the head of the coming men, and he ran so fast that he was almost out of breath when he overtook Harry, who was striding towards his fallen father.

"It was a wild thing to do," he said.

"He died like a MAN," replied Harry, between his teeth, "and I will die, too, rather than pay tribute-money to that gang."

"Heaven help you!" muttered Farley, "but you are a plucky lad."

It was all over with brave Adam Foster.

He died, as other brave men have died, in rebellion against tyranny. The proud spirit, that would not permit him to endure injustice and wrong, had fled from as noble a form as ever bore the name of man.

They gathered around him without a word, as his son Harry knelt by his side, and, raising his well-formed, massive head, with its rich masses of iron-grey hair, he kissed the quiet face.

They looked at the youth's stern face and tearless eyes wonderingly—a passionate outburst they would have understood, but this silent grief was beyond them.

Harry signed to the men to help him to carry his father home, and they raised him from the ground. Not a word broke in upon the tramp, tramp of their feet, as they steadily marched to the hut.

"Place him there," Harry said, pointing to a small patch of greensward.

They would have helped to dig his grave, but the youth would have no other hand but his perform the office.

As they were moving away, he suddenly addressed them:

"For you he died," Harry said. "Will you not now make a stand against those murderous villains?"

For a moment there was a silence; the men looked at each other in a shamefaced way. Then Farley spoke:

"We can but die," he said. "Tell us what to do."

"Not now," replied Harry, wearily. "Come to-morrow."

So they left him, and, alone, he dug the grave for his loved and honoured father. When it was deep enough, he raised him in his arms and laid him down. Then he went to the door and opened it.

"Dick," he said, "come and see the last of him."

The boy came out, his eyes red with weeping, and the moment he looked upon his dead father the tears burst forth afresh. Harry put his arm around his neck, and so for awhile they stood by the grave.

"To think that it should come to this," Harry said, softly. "He came here to win wealth to replace that which he had lost, and has found a grave. Woe to you, ruffians and murderers!" he cried with sudden passion, shaking his clenched hand towards the Red Robins' retreat. "If no other hand but mine is raised against you, the penalty for this day's work shall be paid."

Slowly he filled in the grave, softly patting the earth down, and finally, when the level was reached, laid the turf upon it. The superfluous soil he scattered around.

He went into the hut and was seen no more.

That night the Red Robins were once more upon the plain, not to gather in blackmail, but to exterminate the one family they had for some time believed to be dangerous.

They came on foot at midnight, broke into the hut, awaking Harry from a fevered sleep. Ere he had fully realized the nature of this intrusion his arms were bound to his side.

Little Dick was also a prisoner, and they were dragged out of their humble home and carried away to the mountain.

What bitter reproaches Harry heaped upon himself for not being more wary. But the quick second coming of the Red Robins was so unusual, that he was completely taken by surprise.

When they had been guilty of violence before, they had not showed for days and sometimes weeks afterwards.

Larry Turrell, their leader, used to say, "Give 'em time to digest what's been done. We shall have no trouble the next time we go down."

He was right. Digesting the deeds of the Red Robins led to the greater pliancy of the survivors.

Up, up, under the cold moonlight these men dragged their two prisoners with bound arms, toiling along until the light of the cold orb of night changed to the rays of dawn.

Then they came to a spot near the great rent that divided the mountain in two, and then they halted by a collection of wooden huts.

This was the lair of the Red Robins, and, as they approached it, a tall, burly, bearded man emerged from one of the huts.

It was Larry Turrell, the leader of the gang.

"What ho! my lads," he said. "So good luck has been yours!"

The captors of Harry and his brother were ten in number, a strong band to send against two, and one a mere boy.

Harry looked around him, scanning their faces closely.

Larry Turrell marked the look, and laughed loudly.

"You will know us again," he said.

"Yes," replied Harry, briefly.

"In the next world, but not in this," said Larry, and all his followers roared at the jest.

After this there was a silence.

The leader of the Red Robins stood with folded arms, meditating awhile. Then he raised his head and called out:

"Rigault!"

A swarthy wiry-looking man, a half-breed between an Italian and a Frenchman, advanced. The others kept close guard over the prisoners.

"We are running short of powder," said Larry. "It would be a pity to waste any on them. Bind their legs and bowl them over the precipice. They will find a halting place two thousand feet below."

The moment Harry Foster heard the cruel demon his heart sank within him—not for himself, but for his fair-haired brother.

He turned his eyes towards him, and saw a pride and resolution in his young face that he was not prepared for.

"Do not think of me, Harry," the boy said. "I can but die."

"Larry Turrell," cried Harry, "a word with you."

"A thousand if you wish it," replied the Red Robin leader, with mock courtesy.

"Spare HIM !" cried Harry, pointing to his brother, "and do what you will with me !"

"That is what we intend to do," said Turrell, politely. "You haven't been long at the diggings, and you've given us more bounce than the whole of the rest. You and your father came between us and our dues. I've heard about you as well as seen, and we went down to the diggings yesterday to put a stop to it. Now, my lads, finish the job, and we'll get to breakfast."

Harry made a violent effort to set his arms free, and succeeded in slacking the rope a little, but half a dozen men threw themselves upon him and dashed him to the ground.

Then a fierce and terrible struggle took place. Harry, with his legs only, fought for his life, but numbers prevailed, and they securely bound him so that he lay helpless.

"Carry them a little lower down," cried Larry Turrell; "there's a fine slope for a run there. Now, my lads, be smart !"

Some of the men held back.

The work was too dastardly—too horrible even for them—but there were three not only ready but eager to do the deed.

Let us here record their names, as they will figure prominently in our story. A detailed description of their appearances can be given by-and-by.

Dan Crashleigh, English born, but reared at the Cape; Rigault, the French half-breed ; and Espardo, a Spaniard.

These men, under the direction of Larry Turrell, dragged the helpless brothers to the top of a steep slope that terminated on the great rift in the mountain.

The other men, with white faces, followed slowly after, and stopped on higher ground.

"Ready ?" cried Larry.

"Ready," responded the other men.

"Away they go !"

Not a groan or cry, or word of appeal, came from the young victims. Those who looked upon their faces remembered them for long afterwards.

On the face of Harry there was the darkness of the bitterness that was in his heart; on the face of Little Dick shone the light of a martyr's resolution.

Away!

Down they went with a terrible rush, turning over and over carrying with them a number of loose stones, but no cry from either.

They reached the edge of the precipice, and bounded over. Not a sound from the brothers.

In the dread silence of a moment or so that followed more than one man heard the beating of his heart.

Then a thud was heard, the crash of branches, another thud, and all was still.

The four men mainly responsible for this cowardly crime put on an air of bravado as they ascended the slope. Larry Turrell's face had a smile upon it.

"To breakfast, lads," he said. "We shall have no trouble in collecting the Red Robin tribute to-morrow."

CHAPTER II.

SMUDGE AND HIS MASTER—THE VEILED CAPTAIN LEAVES A LETTER—LARRY TURRELL DOES NOT UNDERSTAND IT.

IT was a year later, and great changes had come to Sweet Water Plain.

The community of gold diggers were gone, scared away by the Red Robins, whose numbers had been augmented by ruffians drawn to the Great Cone Mountain as the needle to the pole.

In the society, and under the rule of, Larry Turrell they found their affinity.

Farley and the other diggers were not kept long in ignorance of the fate of the two brothers, and, as Larry Turrell declared, the tribute-money or blackmail was paid without demur.

But ere long the honest gold-seekers began to whisper together, and one fine morning the whole body disappeared.

They had gone in the night—men, women, and children—taking all that was portable with them.

Larry Turrell was at first taken aback by this movement, but he soon turned it to account.

Dividing his men into two parties, he set one to work gold-digging, while he, with the other, went further afield in search of plunder.

Sometimes he would be absent for a week or more, sometimes only for a day or two ; but, short or long as his journey might be, he always came back with plunder.

Then at night, around the fires lighted on the mountain, his men would lie about smoking, drinking, and telling stories of their evil work, rejoicing over such deeds as only fiends could dream of.

Larry Turrell lived like a monarch among them.

His strength, his daring, his ready resource in time of danger, and, above all, his resolution in punishing the men who dared to be refractory, secured him the post of leader through all.

He lived at home, in a hut high above all the rest, near the top of the Great Cone, with one attendant only, a man whom he called Smudge.

Whether it was his real name or not nobody knew, but he had been Smudge ever since he had been a member of the Red Robin band, which was as long as the band existed.

Smudge was the very antipodes of his master.

His coward heart, weak as water, kept him in perpetual terror. He obeyed Larry like a dog, while he loathed and feared him.

Incapable of committing an atrocious deed from sheer want of nerve, he had been a witness of many a crime done by the bolder and more brutal men about him.

He saw Harry and little Dick, bound and helpless, sent to their dreadful doom.

At night he was haunted by the memory of it. In his dreams he went through the scene again and again. His waking and sleeping hours were one dreadful string of fears and ghastly visions.

But, in time, each vision in turn faded, its place being taken by some new horror.

Even the memory of that memorable scene we have attempted to describe was growing dim, when, one morning, he came out of the hut to get a drink of water.

There was a spring a little lower down which, in winter or summer, never ran dry. So near the mountain top, this may be considered phenomenal, but like instances are not at all rare.

Smudge had been drinking overnight, and was thirsty. His rest had been one long nightmare, and his nerves were in a horrible "jumpy" condition.

As he left the hut, he looked upward, more from habit than anything else, and, to his amazement, saw a strange figure a few yards away.

It was that of a man, simply attired in an easy-fitting naval officer's uniform, a novel attire in those parts, but over and beyond this there was something still more amazing.

The face of the stranger was covered with a veil, made of a soft, shining, silken material.

Through it could be seen the gleam of a pair of bright eyes, and the outlines of a well-formed nose and mouth were faintly visible.

Altogether, there was something in this figure strangely impressive and disquieting, especially to the nerveless Smudge.

For a moment there was no movement on the part of either.

Then the stranger slowly raised his right hand, and beckoned for Smudge to come to him

As that wretched person afterwards declared, he "was drawn to the strange figure as if there had been a rope round his neck "

Terror, in this case, acted like a magnet.

Almost breathless, and entirely speechless, Smudge tottered up to within two or three feet of the stranger, and topped, with his glaring eyes fixed on the veiled face.

Now the two eyes gleamed like jewels shrouded in a semi-luminous mist Smudge could only look at them and tremble.

Not a word did the stranger say, but, taking out a sealed packet from his breast, he held it to Smudge, who took it, as if it had been red-hot, between his finger and thumb.

Then the veiled stranger pointed for him to return, and Smudge, swinging round on one leg, like a weathercock suddenly twisted with a puff of wind, tottered back.

On reaching the hut he laid hold of the doorpost, and, against his will, as it seemed to him, looked upward.

The veiled stranger was gone !

Whither had he taken himself? There was no adjacent

hiding-place, and, according to Smudge's view of the matter, he must have melted away, sunk into the mountain, or shot up into the clouds.

Smudge gets a bit of a shock.

"It was a *ghost*," he gasped.

But there was a very palpable missive left in his hands, an

envelope addressed to "Larry Turrell, Chief of the Red Robins."

"I don't think that I durst give it to him," muttered Smudge. "I wonder if it smells of sulphur?"

He put it gingerly to his nose, but there was no sulphurous aroma about it.

"It doesn't come from THERE," said Smudge, "and it isn't heavy."

"Hallo, there! you, Smudge!" roared Larry from an inner room of the hut.

"Here, sir," replied Smudge, dropping the letter on the floor in his fright.

"Bring me a nip of whisky, will you?"

"Coming, sir."

Smudge took down a bottle and a glass from a shelf near the rude hearth, and, picking up the missive, entered the ch m er of his lord and master.

It was rudely furnished like all the places on the mountain, but come attempts had been made to give it the appearance of c mfort.

The ground was nearly covered with the skins of various animals, and Larry Turrell's couch was a heap of rugs and blankets, making it a soft and luxurious resting-place.

The Red Robin chief was sitting up, with evidence of the past night's debauch in his bloodshot eyes and parched lips.

"Pour out, can't you?" he said fiercely. "Where have you been? I called for you twice before."

"I—I—have been to the spring," replied Smudge, "that is I haven't—I was going—I—I——"

He dropped the letter on the bed, and, backing a step, proceeded to pour out the whisky, putting some into the glass and as much on the floor.

"What's this?" demanded Larry.

"Left—fo-or—you—by—a gentle-ma-a-an," stammered Smudge.

"We are all gentlemen on the Great Cone," said the Red Robin chief, fiercely. "Who was it?"

"I—I—don't know."

"You don't know? Give me that whisky."

He snatched the glass from the hand of his trembling servitor, emptied it, and tossed the glass upon the floor.

Then he took up the envelope, tore it open, and extracted from it a small slip of paper.

On it these words were written in a large bold hand:

"The Red Robins have been tried and condemned."

That was all. The Red Robin chief stared at it, then at Smudge, and then at the letter again.

"Whose joke is this, you white-livered hound?" he demanded.

"It isn't a joke," replied Smudge. "I don't see how it could be, seeing he wore a veil."

"Wore a veil! What do you mean?" demanded **Larry Turrell**. "A veil! Who wears veils? Give me an axe or something to throw at you. I'll teach you to play pranks with me!"

"It isn't a prank," cried Smudge, falling upon his knees. "Give me time, and I'll tell you all about it. I'm always being shaken up, but I never had such a shaking up as I've had this morning."

Then, as well as his condition would permit, he told the story of his meeting with the veiled stranger, his master listening with a frowning, puzzled face.

"It isn't one of the lads," Smudge heard him mutter. "Who then is it?"

No satisfactory solution of the mystery was to be got then, so he had a second nip of whisky and dressed.

"Get breakfast, and go and bring up the boys here," he said. "I'll get at the bottom of this before sunset, or I'm not Larry Turrell. Smart, now! and woe to you if this is **any** joke in which you've got a hand."

Smudge protested, with tears in his eyes, that he had nothing to do with it.

"I haven't a joke in me," he said. "Do I look as if I had?"

"Confound you—no!" replied his master.

Smudge prepared breakfast, which consisted of coffee, smoked deer-meat, a little bread, and the inevitable whisky.

As soon as Larry Turrell had fairly started with it, Smudge set off down the mountain to summon the Red Robins into the presence of their chief.

It was a very unusual thing, especially as they had only the day before returned from a marauding expedition, and the curiosity of the Red Robins was aroused.

But Smudge did not satisfy it.

He felt it would be best for his tyrant master to explain the matter to them, and confined himself to calling them together.

Among the foremost to arrive at the hut of the chief were Dan Crashleigh, Rigault, and Espardo, who, with the confidence of trusted and favoured men, entered the hut. The rest remained outside.

The Red Robin chief was still busy with his breakfast. He gave them a careless nod, and pointed to the whisky bottle.

"Have a drink," he said, "and then read what is on that bit of paper."

He affected a nonchalant air, which was not in harmony with his feelings.

Fear he did not absolutely feel, but the story of the veiled stranger certainly puzzled and disturbed him.

They drank some whisky, read the paper, and looked at their leader amazed.

"Smudge hasn't told you anything?" he said.

"No," they replied.

"Then let him tell it now. Here, Smudge, where are you?"

This worthy appeared in the doorway, and, in obedience to the commands of his master, repeated his story.

It had a visibly disturbing effect on all but Larry Turrell, who still kept up his nonchalant air.

"Anybody else seen this joker?" he asked.

They all answered, "No."

"Then keep your eyes open, lads," said the Red Robin chief; "and if you sight him shoot him down first, and ask who he is afterwards."

CHAPTER III.

THE DAWN OF A REIGN OF TERROR.

WHATEVER indifference to the story of the veiled figure Larry Turrell showed in public, in private he brooded over it, wondering, as well he might, who it was, and what had brought him there to threaten the Red Robin band.

He tried to persuade himself that it was one of his own men playing a prank to frighten Smudge, who was the butt of them all, but it would not do. The dress alone negatived the theory.

THE VEILED CAPTAIN, WITH HIS RIFLE SLUNG TO HIS SIDE, DEFIED THE RED ROBINS AS HE DISAPPEARED.

The coming and departure of the stranger, unseen by all save Smudge, was also puzzling, and not a little alarming.

If he were in hiding upon the mountain he might be looked for again at any moment. He might come and play the assassin in the right time!

Again, the wording of the letter, "The Red Robins have been tried and condemned," was vague but significant.

Who had tried and who had condemned them, when there was virtually no law in the land?

"It's a confounded joke—it must be," Larry said, and tried to dismiss it from his mind.

But it haunted him, especially at night when he was alone, for Smudge, in his eyes, did not count.

In the arrogance of his nature, as leader of the band, he had chosen to live high up above his followers. They herded together below; his hut was isolated.

And there he must continue to live unless he chose to show the white feather, which would be fatal to his leadership.

If he changed his abode to one in the midst of his men, they would laugh at him, despise him, and his power would be gone.

No; he must remain where he was when at home, and keep a wary eye for the foe who had so strangely announced his coming.

When night came on, he barred the door with his own hand, and made Smudge brew him some whisky toddy.

"And make enough for yourself, my lad," he said. "We will have a merry hour together."

Smudge, nothing loth, made a jug of punch, and, with it, both in a measure drowned their fears.

But not wholly so.

There are thousands of men who will fight bravely enough in the heat of battle, but who would shrink cowed at the threat of an assassin.

To feel that someone is lurking about, bent on taking your life, will try the stoutest heart; and only the bravest of men can go about under such conditions without fear.

Larry Turrell was a ruffian, bold in his way, but, like all bullies, he had a soft spot in his heart.

In a time of terror any companion is welcome, and Smudge, who usually slept in an outer room, was commanded to bring a rug and lie like a dog at the foot of his master's couch. Larry Turrell lay down with a revolver on each side of him and prepared to sleep.

It was rather a rough night; the wind was high, and there was some rain. He could hear it pattering on the roof as he had heard it a hundred times before, and found nothing ominous in it.

Now it had the sound of an enemy's footsteps in his listening ears.

Smudge, living in a chronic state of fear, was no worse than usual, and soon fell asleep. It was a good two hours later when his master closed his eyes.

It was daylight when they both awakened by a knocking at the door.

Larry sprang up, and grasped both his pistols.

"Who's there?" he cried.

"It is I—Rigault," was the reply.

Larry rose up, and bade Smudge open the door. When this was done, the half-breed was seen standing in the doorway with a troubled face.

"We have been waiting for you to wake," he said; "half the morning is gone. The man with the veil has been busy in the night."

"What do you mean?" asked Larry, yawning, so as to show an indifference he did not feel.

"He nailed a notice on the long hut," said Rigault; "and here it is."

Rigault took a paper from his breast, and tossed it on the table, then looked round, as if in sudden fear of seeing an enemy behind him.

"Read it, Smudge," said Larry Turrell; "I can't be bothered with such trash."

Smudge, in a state of aspen-like shivering, opened the paper and read:

"Five of the band will be called upon to die. The Veiled Captain will come for them at a time of his own choosing."

"Is that all?" said Turrell, laughing. "On my soul! it is a most excellent jest."

"Come out here," said Rigault, fiercely, "and read another joke intended to amuse *you*."

Turrell went out, and Rigault pointed to a paper fastened to the wooden wall of the hut.

On it, written in a bold and clear hand, were these ominous words :

"In turn, all shall be taken from you, and you will be the last to die. Flight will be in vain. In no corner of the earth will you be safe from the avenging hand of the

"VEILED CAPTAIN."

"Can any man here write like that?" demanded Rigault; "and see here, below, a seal—a flaming sword. Who has such a thing among us?"

Larry Turrell did not immediately answer him.

Bending down, he saw that the strange, alarming notice was not written on paper but parchment, and had been executed with all the care exercised on an important legal document.

"I don't know what it means," he said, at last.

"It means this, that there are vigilants abroad," said Rigault.

"Vigilants!" cried Turrell. "Why, WE are vigilants. Pshaw! man, it is only some fool out here, larking a bit, trying the bogey game. I'll come down and have a talk with you after breakfast, or stay and have some with me, as I am the last to die. Ha-ha! you will be safe at present from the foe!"

Rigault gloomily assented, and, during the rough morning meal, Larry Turrell did most of the talking. Afterwards they went down to the village, as the collection of huts were called, Turrell taking his rifle with him.

Many of the men, whose duty it was to be in the gold diggings, had gone down, but the rest were standing about in groups, each with his rifle and otherwise armed.

The strange notice was under discussion, and, as the two men appeared, troubled eyes were turned upon them.

"My lads!" said Turrell, "what is the meaning of these long faces? Come! it is some daring fool trying to scare us, and a mighty big laugh he will have over it. See here— I have been favoured with a special notice.

He was drawing it from his breast when the clashing of a horse's hoofs were heard on the southern side of the Great Cone.

The huts had been erected near the great rent in the

mountain, just where it was narrowest. It was here where the tremendous rift came to a point, as it were, and a distance of about sixteen feet alone separated one part from another.

At this point, too, the road up the mountain wound behind a large rock, and by that way Larry Turrell and Rigault had just come.

From thence, too, came the sound of horses' hoofs.

The men looked at each other in blank amazement.

Their horses were kept in sheds on a small plateau a quarter of a mile lower down. Who, then, could it be who was riding from above?

They were not long left in doubt.

Round the rock, at an easy trot, came a fine horse, as near thoroughbred as anything ever seen in these parts—a splendid creature.

But the men did not look at the horse, as the rider claimed their sole attention.

It was the Veiled Captain.

He sat easily in his saddle, with a rifle slung at his back, and the silken veil clinging close to his face, giving the outline of his features, but no clue to their identity.

Apparently without heeding the men, he rode straight for the narrowest part of the great rift in the mountain, with the evident intention of risking the leap.

The amazement of the men overwhelmed them.

Larry Turrell was the first to recover.

"Confound it!" he cried, "will you let him go? Bring him down!"

Half-a-dozen rifles were brought to the level, and, as the gallant horse fearlessly bounded across the gulf, the triggers were pulled, and the Veiled Captain threw up an arm in derision.

All had missed.

Possibly the hurried way they aimed, and the state of their nerves, had a good deal to do with it; but the strange rider and his horse got across unharmed.

Nay, more. The moment they were over, the Veiled Captain drew rein, leaped from the saddle, and unslung his rifle.

The horse, trained to the work evidently, lay down, and his master knelt behind him.

With a quick aim he fired, and Larry Turrell felt the bullet whistle near him.

He, with the rest had suddenly shown a desire to get under cover, and was bolting into one of the huts when the Veiled Captain fired.

A burst of laughter followed the shot.

Then the horse leaped up, his rider sprang again into the saddle, and they vanished down the rough side of Eagle Craig.

Larry Turrell took off his hat, and looked at it.

The bullet had cut its way through the crown, within an inch of his head.

"Well, I'll be——no, I won't! What is it? Who is it?" he exclaimed.

The hut was half full of men, and none could answer him for the moment.

At last Rigault said:

"Whoever it is, he is not to be sneezed at or coughed down, and so I think one of us had better get ready for the end."

"He can't shoot!" said Turrell, rather feebly.

"Not shoot!" cried Rigault. "Are you mad? He could have settled you if he had liked. Do you forget you are to be the LAST?"

And Turrell turned away with a livid face. Was it a thing he was likely just then to forget?

CHAPTER IV.

LARRY TURRELL GOES ON AN EXPEDITION—THE RETURN
—BLACKMAIL—THE DOOMED FIVE.

THE half of the mountain known as Eagle Craig had never been explored by the Red Robins. It had been looked on as inaccessible.

On the side nearest the goldfield it rose up almost like a wall, and it was at that end where the ravine was very narrow, rough, and considered almost impassable.

On the other side of the mountain was a vast prairie, where the wild cattle roamed, scarce heeded by man.

It gave out no promise of gold, and adventurers had hitherto simply glanced at it, and turned to the rougher ground on the right or left.

But now the attention of Larry Turrell and his men was directed towards this quarter.

It was thought probable that the strange being who called

With a quick aim he fired.

himself the Veiled Captain had come from that direction, and a watch was set upon the summit.

But several days passed, and there were no signs of a foe.

Then the Red Robins began to take heart again.

After all, they might have been the victims of some jesting, daring adventurer, who was, perhaps, "covering" some great find away in the rocky district.

As yet, nobody had suffered, and, with the audacity of

people who see no possible danger, they began to laugh at the notices so strangely posted in their midst.

"It's a party that has struck a rich vein," said Turrell, one morning, "and wants to keep us at home. We will go out, boys, and find them. Then they shall pay a levy for their little joke."

The Red Robins assented, and the working party was sent below, and the usual watching body despatched to the summit.

Up to the present it had consisted of six men, but on that occasion, by the indisposition of one, it was reduced to five.

This happened after Turrell had departed with the portion of his gang called his "war party."

They rode down from the mountain and departed on their way, with provisions for the day—with jest and laughter on their lips.

The working party went to the diggings, and for two hours all went on as usual. Then their dream of security came to an end.

The deep thud of horses' hoofs was heard, and, looking up, they beheld a mounted body of men deploying so as to surround the diggings.

Each man was well armed, and had his rifle ready to use on the least sign of resistance.

The Red Robins numbered about thirty; the new arrivals about forty. One party was on foot, the other on horseback, and resistance was useless.

And at the head of the new comers was seen the source of their recent terror—the Veiled Captain.

He bestrode the beautiful horse which had so gallantly leaped across the terrible gap in the mountain, and when his band had formed a circuit round, he rode forward, attended by only three men.

"Hands up, every man," he said, with the voice of a silver trumpet. "The man who moves or resists, dies."

They felt that he would keep his word, and mute as mice they stood while he rode forward, and bade them give the results of their labours to his followers.

"It is tribute to the Veiled Captain," he said; "it is your turn to pay it now."

It had been a busy morning, for they were working the richest part of the field just then, and, as each man gave over what he had, his hands and legs were bound with his own scarfs or bits of rope which the invaders had brought with them.

In addition, they were blindfolded, and laid with their faces on the ground.

It was humiliating, but better than death, and they bore it as such men take *any* form of defeat rather than give up their worthless lives.

The terror inspired by that mysterious veiled leader passed all common fear. The murderous knaves, so bold in dealing with the weak and helpless, quailed before him.

Later in the afternoon Turrell and his men returned, to view with amazement the gold-diggers lying like logs upon the ground, silent and helpless.

Their bonds were loosened, they were put upon their feet, and then they told their story, or rather stories, for in only one point did their narratives tally.

And that was, the Veiled Captain had been the leader of a body of men who had swooped down upon them like eagles from the clouds, demanded tribute, and taken it away.

On the point of numbers they varied.

"There were a hundred at least!" cried one, while the others said, "More." A natural exaggeration intended to cover their want of courage in not defending themselves.

"But what were they like?" demanded Turrell, wildly.

On this head they could tell him little, except that they were men of bold bearing, roughly dressed, their leader excepted, and mostly young.

"But where did they come from?" cried Turrell.

No one could tell.

"Which way did they go?"

Again they had nothing to tell him.

Not a shot had been fired, not a man wounded. It was more than humiliating—it was exasperating.

"Look here, lads!" said Turrell, "we've got some rival Robins about here, and the captain's come this veiled move to scare us. Don't be scared. Let us meet them like men, and have it out. We've been masters here for a long time, and I for one am not going to give in."

Ordering them to fall in, he led the way up to the plateau.

where they kept their horses, and where he resolved to bivouac for the night.

"If you have seen so little," he said, "the watch on the top of the Cone must have seen more. Fetch 'em down!"

Rigault took half-a-dozen men as a relief watch and departed. The others gathered wood from the pine trees, and proceeded to light camp fires therewith, to cook their evening meal.

Smudge was commanded by his leader to follow Rigault, and bring down whisky, and a blanket or two from his hut.

Poor Smudge!

He was in a terrible knock-kneed condition. The terror inspired by what he heard made him as limp as a herring, and he crawled away like a coward going to execution.

Ere he had gone far he met a man crawling towards him, and was turning to fly, when he recognised him as one of the gang, named Stevens.

This was the sixth member of the watch who had been left behind through indisposition.

"Hallo!" exclaimed Smudge, "where's the rest?"

"Up there," replied Stevens, "and likely to stop there unless they are helped down."

"What do you mean?" asked Smudge, with a curious dropping action, the outcome of a little extra weakness in his ever-failing knees.

"As I lay huddled up with pain," said Stevens,—"for I've had a touch of colic to-day,—I saw twelve men go by. They were led by the Veiled Captain."

"Oh, Lor'!" exclaimed Smudge, sitting down plump, "don't, please!"

"It's true," said Stevens. "They looked at me through the open door, and one of them spoke to their leader. 'Not a sick man,' I heard him say; 'but his turn will come.' Then they passed on"

With trembling hands Smudge drew out a handkerchief and wiped his forehead, wet with the dew of fear.

"After that," proceeded Stevens, "they went away, as *silently as ghosts*. Their footsteps made no sound, and I felt—I can't tell you how. Anyway it cured my colic, and I got up to shut the door."

"But I didn't do it at once," Stevens went on, after a

pause. "I'd got a sort of fascination on me, and I just peeped out, and tried to see what had become of them; but they were gone, so I stole back and lay quite still for an hour—it might be more."

"Or less," said Smudge. "You can't have reckoned time, I couldn't."

"Well," said Stevens, "some time passed, and, thinking I could go out and make a move for the plain, I opened the door. Just then I heard—faintly of course—cries right up at the top of the Cone."

Smudge wriggled like a worm on the hook, and gasped like the fish just landed with the aid of the worm.

"I couldn't see anything," said Stevens, "for there's so many jutting rocks in the way, but I plainly heard the cry, 'Mercy! mercy!' I went back in a hurry, shut myself in, and came out no more until I saw, through a crack in the door, Rigault and the others coming up."

"Have you told Rigault?" asked Smudge.

"No; he's not a pleasant chap to talk to," replied Stevens, "and I thought, if there was anything wrong, he had better go and find it out for himself."

"It's a horrible thing," said Smudge; "and worse because we don't know what it is. Stevens, you are a good sort of fellow!"

"Thank you for nothing! What do you want?"

"I am going up for some rugs and the captain's whisky. Come with me. We are going to camp on the plateau to-night."

Stevens, after a little hesitation, to be expected under the circumstances, consented, and they went up together.

The rugs and whisky were obtained, a nip of the latter being taken by each out of the bottle, and they were about to descend again when Rigault and his men came hurrying down.

Their faces were white under the tan, and they looked like men who had had more than an ordinary scare.

"What's the matter?" asked Stevens.

"Get out of the way!" cried Rigault.

No other answer was vouchsafed him, and the men, following Rigault with hasty steps, hurried down the mountain side.

"What now!" cried Stevens, staring at Smudge in dismay.

His nerveless companion could only open his mouth, and point downwards.

The action was expressive, and, with terror as a stimulant, they followed in the wake of those who had just passed by.

Like drunken men they blundered over many an obstacle without falling, and without injury to themselves or the rugs or whisky arrived at the plateau.

There they found Rigault, and those who had accompanied him, standing breathless in the midst of the men, all eager to hear the cause of their rapid return.

Larry Turrell, with his rifle in his hand, the stock resting on the ground, stood a little apart, with an assumption of bravado that was belied by his quivering lip and roving eye.

Instinctively he had guessed what Rigault had to tell.

At length the story came—brief, but terrible.

" All dead—shot through the heart," said Rigault.

" All ?" echoed Turrell.

" The whole five."

" There were six."

" No," said Stevens, advancing , " I was to have gone, but——"

Turrell brought his rifle to the present, and was about to fire, when Stevens fell on his knees.

" I know nothing of it," he said. " I was taken ill, and they left me behind at the last moment."

" And suppose he was there—what then ?" said Espardo, the Spaniard. " Was not five the number written ? "

" A curse upon you all ! " said Turrell, in a sudden transport of fury. " Somebody here is playing a double game. Who is it ? Stand out !"

" You talk like a fool," said Crashleigh. " What sense would there be in shooting each other ? "

" I can stand a foe who comes out and meets me face to face," said Turrell ; " but this veiled man, or devil, who comes and goes like a will-o'-the-wisp, drives me mad ! "

" And makes a coward of you," added Crashleigh, coolly.

Turrell turned angrily upon him, but the other met his gaze unflinchingly.

" We are no foes, at least," said Turrell, softening down ; " and if I have one here, let him go. He shall depart without a hair of his head being touched. I swear it !"

No man stirred.

"So far so well," said Turrell, drawing a deep breath. "If we keep together and be vigilant we may yet catch our secret foe napping. He is not far away. The Eagle Craig seems to be his home. Rather than be cut off in twos and threes we will seek him there——"

"Brave talk," interposed Rigault; "but how will you get there? It has the reputation of being inaccessible."

"It cannot be," said Turrell. "It is there he hides, and some-how he comes and goes. Boys, we are most of us old trappers, and know how to use our eyes. Let us wait a bit and watch."

"Easily said," muttered Crashleigh; "but no man is safe here. Let us clear out."

"And go where?" asked Rigault. "How many men are there here without a price upon their heads?"

There was an uneasy movement among the men, but none stood forward to declare themselves free.

"No," continued Rigault; "it won't do. To go back from whence we came would put us out of the range of the Veiled Captain at the cost of our lives. To go further ahead would be to die like dogs in a desert. We must remain here, and, as Larry Turrell says, try to get the upper hand of this veiled man, or fiend."

The men listened in silence.

There was no cheering, no enthusiastic assent to his declaration. They all felt like men under the extreme sentence of the law.

The fires were made up, and they gathered round them, gloomily whispering together, while Larry and his chief lieutenants, Crashleigh, Rigault, and Espardo sat apart engaged in earnest conversation.

Only one theme was under discussion.

The Veiled Captain.

Who was he? What was he?

Would he be able to carry out his threats; and were they indeed all doomed men?

Whose face was it behind the Veil?

It was dealing with the UNKNOWN that put new terrors into the startling episode!

"Who is this man that can come and go at will, as it

seems to me?" Larry Turrell asked himself—many times that day.

Then a superstitious fear began to work upon him! "Might it not be something more than mortal, which had come to destroy the band?"

Rigault, Crashleigh, Espardo, all daring ruffians, began now to feel the terror they had long inspired on others.

It could not have been raised by an ordinary foe.

But the Avenger coming as he did inspired them with a secret dread, none the less hard to bear because they dare not speak of it to each other.

Henceforth there was to be no dividing among them; all were to work in the fields at one time, and at another to go in a body on the marauding expeditions so essential to them.

Three days passed, and the veiled foe was neither seen nor heard of. The watchful eyes and ears showed no trace of him or his followers.

Twenty miles away there was a halting-stage for those who were penetrating into the interior of the country northward. There, as Larry Turrell knew, a spirit store had been set up by one of those enterprising men who will go anywhere and live anyhow, so long as they can make money.

"We must have action," said Turrell to Crashleigh; "this skulking and moving about will make cowards of us all."

"It seems to be touching some of 'em up a bit," Crashleigh replied. "It is no use blinking facts, Turrell, the hearts of the men are softening.'

The band left an hour afterwards, riding across the goldfield with their eyes roaming furtively about in search of their dreaded foe.

But there were no signs of the Veiled Captain.

The morning was fine and the air still. Not a sound, save their own voices and the tread of their horses' hoofs, fell upon the ears of the Red Robins.

In silence they rode, until five miles lay between them and the Great Cone.

Then they began to gather heart again, and talked a little. Another five miles covered, and they were themselves again.

Rude laughter and coarse jest echoed in the place. Suddenly the voice of Turrell was heard.

"There are emigrants ahead of us," he cried, pointing to a line of moving figures in the horizon.

With a yell of delight they put spurs to their horses, and dashed forward, the moving figures advancing towards them.

In a little time Larry Turrell saw that he had made a mistake. The strangers were no emigrants, but a body of horsemen.

"Halt!" he cried, and they all reined up. "Steady, lads. I don't like the look of that lot. Who is it in front with a white face? Wheel sharp there. It is the veiled fiend. Ride for your lives.

CHAPTER V.

THE FLIGHT OF COWARDS—THE VEILED CAPTAIN'S RETREAT —ESPARDO IS NAMED.

THE Red Robins in their sudden flight were like wild animals under the influence or the terror that leads to a stampede. They lost all reason and sense, and madly rode away with the thunder of pursuing hoofs in their ears.

But it was all imagination.

The Veiled Captain was not pursuing them.

He rode after them for a few hundred yards, and then reined up. His men followed his example, and shouted with laughter.

"See!" he cried, "what curs they are. They are hardly worth calling foes. What say you, Hal?"

He addressed a young fellow who had reined up close behind him, a fine specimen of manhood, well built, lithe and strong, with the light of laughter in his eyes.

"It makes me blush," he replied, "to think that any of us ever stood in fear of them. But it was the women and children that made us cowards."

"And you were not organised," said the Veiled Captain, quietly, "while they were. That made all the difference."

"I wanted to have a slash at them to-day," said Hal, loosening his belt, "but if you say no—there's an end of it."

"What I have designed," said the Veiled Captain, "I will

carry out to the letter. Piecemeal, I will break up the band, leaving Turrell till the last."

"Your word is law," said Hal, doffing his hat.

"Now, my men," cried the Veiled Captain, "home."

The men answered with a shout, and, touching their gallant horses with the spur, they rode on at a smart pace, not deigning even to look towards the Red Robins still flying in the distance.

Behind each man, strapped to the saddle, was a package, or a small cask, and the band had evidently been out for provisions, obtained honestly enough, as we shall soon see.

They rode straight back to the rift in the Great Cone, and, dismounting, led their horses over the rough ground.

It will be remembered that on this side of the mountain the huge rent was at its narrowest, and so uninviting was its approach that it had never been explored by the Red Robins, but the horses of the Veiled Captain's band, though they slipped here and there as they traversed the ascending ground, reached the ravine in safety.

They entered one by one through the narrow way, and here, for a time, the path they trod was gloomy.

On either side rose the tremendous cliffs almost as straight as a wall, but with jutting rocks and trees here and there, which seemed to deepen the twilight of the place.

The Veiled Captain led the way.

Once within the ravine, he remounted his horse, and rode on at a walking pace. Close beside him was his lieutenant, whom he called Hal.

The ground was still rough, and few horsemen would have cared to ride over it, but both men and horses of the band appeared to be used to it.

One by one the men mounted and rode behind their leader, no man speaking; the only sound being the occasional rattle of arms, and the pattering of the horses' hoofs.

As the ravine widened its beauty became apparent, for presently the earth was covered with a thick moss that deadened the sound of hoofs, and the rocks on either side were clothed with trees and shrubs.

Here and there the mountain-sides leaned inward until they formed almost a complete arch overhead, and, in sheltered corners inaccessible to man the eagles, from which that side of the mountain took its name, lived and reared their young.

On rode the Veiled Captain until he came to one of these shadowed places, with rugged rocks hanging overhead.

At this spot the moss was so thick and close that it was as soft and springy as half-a-dozen Brussels carpets piled one above another.

No view of the spot could be obtained from above. It was as secluded as if it were in the bowels of the earth.

The Veiled Captain leaped down, and Hal took his horse's rein.

As the other men came up they dismounted, and loosened the packages they had carried behind, piling them in a heap upon the ground.

It was quickly done, and the saddles and bridles were then removed.

On the left, in the side of the mountain, was what looked like an ordinary crack in a rock, wide enough to allow a man to easily penetrate it.

One of the men passed in, and, after a short delay, returned with an armful of tethering ropes, such as are used to secure grazing cattle.

These were for the horses, and, being put on, half the men led the animals away two by two; the other half of the band remained behind.

Not a word was uttered.

Perfect discipline prevailed.

When the horses were gone, the Veiled Captain passed through the rift in the rocks, followed by one of the men, who struck a match and lighted a candle he took from a niche.

With this he passed on, lighting as he went, until at least a score of candles were burning in one of the most charming grottoes ever seen by man.

It was one mass of glistening crystal, sparkling as if the fantastically-shaped wall were a mass of diamonds.

Huge crystals hung like chandeliers from the roof, fantastic masses jutted from the sides, the very floor was covered with sparkling atoms, making the place to the eye something like a dream of fairyland.

But the realities of life were there also.

THE VEILED CAPTAIN.

Arms, food, rugs, cooking utensils, and other appurtenances of semi-civilisation, were stored away in various recesses formed by Nature's hand, and at the far end was a raised platform, also Nature's work, on which there was a curious resemblance to a crystal throne not fashioned by the hand of man.

Such, in brief, was the Veiled Captain's haunt.

Walking with a measured step to the platform, he lay down, resting on his elbow, watching his men at work storing away the necessaries they had brought back with them.

When it was done, they retired and left him alone.

Then he rose up and slowly paced to and fro with his hands clasped behind him.

Suddenly he raised his right hand and uttered a short sharp cry—a cry of triumph mingled with pain.

"Already the dead are half-avenged. I triumph. Their coward hearts are hollow. In this lawless land *I* am the law. I hold the sword that hangs suspended over them. It is I who shall decree the hour of its falling."

Then, in a moment, his mood changed. His head was bowed down, and he clasped his hands tightly over his heart.

"The memory of my loved ones," he moaned—"it is almost too hard to bear. Blood-stained ruffians"—he was roused again, and his voice echoed through the crystal cave —"cunning and cruel, why do I spare you for an hour?"

The entrance of his lieutenant checked his outburst of passion, and in a moment he was cool again. Hal looked quickly at his leader, and seemed to have the power of reading the emotions behind the veil.

"Recalling the past?" he said. "Why do you give way to these paroxysms? Strong as you are, they may one day weaken—perhaps destroy you."

"Hal," said the Veiled Captain, softly, "it is over. But they will come at times in spite of me. Like a cyclone, they sweep through my whole nature; but do not fear. They will not kill me—I am sturdy and strong. Feel my pulse."

Hal laid his hand on the wrist extended towards him, and held it there for awhile.

"Yes," he said "there is no fear here, but I know that it will not always be so."

"I will go on to the end," replied the Veiled Captain "and when my work is done, what matters what comes to me?"

"I will not try to reason with you on that head," said Hal; "by-and-by I hope to see you happier. Is there not something to be done to-day?"

"Yes," returned the Veiled Captain, "and for me to do. For the rest, let the day be an idle one."

"Idle, and with the mine to work!" said Hal. "No, I think not."

"I will come with you and see how it goes on," said the Veiled Captain.

They left the grotto, and, outside, the men had gathered together with picks and spades, silent as before.

This was another proof of the perfect discipline.

Ordinary conversation could have been heard on the mountain above, in the retreat of the Red Robins.

The Veiled Captain looked at them, and, through the veil, his eyes flashed proudly.

With the motion of his hand he bade them follow him, and led the way some two or three hundred yards up the ravine.

There the aspect of the place was changed.

The moss was gone, and in its place was a spread of smooth light-yellow sand, into which a small cascade from above trickled and disappeared.

On one side there was a long narrow trench, dug as systematically as a garden is worked, and close to the cascade stood a digger's rocker used to wash the earth by the seekers of gold.

Under that flooring of sand lay one of the richest veins of gold ever discovered and worked by man.

A number of the men stepped into the trench and began to dig the soft soil, casting it into wicker baskets, which others took up and carried to the rocker.

Of course there were some slight sounds made, but the operations on the whole were carried on in strange silence.

Questions were asked and answered in dumb show. There was nothing to betray the secret of their labour to anyone upon either side of the mountain.

After watching them for awhile the Veiled Captain walked slowly away and disappeared. Still the men worked on in silence.

For two hours the spade and the rocker were never still. Gold in amazing quantities was found in dust and nuggets in various sizes. Then, at a signal from Hal, the labour ceased.

The gold was put into a linen bag, and deposited in the grotto. Then in a body the men made their way up the ravine.

Not a word was said until they had reached the plain on the other side, and here, under the shelter of the cliff, well out of the sight of Larry Turrell or anyone on the summit of the mountain, they came to a regular camp.

There were huts built close to the rocks, and at some of the doors women and children were waiting for the coming of the men.

Joyous but subdued greetings were exchanged between the married men and their dear ones.

A wonderfully pretty girl came forward and threw her arms about Hal's neck.

"Safe again," she said.

"All right," he replied, "don't be anxious, Lucia. No harm will come to the Captain."

The girl blushed a rosy red and turned her face away.

"I did not speak of him," she said softly.

"No, sis," said Hal, patting her cheek, "but he was in your thoughts."

"I wish he would not stop in the ravine alone," said Lucia.

"He will do so," said Hal. "He will keep his vow, to eat and drink with no man until the Red Robins are exterminated."

"Let them be exterminated, then, at once," said Lucia, stamping her foot.

"In HIS time, not ours," said Hal; "but come, I am hungry, let us go in and see what good things you have ready for me."

Lucia put her hand through his arm, and together they disappeared within one of the huts.

Leaving the band to the enjoyment of rest and good fare, we will turn for awhile to the Red Robins again.

Late in the afternoon they came riding home with their

heads drooping.   Shame and humiliation covered them like a garment.

First of all, their wild flight had been checked by Larry Turrell, when he found they were not pursued, and, like all men who feel they have made themselves ridiculous, they felt it very bitterly.

Then, when they turned and rode to the spirit-store, they found their coming was expected.

The place was closed, and the sight of several rifle muzzles peeping through openings in the wooden walls led them to think that discretion was the better part of valour.

Without their whiskey, they returned, angry with them-selves.   No whipped cur ever went home more shamefaced than these once blustering ruffians—one and all.

Scarcely exchanging a word, they rode up to the plateau where they kept their horses, and dismounted.

Barely had they done so when a cry from Smudge turned all eyes in his direction.

He was standing by the door of the nearest hut, pointing to a strip of parchment nailed to it.

In a body they hurried forward, and read, in the dreaded and now familiar hand, these words:

"Espardo the Spaniard's hour is at hand."

CHAPTER VI.

THE ATTEMPTED FLIGHT—ACROSS THE GREAT CONE AT NIGHT—ESPARDO'S HOUR—THE VEILED CAPTAIN.

THERE was no signature, nor was there need of one; for who but the Veiled Captain, or a messenger from him, could have placed it there?

Espardo read it with the rest, and his swarthy skin blanched to a leaden hue.

In all the band there was no ruffian more cruel. In his ears the cry for mercy had many times been shrieked in vain. Those long sinewy hands of his were trebly dyed with blood.

Acting upon some strange impulse, the other men fell away from him, until he stood alone like some pariah and outcast. His dark eyes flashed angrily.

"Is this what you call a brotherhood?" he asked. "Have we not sworn to stand by each other through all?"

" Why, that's true enough," said Larry Turrell. "Come lads! Espardo is not to be thrown to the veiled man or devil, like a bone to a dog. He shall not be taken from us without a struggle."

The men feebly cheered this sentiment, and once more gathered about Espardo, vowing, in troubled tones, that they would stand by him.

Even Smudge had a word to say.

"D-o-o-on't fear!" he said, "we will pro-o-o-tect you," a promise that gave rise to a roar of laughter.

It had the usual effect.

The gloom was temporarily dispersed, and Larry Turrell harangued the men in the old style.

What was there to fear? Why should they shrink from a man simply because he did not show his face. If THEY kept a good look-out perhaps HE would be caught napping.

Once more their courage rose high, and they talked of settling the question of supremacy the next time they came across the Veiled Captain and his men.

The only man who did not rally in the least was Espardo.

He FELT he was doomed and that no man could save him.

After the fires were lighted and the usual cooking in progress, he squatted on the ground, clasping his knees with his hands, and his eyes fixed upon the horizon.

Who was this dreaded foe?

He called back to memory the forms and faces of many men he had wronged, but none would answer to that of the Veiled Captain.

" Can the grave give up it's dead?" he asked himself with a shudder.

Turrell, Crashleigh and Rigault came up to him in a body, and tried to rally him from his gloom.

He was one of them, a leader and a brother in many a daring outrage, a willing assistant in many a ghastly crime.

" Cheer up, lad," said Turrell, " he hasn't got you yet!"

" But he will get at me some time if I remain here," replied Espardo. "I must fly!"

" Where to?" asked Crashleigh.

"I care not," replied Espardo, "so that I get away from here. I will go on foot. On the other side of the mountain there's a wide land. If once I got there I could throw him off the scent."

"It's a good idea," said Turrell, softly, "and hark ye. Why should we not all go?"

"All the men," said Rigault?

"No, no, by ourselves. The whole band could not move without attracting attention. Let us talk it over by-and-by. For the present mum!"

The night came, the fires were put out, and the men crowded into the limited accommodation of the few huts. The fact of the four leaders keeping together excited no suspicion.

"They mean to stick to Espardo," the men said.

Smudge was told by his master that his services would be dispensed with, and he of all the band suspected that something was in the wind.

Fools often exhibit a shrewdness that astonishes wiser men. He lay close in one of the low sheds where the horses were stabled until it was dark, and then crept out to the hut where Larry Turrell and his lieutenants were.

Lying down close to the door, Smudge could hear them talking in an undertone, and with a great effort distinguished a few scattered words:

"The—other side—get away—the men—who will suspect—at the most—die!"

"They are going away," thought Smudge in a terror.

Without a leader the band indeed was doomed.

"I'll follow 'em," thought Smudge, "until it's safe to show myself. They are sure to want somebody to cook and wait upon 'em. They won't kill me."

He drew back and lay in a hollow behind a clump of rock to wait and watch.

It was a clear night, although there was no moon.

Overhead, the sky was thickly studded with stars that shed a soft light upon the earth. No wind was stirring, and the men had gone to rest, or were wrapped in thought.

Save for an occasional restless movement of one of the horses, absolute silence reigned.

Doggedly Smudge waited, and when about two hours had

elapsed the door of the hut was softly opened, and Larry Turrell appeared.

His footsteps made no sound.

Then, one by one, the other three appeared, and no sound accompanied their movements. With some soft material they had muffled their boots.

They turned upwards, going away as silently as shadows. Smudge guessed the direction in which they were going.

He could follow them easily, as there was only one clear track to the summit of the mountain, and an easy one.

On the other side, as he knew, the way was rugged and perilous, and not to be travelled in so weak a light.

At two in the morning the moon arose, and with her aid they could pursue their way.

Taking a hint from his leader, Smudge tore his handkerchief in two and muffled his boots. Then he went upon their trail.

Nothing occurred to check the progress of Larry and his friends, or their lone follower. Larry's old home was reached, and then a halt took place.

The four men entered the hut, where Larry routed out some whiskey in half-empty bottles, which they drank, and, after a while, resumed their journey.

The summit of the Great Cone was reached, and Smudge, half dead with fear and cold, heard Larry Turrell say:

"We must wait here for the moon, unless we want our necks broken."

It was a weary hour that followed, broken only by the whispers of the men. Then, at last, the moon peeped up above the horizon, and gave her waning rays to the fugitives.

The descent was slow and arduous.

They had to seek a path, for of this side of the Great Cone they knew very little. More than once they had to turn back and choose a new route, to the great terror and peril of Smudge.

But he escaped detection, and when the dawn came the descent was nearly accomplished.

The level plain lay about two hundred feet below.

Far as the eye could reach, no living thing was in sight. Dotted about the plain there were clumps of bushes, and here and there a huge boulder stood up in the earth like some huge thunderbolt hurled from the sky.

"We have yet some hours before we are missed," said Turrell. "If we push on we shall, in two hours, be out of reach of danger."

They started again, and speedily reached the plain. Smudge felt that he could not as yet follow them in safety, so remained in hiding upon the hill behind, but with his eyes fixed on those he had followed through the night.

They strode on hurriedly, like men who see a goal that must be quickly reached, walking with their rifles at the trail.

Each man seemed to think of himself alone, and Espardo soon began to lag a little.

Once Larry Turrell looked back, and impatiently beckoned him on. He answered with a spurt, but soon lagged again.

In this way half-a-mile was traversed, and then another figure appeared upon the plain.

It was that of the Veiled Captain.

Rifle in hand, he appeared suddenly from behind a spur of the mountain, and strode with the swiftness of an avenging spirit over the ground.

To the terrified Smudge he seemed to glide, to fly along.

The fugitives did not see or hear him, and he rapidly overhauled the lagging Espardo. Ere another half-mile was completed, he was upon him.

At the last moment the doomed Spaniard heard him.

He faced about, saw the veiled figure, and uttered a cry that a few moments later reached the ears of Smudge.

But, ere the terror-stricken watcher heard it, the Spaniard was cast to the ground, and the foot of the Veiled Captain placed upon him.

The cry of Espardo had caused the other three fugitives to turn, and then they saw the Spaniard under the feet of their dreaded foe.

He held his rifle lightly poised, ready to shoot.

"Back to your den, you curs," rang out that clarion voice.

And then he covered them with his rifle, fired, and sent a bullet whistling between the heads of Turrell and Crashleigh.

"He's at our mercy," cried Turrell: "come on!"

"Steady!" shouted Rigault; "look yonder!"

He pointed towards the Eagle's Craig, and his amazed companions saw a number of horsemen deploying into the plain with the evident object of working round and preventing their flight.

"Curses," cried Turrell, "let us get back. We can't save Espardo!"

The instinct of self-preservation is always strong, and never stronger than in such men. They made a little detour, and fled back to the Great Cone.

Then the Veiled Captain uncoiled a short strong rope from his waist, and bound the half-stunned Espardo.

"Rise," he said, and come with me.

"Who are you?" cried Espardo. "Are you man or fiend?"

"You will know who I am before you die!" was the answer. "Come. There is yet one more chance for your wretched life. We are not assassins."

Espardo rose up, and, with tottering steps, walked along side his captor, the horsemen swiftly closing in and forming a cordon through which, if the Spaniard had attempted it, there was no escape.

To Smudge it was like some wonderful dream.

He saw Espardo led away to his doom, with his hand upon his heart, the image of despair, and when he and his escort had disappeared behind the spur of the mountain, he turned his wild eyes in the direction of his master and two remaining friends.

They had reached the mountain, and were returning by the way they left it, presenting the appearance of men who hasten away from some great convulsion of nature.

On they came, and Smudge did not stir until they were near him. Then he rose up, and, spreading out his hands, cried:

"Master, it's no use. There's no escape. We are all doomed men."

CHAPTER VII.

THE TRIAL AND SENTENCE ON ESPARDO—THE CAPTAIN ON THE CRAIG.

EVENING was at hand, and twilight rested on the ravine— a soft, soul-moving light, such as poets love, though it makes them sad. The sun had sunk over the Great Cone, and night would soon be there. By the grotto, the Veiled Captain and his men had assembled with a prisoner in their midst.

It was Espardo, the remorseless, cruel Spaniard, who had shown no mercy to others, and now had none himself to hope from man.

The Veiled Captain sat upon a rough camp-stool. Facing him was Espardo, under the care of two armed men, of whom Hal was one. The rest formed a semicircle around.

"Espardo," said the Veiled Captain, "you have had a day to reflect upon the past, and now the hour of your punishment is at hand. Have you anything to say why the murderer's doom should not be yours?"

Espardo licked his dry lips, and, after a few moments' silence, answered huskily:

"If there is anything to do to save my life," he said, "I would do it."

"Do you deny the charges made against you?" asked the Veiled Captain.

"They are not proved against me," Espardo said.

"Michael Warren," said the Veiled Captain, "stand forth!"

A man of middle life, with a white, sad face, stepped out from the ranks and confronted Espardo.

"Do you know that man?" asked the Veiled Captain.

Espardo's lips quivered.

"We have met before," he said.

"And met where?" asked the Veiled Captain. "In his lone house, where he found his wife and child murdered by you, and he, an unarmed man, you left for dead. Do you deny it?"

"No," Espardo said, as his head sank upon his breast.

"Enough, then," said the Veiled Captain sternly, "let this charge stand as a type of many that could be brought against you. Your fate is sealed."

"You have no right to kill me," Espardo said.

"In a land where there is no law," said the Veiled Captain, sternly, "somebody must lay the foundation for it. I do it here, and do it my own way, to strike terror into the hearts of plunderers and assassins. To destroy you all at once would avail little: other bands would spring up, and the old system of plunder go on.   But I have said it shall come to an end, and for that end I work."

"You will know who I am before you die."

"Who are you?" cried Espardo, wildly.   "I hear your voice, but I cannot see your face."

"You shall know in a few minutes," was the answer, "as

all your vile brethren on yon mountain shall know when their time comes. Espardo, I will be more merciful to you than you have been to others, and give you a choice of death. The rifle and the rope are ready—make your choice."

The eyes of Espardo travelled round the half-circle of men about him, hoping to find one gleam of pity, but every eye was coldly staring at him.

"I will be shot," he said, with an effort; "but one last word. Let me live, and I will be your slave. No dog would serve you as I will——"

"Silence! bring him hither!" said the Veiled Captain.

They brought him up to the Veiled Captain and left him standing before him, every man turning his head away.

Then the veil was raised a little, and Espardo saw a face that least of all faces in this world he expected to see.

A piercing cry rang from his lips.

"Can the grave give up its dead?" he cried.

"Hal," said the Veiled Captain, "take him away. Have lots drawn for those who are to carry out the sentence. Let them aim well, so that there be no needless torture. Remember that here we act in the spirit of the laws that govern our great country. Away with him!"

Espardo suddenly sank upon his knees.

"I cannot—I dare not—die," he cried.

The Veiled Captain turned away, and Hal signalled to some of the men to raise the Spaniard to his feet.

They did so, but he could not stand without assistance.

"I never meant to do half what I have done," he said; "it was Larry Turrell who led me into it."

They made him no answer.

In silence he was half led, half dragged away further up the ravine until they came to an open spot midway between the grotto and the encampment of women and children.

Here they halted, and Espardo was put against the rocks facing them. Hal bound his eyes with a handkerchief.

"Mercy!" gasped the Spaniard.

No reply was vouchsafed him. Hal stepped back, and, taking a bag from his pocket, drew out a small pebble, which he held close in his hand until the bag had passed round.

When all had drawn, the men, by a simultaneous movement, extended their hands.   Six had drawn black stones, the rest were white.

Those who had drawn the black stones stepped out, rifle in hand, and formed a line about ten paces from Espardo.

The others drew back.

Not a word, not a sound, save the slight rattle of arms and scraping of feet upon the soft soil.

The rifles were levelled, and the lips of Espardo were seen to move.

" Mer——"

Hal waved his hand, and, as one weapon, the rifles were fired.

A true aim had been taken, and Espardo fell forward on his face.

The noise made by the weapons echoed up and away over Eagle Craig, on the summit of which the rays of the setting sun rested still.

Hal looked up, and far overhead, on a jutting crag, saw the figure of his leader—the Veiled Captain—standing still as a statue.

Hal raised his hand, and there was a movement in reply. Then some of the men brought out spades from a nook hard by, and rapidly a shallow grave was dug.

In this they laid all that remained of Espardo, filled it in, beat it smooth, and scattered the spare sand around.

All was done in silence, and without a word they fell in, and marched away to their camp, headed by Hal.

There, as before, the women were waiting, and foremost among them was the pretty Lucia.

" I heard the rifles," she said, with a shudder.

" Yes ; justice has been dealt to one," replied Hal, " and the Captain has gone up to Eagle Craig to brood.   Killing is not congenial work to him, but now that he has set his hand to the plough he will not go back ; nor will he halt until ruffianism, plunder, and murder have been banished from the land."

CHAPTER VIII.

LEAVE TO TAKE A JOURNEY—TURRELL'S BASENESS—A
STARTLING DEFIANCE—HOME LIKE A WHIPPED DOG.

"WHAT is it that makes white-livered curs of us all?" asked
Larry Turrell, in a paroxysm of helpless humiliation.

He had returned to his band, and accounted for his absence
by saying that he, Crashleigh, Rigault, and Smudge had been
to the summit of the Great Cone to look around.

Of Espardo they professed to know nothing.

"It would never do to tell the truth," he said, "and it
would be difficult to get up a lie that would work, unless we
simply say that we left him here walking up and down, and
probably he fell over the cliff."

The men heard his story and said nothing.

They did not believe it, and, being unable to refute it, wisely
remained dumb.

Two days had passed when Larry Turrell made the above
recorded wailing utterance to Rigault.

The pair were standing near the slope, down which poor
Harry Foster and his brother, Little Dick, had been remorselessly thrown. They were indeed standing almost on the very
spot where they stood on that memorable occasion, but,
strange to say, no thought of the crime entered their heads.

"It is the mystery that hangs about him," replied Rigault.
"I'd like to get a look at his face."

"There was a time," said his companion, "when Larry
Turrell was afraid of no man, but latterly I've had dreams
——"

"Dreams! Bosh! rubbish!"

"You may say so, Rigault," replied Larry Turrell; "but if
you had such dreams as mine you would sing a different song.
They come every night now, and they are like a foretaste
of the tortures the parsons tell us are in store for the wicked."

"Parsons tell lies!" returned Rigault, with a contemptuous
curl of his lip.

" Don't make too sure of that," replied Turrell, " but any-way I'm having a rough time of it."

"And the whisky's quite out," said Rigault; "so that, with bad spirits and no spirits, we are in a pretty plight."

"Some must be got, if we die for it," said Turrell. "To-morrow we will have another try at the shanty yonder."

" I'm game," replied Rigault. "Anyway we can't stay up here and starve for a drink."

The men were ready to go. As things were, the majority felt that the sooner they were put out of their misery the better. No man among them felt safe for an hour, and it was the constant *suspense* that racked them.

That night the Veiled Captain, or one of his commissioners, visited the Red Robins again.

Nailed to the door of the hut wherein Turrell and his two remaining lieutenants slept, another parchment was found in the morning

The message this time was laconic, but not threatening.

" You may get food and drink *if you pay for it*."

" Well ! I am more than bothered," said Turrell, when his attention was called to it. "What do you say to it, Rigault ?"

"Well! he heard us talking," was all Rigault could say.

"How ?"

"I don't know."

It was very puzzling, and, in a way, as terrifying as all that had gone before.

What manner of man was it who seemed to have the power of being ever present with them ; who came and went at will ; who, apparently never slept ?

" Well ! it's kind of him," said Crashleigh, with a dry smile ; " and, as we have a little gold dust, I suppose we had better pay."

"I'll see when we get there," said Turrell, between his teeth.

It was horribly galling to be thus ordered to do things so foreign to his creed and nature, but he was obedient at the start, and took a small bag of gold-dust to pay for what he needed, if there was no help for it,

As they had a long way to ride, they started early, and,

with watchful eyes, rode away over the plain. No dreaded foe appeared.

As they got away from the Great Cone they gave their horses the rein and galloped on at a great pace, much to the dismay of Smudge, who was only a second-rate horseman.

On they rode, until the mountain was like a cloud in the distance, and nobody they had cause to fear was in sight.

Then, as before, their hearts grew bolder.

It was the old story over again; a very good sample of mankind in general. Larry Turrell struck up a coarse drinking song, and his men joined in chorus.

After two hours' hard riding, they struck a trail made by emigrants going inland, and they followed it until they saw two or three huts of considerable size in the distance.

This was their destination—the "stage" as it was called—where the whisky shanty was, with accommodation of a limited nature for man and beast.

"Halt!" cried Larry Turrell.

The men reined up, and a consultation ensued. Possibly a trap might have been laid for them, and it was necessary to proceed with caution.

With rifles slung at their backs to show their peaceful intentions, they presently proceeded, Larry Turrell leading the way.

As they drew near they saw that they had little to fear.

Outside the largest hut two little children were playing, and hard by a woman was washing some linen in a tub.

"Hurrah, boys!" cried Turrell, "we've got a clear field to-day."

And so they had.

No strangers were there that day, and the only man in the place was the store-owner, who came out as they cantered up, and gave them a quiet "good-day."

He was a short, thick-set man, with the face and physique of a prize-fighter of the better sort, quiet, cool, and courageous.

Over the entrance to the saloon was a board, with a rough inscription upon it.

The Red Robins reined up, and dropped from their saddles the two children running to their mother. She looked up quietly, and went on with her washing.

"Nice day, gentlemen," said Ben Barker.

"Good enough for us," replied Larry Turrell, with a laugh, which was echoed by his men. "Now then, drinks all—whisky, and never mind the water."

Ben brought out a keg and some tin mugs, and proceeded to give a drink to all. When it was done, Larry asked him how much whisky he had in stock.

"About four kegs," Ben replied, "and I expect some more to-morrow."

"We will take all you've got," replied Larry, and laughed again.

"Who will pay?" asked Ben.

"The Veiled Captain," said Larry, and, as if this were the best joke of all, the men roared with laughter.

Ben Barker looked at him steadily.

"I think, Mister Turrell," he said, "you had better run straight with me."

"Just what I'm doing," replied Larry. "We want the whisky, and we mean to have it."

"Very well, gentlemen," said Ben, quietly, "I've got to give in, I suppose. I can't stand against you all. There's the kegs in the corner, help yourselves"

The kegs were seized, and four of the Red Robins took charge of them.

Then Larry Turrell asked for something to eat.

"Well!" said Ben, "I'm short of food—in fact, I'm right run out. The consignment I expected is late, and there's the children to think of."

"Oh! hang the children!" said Larry, savagely. "Give us what you've got!"

"Very well," returned Ben, as quietly as before, "if you say so, it must be done."

Three loaves of bread, a handful of biscuits, and a ham was all he had, and he brought them out. The hungry men soon disposed of them, and then proceeded to ransack the place.

There was not much to look over, and their search soon

ceased; then, having opened one of the kegs, they had another drink all round, and were **about to** remount, when Crashleigh made a suggestion:

"Why not fire the darned place?" he **said**.

By this time the storekeeper's wife had gone into the house, taking the children with her. Crashleigh's suggestion was received with a shout of approval.

Ben Barker walked to the far corner of the bar, and struck a match.

"Clear away!" he cried. "I'll fire the place for you. I've got a powder-mine here, and I think that I'd better blow the lot to smithereens than trust to your mercy. We are prepared for you, and WE are ready to die!"

The Red Robins, almost to a man, leaped into their saddles, and urged their horses some yards away. Larry Turrell called on them to stop.

"It's his brag," he cried.

"It isn't, as I live!" replied Ben, with close-set lips. "The first man who comes inside this bar will go sky-high with me!"

The first man did not advance. After all, they had got all there was to have, and they were not willing to run the risk of so terrible a death.

Larry Turrell got slowly into the saddle and joined his men.

"It would be a fool's game," he said, "for he looks as if he meant it, and we've got what we wanted. Home, my lads!"

With all their success they felt uncommonly small as they rode away, followed by a shout of laughter from Ben Barker.

Larry turned in the saddle and shook his fist at him.

"You keep a sharp lookout," he cried, "we shall come again."

"Do," replied Ben, derisively, "and maybe I shall have a few friends with me to give you a welcome."

The Red Robins put spurs to their horses and rode **away**, Turrell lagging behind.

So they went on until they were nearing home, and then the thundering of horses' hoofs was heard behind them.

Larry turned and saw the dreaded foe advancing—a line of horsemen, headed by the Veiled Captain.

His men looked back also and saw the unexpected sight Into the heart of each man there entered the question :

"How came they here?"

Immediately they fled at their topmost speed, riding away from their leader, who, being a heavy weight, and riding a tired horse, rapidly lost ground.

"Stop, you curs!" roared Larry. "Are you going to leave me alone?"

If they heard, they did not heed him, and rode on. He beat his horse, and urged it on with wild cries, but he lost ground.

The thunder of the pursuers increased in volume in his ears.

Better mounted, and on fresher horses, they gained on him rapidly.

Then, in a moment, as it seemed, he was in the midst of them, but, to his amazement, they went thundering by.

His wild eyes looked out for the Veiled Captain, but he saw him not. Turning again in the saddle, he beheld him about fifty yards in the rear, loosening a lasso that hung on the pommel of his saddle.

"For ME," thought Larry, and, forgetful of the promise that he was to be the LAST, he saw death advancing.

His hands seemed palsied, for their efforts to work the reins were almost fruitless. He thought of his rifle, but had no power to unsling it.

So great was the terror with which this unknown foe inspired him.

Not a word, not a cry, came from the Veiled Captain.

Sitting easily in the saddle, he rode in pursuit, gathering up the lasso, until he had it ready for a throw.

Then he twirled it two or three times over his head, as he urged his horse on by a pressure of his knees.

In a minute or two he was within casting distance, and then it came whizzing through the air.

Larry heard it, and his heart grew sick within him.

The fatal loop settled about his shoulders, tightened, and then, with a jerk, he was thrown from the saddle

His horse galloped a few yards farther on, and then gladly stopped, tired out with its day's work.

Half-stunned, Larry Turrell lay upon the ground, but he was sufficiently conscious to know what took place.

The Veiled Captain reined up close by, and dropped from the saddle.

"All's over!" thought Turrell, and his mouth opened to gasp a prayer for mercy.

But his hour had not yet arrived.

The Veiled Captain knelt down by his side and searched his pocket, quickly finding the small bag of gold-dust.

Then he spoke.

"I take this," he said, "to pay Ben Barker for the whisky you robbed him of to-day. You see now how vain it is to hope, by tricks, to get the better of *me!* Lie there like a dog!"

Casting the end of the lasso carelessly down, he remounted and rode away.

The feelings of Larry Turrell were of a mixed nature.

He was glad that his life had been spared, but the feeling of littleness that came over him took the form of torture.

While the Veiled Captain was searching him he had endeavoured to make out the face behind the veil.

But the veil was made of some material that was very baffling. It only gave the dimmest of outlines of the face, while the wearer, it was clear, could see with tolerable distinctness.

The voice, too! Where had he heard it before?

It was like, and yet unlike, a voice with which he had at one time been familiar, but he could not locate it or recall its owner.

Crushed by the weight of this fresh humiliation, he lay upon the ground, quite still, and presently his horse came slowly up, nibbling the coarse grass that grew upon the plain.

He called to it softly by name, but it went on eating, unheeding him.

Hitherto, it had always been obedient to his call.

"Like all who know me now," he thought bitterly, "it despises me. Why did I not stand my ground, and *have it out?* In height, in strength, I am more than a match for this veiled fiend. but——"

He stopped short, and tears of mortification ran from his eyes.

Mystified, beaten, dismayed at every point, he felt that he was making one at a game in which he was no better than a frightened child.

He brooded on, until he thought he might make an effort to rise.

Raising his head he looked slowly around him.

He was alone.

In the far distance, towards the Cone Mountains, he thought he could distinguish horses and men, but was not sure. With an effort he got upon his knees.

Then he strove to release himself from the lasso.

But it was not to be moved by any efforts made by him.

He did not remember the Veiled Captain knotting it behind his back, but he might have done so. Anyhow, there he was, with his arms securely held to his side.

His horse was standing very quietly, and allowed him to approach.

Then, after two or three efforts, he succeeded in getting into the saddle, to find that the reins had fallen over the horse's head, and were not to be got at without dismounting again.

He would not risk that, but urged the animal on with knees and voice, and presently it turned homeward, walking slowly, stopping here and there to nibble the grass, until it was urged on again.

In this degraded fashion did the once terrible leader of the Red Robin Band return slowly to the foot of the Great Cone, where he dismounted, and, having got hold of the reins, led the horse up the rugged path, the lasso, evidence of his galling defeat, trailing in the rear.

For some distance his way was a lonely one, for as far as he could see none of his men had returned. Then the fear entered his mind that they had all been slain by the foe.

But as he drew near the plateau where the horses were stabled he heard the sounds of moving men and voices, and stopped.

His men, or some of them at least, had returned. Could he

—dare he face them in his miserable bound condition ?

Then arose the fear that it might not be his own men who were moving about, but the followers of the Veiled Captain.

He would have left his horse if he could have tethered it to anything, and gone on stealthily alone, but there was nothing to secure it to.

To leave it with the hope that it could not follow him would only end in one way. Accustomed to the track it would surely go on behind him.

He sat down to think what he should do, and after a few moments' puzzled thought he decided to let the horse go on alone.

He would then soon learn whether it were friend or foe upon the plateau.

The horse needed little urging. Being set free, a soft word sent it on at a smart walking pace, scrambling up the rough parts of the road with a noise and clatter that was soon heard above.

Larry Turrell heard shouts of alarm, and a faint noise of the closing of doors. Then he knew that it was his men above, and they were hiding in the huts fearing the advance of the enemy.

Despite his own miserable condition, he laughed. The terror, which was so serious a thing in himself, was rather amusing when found in others.

" All alike," he muttered, "I can hope for no real help from them. I'll have another run for it, and go alone."

He rose up, and slowly proceeded up the narrow road until he came within sight of the plateau. It was deserted, and all the doors of the huts closed.

He was not sorry to see it, as it gave him a chance of getting into the place he had recently made his home, without being observed. Smudge, perhaps, would be there, and would sever the lasso before the others had an opportunity of seeing it.

For Smudge's opinion he did not care a rap, but he little thought that the cowardice of his follower would eventually be the means of exposing him.

Smudge was inside the hut, quaking all over. Larry had guessed aright ; the return of his horse, riderless, had led his men to think that the enemy was near.

Of all the Red Robin band none, indeed, had been hurt. They were pursued as far as the base of the mountain, and then the Veiled Captain's men reined up, with derisive laughter on their lips, and turned towards the gap, disappearing one by one, unseen by the Red Robins.

They were now in the huts, ready, like rats in a corner, to sell their lives as dearly as possible.

Smudge was alone.

When the alarm was raised, he dashed into his master's hut, and nobody followed him.

With the few rough bits of furniture, he put up a feeble barricade against the door. then seized a rifle which stood in a corner, and loaded it.

"I'll shoot the first man who comes in here," he said wildly.

The first man to enter was Larry Turrell.

He came up, and tried the door by leaning against it. Then he called to Smudge by name, and, getting no answer, he raised his foot, and kicked in the door.

As he strode in, Smudge, blind with terror, raised the rifle, and fired point-blank at him. Larry Turrell staggered back, and fell heavily to the ground.

CHAPTER IX.
ONLY FAINTED--THE VEILED CAPTAIN AND BEN BARKER— LUCIA MISSING.

No sooner had Larry Turrell fallen than Smudge saw the mistake he had made, and, with a wild cry, he threw himself down by the side of his tyrant master.

It was strange that he should feel, for a moment, sorry for what he had done, but it was so, and his moans and cries were heard by all around.

"Help! help!" he shrieked. "I've shot the captain! Oh! oh!"

The doors of the huts opened, and the men came hurrying out to gather round the prostrate form of their giant leader.

The lasso was still about his arms, and he lay quite still There was no sign of a wound upon him.

The men stared at the strange figure in amazement, and then at each other. Rigault knelt by the side of his leader.

"Where did you hit him?" he asked Smudge.

"I—I don't know," stammered Smudge, "and, now I think of it, I don't remember putting a bullet in the gun."

The men chuckled, and a faint smile passed over Rigault's face.

"He's not dead, but only fainted," he said. "The captain's a bit unstrung."

This was, indeed, the fact.

Larry Turrell, wearied, worn, and fatigued, had yielded to a sudden shock, and fainted away.

They brought him round, and, having cut the lasso, which had been skilfully knotted behind him, they put him on one of the rough seats in the hut.

He drank some whisky, and the stimulant helped him round so that he could speak.

"Am I hit anywhere?" he asked. "I don't feel it."

"There was only powder in the rifle," Rigault answered. "Come, captain, don't look so sheepish; we forgive you. There is no man here who can point a finger at you. Those fellows drove us this morning like sheep, and, as far as I can see, they did it for fun. I'm hanged if I can make it out."

"You will very likely be hanged when you do make it out," remarked Crashleigh, with a grim smile.

"Well, boys!" said Larry Turrell, "it seems we've got the very Old One to deal with; but we won't give in. I'll think out something to get the better of him, yet!"

Leaving him to cheer his men to the best of his ability, we will follow the Veiled Captain, who, after lassoing Larry Turrell, rode away in the direction of Ben Barker' store.

He did not draw rein until he was up to its door, and Ben was there, ready to take the bridle.

"I won't stop now, Ben," he said; "I've simply brought you the gold for your whisky, as I said I would."

"Bully for you, captain!" replied Ben; "but won't you have a drink? Forgive me—one!"

The Veiled Captain shook his head.

"You know my vow," he said, "never to eat or drink with man while a Red Robin is alive."

"Destroy the nest, sir," said Ben; "smoke 'em out and smash 'em like wasps!"

"All in good time," replied the Veiled Captain. "Ah! here is your wife and little boy. How do you do, Mrs Barker?"

Crushed by a fresh humiliation.

"I'm well, sir," the woman replied, as she came forward. The Veiled Captain held out his arms.

"Give me the boy up here,' he said.

The mother lifted up the child, who gazed wonderingly at the veiled face.

" Are you not afraid of me ?"

" No," replied the boy ; " you are kind, I am sure."

" Would you like to ride away with me ?" the Veiled Captain asked.

The child looked anxiously towards his mother, but he turned back again and said :

" I am not afraid of you."

" Here, take him ! " said the Veiled Captain ; " he is made of the right stuff."

The child's mother, as she took him, raised her eyes to the veiled face.

" I hope you will be happy—one day. Heaven bless you !"

" The ' one day ' may never come," he said.   Then, with a wave of the hand and a kindly nod to the child, he turned his horse round, and rode away.

" A good fellow, a brave fellow ! " said Ben, enthusiastically. " As gentle as a woman if let alone, but, roused, who shall turn him from the path he chooses to take ? "

" No woman could help loving him," Mrs. Barker said ; " if he asked me, Ben, I am sure I should run away from you."

" But he won't ask you," replied Ben, good-humouredly, " and I'm not afraid. He's got no woman in his head just now."

" But there is a woman who has him in her heart," was the reply.

The Veiled Captain rode back, and late in the afternoon again reached the Great Cone Mountain.

After a glance upward, he dismounted by the narrow rift and led his horse over the rough ground.

On entering the ravine he gave his horse the rein and walked slowly on alone.

The horse after a glance back at him trotted on ahead, and it was soon out of sight.

Evening was coming on, and, during the day, the Veiled Captain had neither eaten nor drunk. Coming to a small spring, he knelt down and took a long draught of pure water, and walked on till he came to a spot where nature had fashioned some rude steps in the rock on the side called Eagle's Craig.

Up there he went with a quick light step, until he came to

a sort of landing-stage.   Here he paused, and turned his face towards the Red Robins' haunt.

Smoke was rising from two or three of the huts, but he could see no movement outside, and he resumed his way.

Up, up—by a path that was sometimes tolerably easy to one accustomed to mountain-climbing, sometimes so perilous that the least false step would have hurled him a thousand feet down—up he went.

Below the gloom was gathering, but above the light of the sun still shone.   The cleft summit of the Great Cone looked like a rudely carved and gilded bishop's mitre.   Up, up he went, almost to the very summit, and then in a recess where many an eagle had built its nest the Veiled Captain found food and wine awaiting him.

There he sat down, out of sight and earshot, to eat his evening meal alone, in the afterglow of the sun that had gone down, and there he remained until the sky was a blue-black and studded with untold stars.   Then he slept.

The night passed, and the dawn found him descending on the other side, by a way that only a man with the strongest nerve would attempt to traverse.

Over rugged rocks, down steep inclines with scarce a projection for hand or foot hold, but cool through all—never once losing his head, and reaching tolerably level ground at last in safety.

He was now within half-a-mile of the camp where the women and children dwelt.   He knew they would be awake by that time, and the men most probably at breakfast, and he walked on slowly in that direction.

As he surmised, the people were stirring.

Fires were being lighted, and little children, half-dressed, and some of them not dressed at all, were running about and skipping like lambkins at play.

The women were busy over the camp fires cooking, and the men stood about in groups.

As the Veiled Captain drew near he speedily attracted attention, and the men ceased talking.   The women, too, abandoned their work, and the children stopped their play.

In the midst of a silence that was more impressive than

any noisy demonstration, the Veiled Captain walked into their midst.

"Good-morning to all," he said, in his soft, silvery voice.

A murmured "good-morning" came from all, except the little children, who had got together, and were regarding the Veiled Captain with wonderment, but not terror.

"I do not see Hal!" he said.

"Hal has overslept himself," replied one of the men.

As if to confirm this assertion, Hal, at that moment, appeared at the door of his hut, stretching and yawning.

"Hal!"

The young fellow turned, and, with a quick step, came up to his leader.

"Is anything wrong?" he asked. "I did not expect you till noon."

"I slept on the Craig last night," the Veiled Captain replied, "and I had troubled dreams. I am not usually childish in that respect, but they were so vivid that I came on here to see if all was well."

"All is well."

"Where is Lucia?"

Hal cast his eyes round at the women, who had now resumed their cooking operations, but his sister was not there.

"She, as I did, has overslept herself," he said.

He ran back to the hut, and was heard to call upon her by name. Then followed the noise of a hasty knocking at the door, and a further calling to her.

"Something is wrong," muttered the Veiled Captain, as he strode towards the hut.

At the door he met Hal hurrying forth with a wild look in his eyes.

"She is not here," he said.

Immediately all was commotion. The men and women hurried up, and gathered round.

"Be calm, all of you," said the Veiled Captain; "perhaps, after all, there is no reason for anxiety. When was Lucia last seen?"

"Not since last night," replied Hal. "She has been rest-less since the time when your horse came home without you.

In vain I told her it was nothing She feared som th b   u
fallen you. Then, when the night came on, she k p ac   in
and out, until at last I bade her go to rest. She went ut
not to sleep, as I fear now."

"Hal," said the Veiled Captain, "come with me. Fear
not. If Lucia is in peril, I will save her. If wronged or
dead, the vengeance I have laid out for the Red Robins shall
be as nothing to that which I will take."

CHAPTER X.

LUCIA IN CAPTIVITY—SMUDGE ON SENTRY DUTY—A CHANGE IN HIM—OVER THE PRECIPICE—KILL HIM.

ON the previous night Larry Turrell sent Crashleigh with
four men to the summit of the Cone to see if there was any
sign of a camp below.

Judging by his experience on the day when Espardo was
captured, he concluded that the Veiled Captain's quarters were
on the other side of the spur of the mountain. He was so
far right, as the reader knows, as to hit upon the spot where
the women and children were encamped.

Early the next morning Larry Turrell was aroused by a
knocking at the door.

Springing out of bed, he seized his revolvers; but, on being
reassured by hearing the voice of Crashleigh, he laid them
aside again.

Smudge came into his room, rubbing his hands and grinning like an ape.

"Rare news," master, he said, "they've found a woman."

"They! What's that?" asked Larry Turrell.

"A woman, and a pretty one," said Smudge, smacking his
lips. "Young, like a flower."

Larry Turrell tossed on his clothes, and, hastening out,
found that the story was true. Standing by the door was
Crashleigh and his men, with a young woman proudly
erect in their midst.

They had bound her hands behind her, and the bosom of
her dress was slightly torn, evidently during a struggle with
her captors.

The Red Robins stood around, gazing at her with admiring eyes, but she seemed totally indifferent to their coarse, rude gazing.

Larry Turrell looked at her, and she kept her eyes on him unflinchingly.

"Where did you get hold of this pretty bird?" asked Larry Turrell.

"Half way down on the other side of the Cone," replied Crashleigh. "She had been over here in the night, and was making her way back again."

"So," said Larry Turrell, with a grin, "the Veiled Captain is not above the sweets of life. Why, this is a rare capture. Pretty one, have I not seen your face before?"

"It is useless for you to ask me any questions," she replied. "I will not answer you."

"An eaglet," exclaimed Larry, "to be tamed by-and-by. I have a cage for you, pretty bird, and I will softly whistle to you until you will chirp back to me."

"Nay," said Crashleigh, "there are two to that bargain. *I* found her."

"And is not all that is captured mine?" said Turrell.

"No!" replied Crashleigh, boldly.

"Nor is it yours," interposed Rigault; "or anyone's here especially. Spoil has ever been divided, but, for such an one as this, we must draw lots."

"Ay! that's it," cried the men; "draw lots for her."

"And let the man who wins her make her his bride," said Rigault. "By the stars! we will have a rare wedding, and Jumpy Smudge shall be the priest."

The pretty girl, in whom the reader has of course recognised the lost Lucia, looked round upon them all defiantly.

"You may cast lots," she said, "and you may destroy—kill me—but I bid you beware. Think you that the Veiled Captain will let my death go unavenged?"

"Hear her!" cried Turrell. "The Veiled Captain—so we have it at last. Vengeance or no vengeance, we will spoil his joy for many a day to come. Put her within my hut, lads, and let her bide there awhile. Fair play in such a thing as this. Now hurry in; and you, Smudge, are man enough to keep guard over a woman. Load your rifle——"

"And see that you put a bullet in it this time," added Crashleigh, "or the lady might faint."

Turrell glanced at him evilly, but took no further notice of the sarcastic remark. Obeying a movement of his hand, the men pushed Lucia towards the hut, thrust her in with Smudge for a companion, and closed the door.

"Breakfast first," said Turrell, "and fun afterwards. Our Veiled friend has perhaps not missed her yet. By the gods! but it is a rare find."

The men set to work, and in a short space of time break. fast was prepared. Larry Turrell, Crashleigh, and Rigault partook of it together, and talked of their chance of gaining a wife.

"It may be a short honeymoon," said Larry Turrell, "but what of that? I'd not forego it if the fiend afterwards rent me to shreds."

"You are not married yet," grinned Rigault.

As, in such cases, every man thought of himself as the probable winner of the prize, and a strange hilarity prevailed.

The rocks echoed with unseemly jests and coarse laughter.

Smudge, doing duty over the fair Lucia, felt more miserable than ever.

Though he admired Lucia as the rest did, he felt in awe of her, and, while keeping watch, stood back in the gloom in a sneaking way that was particularly his own.

Lucia sat down upon a rude stool at the far end of the room, and for a while there was silence. Presently she spoke:

"Come out of that corner, man," she said, "and look at me."

'If you will excuse me,' replied Smudge, "I'd rather remain here."

"I want to do that to you which I would not do to the others," Lucia said, "make an appeal. If you have one spark of manhood, of kindness, of honour in you, kill me now."

"Kill you?" exclaimed Smudge, aghast.

"Yes," she said. "Place your weapon here, against my brow. and pull the trigger. It will be the kindest act you ever did for man or woman."

"NOW SHE ROLLS!" CRIES TURRELL. "OVER WITH IT!"

"Oh! don't say that" cried Smudge, "nobody will hurt you. Larry Turrell will be kind to you."

A fierce, passionate cry broke from Lucia's lips.

"How dare you talk to me in that way?" she said. "Come here, kill me, I command you!"

"I dursn't do it," said Smudge. "I'm a miserable coward, and if I obeyed you, they would flay me alive."

"Say that I tried to escape, and you did your duty."

"I should be found out; they wouldn't believe me. Besides, it would be so terrible a thing to do, you are so young and pretty——"

"Silence!"

He stopped short, as if he had been shot, and again there was a silence between them. Outside the Red Robins were roaring with merriment.

"Oh! my lost loved ones!" moaned Lucia, "what will you say or think? I pray heaven you may never know my fate!"

A tear rose unbidden to her eye, but she forced it back, and sat with a face that was white and strangely still—the face that the martyrs of the old Roman arena might have worn when awaiting the summons to a meeting with wild beasts.

By-and-by Smudge began to creep towards her, leaving his rifle in the corner.

"I'm very sorry for you," he said, "on my word I am."

She looked at him with doubt in her eyes, but it speedily passed away. The expression in the face of the timid Red Robin was kindly enough.

"I don't belong to this band by choice," he said. "Larry Turrell took me prisoner as I was going inland with some friends. He killed all but me, and my life was spared because he wanted one like me for a servant."

"Why do you remain with them, then?" asked Lucia "Go to the Veiled Captain and tell him your story. He will help you."

"Do you think so?" said Smudge, dismally.

"I'm sure of it; and he would thank you for killing me at such a time as this!"

"Oh! I can't do that!" whined Smudge, shrinking back. "I couldn't do it anyhow! What, put the rifle to such a face as yours, and——oh! it would be too horrible!"

"Then say no more," said Lucia, kindly, "but look out and see what those knaves are doing."

Smudge found a convenient crack in the wall, and proceeded to report.

"They have finished breakfast," he said, "and Larry Turrell is picking up a lot of stones. I can guess what that is for. They are going to draw lots."

Lucia shuddered.

"Now Turrell has got a bag, and the stones are being dropped in one by one, all dark but a single white one, and that's——"

Smudge stopped short. For the first time it then flashed upon him what their drawing meant. Fool and coward as he was, his blood boiled within him.

"I don't think I can stand by and see it done," he gasped. "Oh! how I hate the lot! I'll let fly into the thick of them and run for it."

A frenzy suddenly laid hold of him, and it gave to the coward the momentary courage of the brave man.

"Go and do your worst among them, never mind me," said Lucia. "Do what you will, little or much, in my name, and I will thank you."

Smudge laid hold of the rifle, and, opening the door, stood before his amazed comrades looking like one possessed.

"Stop this game," he said, "I can't stand it. She's too beautiful—she——"

He brought the rifle to the present, and they broke away like sheep when a dog suddenly appears.

"Drop that gun, will you?" cried Larry Turrell.

The answer Smudge gave was to pull the trigger.

One of the men received the bullet in his chest, and stag

gered back to the very verge of the precipice, when he fell and lay half over, dead.

Then Smudge tossed his weapon into the air, and fled down the mountain side.

"Capture him; bring him back!" cried Larry Turrell.

All the men followed but one, and he was so utterly staggered by the sudden outburst of Smudge that he could only stand still and stare.

This man's name was Trant, and he bore some facial resemblance to Smudge, although he was of a different disposition. In his half-frozen state of astonishment his resemblance to Larry Turrell's attendant was remarkable.

None of them had their rifles, nor thought of getting them, but, standing by the hut, they watched Smudge's wild flight down the mountain. He went on at a reckless pace, and none of his pursuers appeared to be able to keep up with, much less overtake, him.

And standing fifty feet above, watching this strange scene, was the Veiled Captain.

Alone he had come to find out if Lucia was captive among his foes, and now he had evidence of his surmise being right. Lucia, with her hands alone bound, could make a move, and now she came out of the hut, bent on escaping from her captors even at the risk of her life.

In a few moments she was on the edge of the precipice, and, turning, faced them boldly.

"Come near me, now, if you dare!" she cried.

"Curse it!" said Larry Turrell, between his teeth, "we shall lose her. Come, pretty one, no tricks. We are not going to hurt you, we——"

He was suddenly tripped up, and thrown to the earth with tremendous force.

A cry burst simultaneously from the lips of Trant, Crashleigh, and Rigault.

Turrell saw a figure—that of the Veiled Captain—glide swiftly and put an arm round Lucia's waist, then face about and point a revolver at the standing men.

Like scared rabbits they fled into the nearest hut.

Lucia had fainted away, but the Veiled Captain, holding

ner lightly in his arms, sank into a sitting position and slipped over the precipice.

Larry Turrell sprang to his feet.

"Come out there!" he roared, "we've got him now, men. Help me to run this rock down. It's a safe game. He's got the girl and we need not fear him."

So rapid had been the succession of incidents that the other men were in a bewildered state, but they heard Larry's voice and obeyed him.

A huge boulder stood within a few feet of the precipice, and the three leaders quickly set it going. Trant stood watching them like a man in a dream.

"Over there—straight as we can run it!" roared Turrell like a madman. "We'll smash him now if he is flesh and blood. Over with it! Quicker! Now she rolls!"

Urging his assistants on with wild cries, Larry Turrell strained every nerve to get the large stone over the precipice.

Disappointed of his prey, burning with fury, and spurred on by his fears, he made a great effort to destroy his enemy.

It was now or never.

If he could not crush his foe then he felt that all future efforts would be fruitless.

He had in his eye the exact spot on which the Veiled Captain quietly dropped with Lucia resting on his right arm, and to that spot he guided the rolling boulder.

OVER!

As it rolled over the side the three men drew back, and stood for a few moments breathless and silent.

Crash, crash! rumble, rumble!

They could hear it going down with a terrible rush, striking in its descent one of the stunted trees growing out of the cliff, then bounding on to some projection, which it broke away, and, with a small avalanche of stones, down it went into the ravine below.

They heard it strike the solid earth, splitting into a thousand pieces, the noise of its fall echoing right and left.

But no sound of human voice, no cry of terror. nothing to indicate that the attempt to crush the Veiled Captain had been successful.

"It hain't touched him," said Crashleigh.

"Then he IS more than mortal," hissed Larry Turrell, "or he's leagued with some power that parsons talk about."

"Let us look over and see what's come to him," suggested Rigault.

"You may," said Turrell, with an oath; "but I'll not waste any time. He's safe enough. You can't trick him. He's here to destroy us, and he'll do it. Make up your minds, we are all doomed men!"

Muttering to himself Larry Turrell walked gloomily to his hut, and entering, shut himself in.

Crashleigh and Rigault drew cautiously near the precipice, and the latter, throwing himself down at full length, peered over.

"Safe! as Larry said," he whispered. "Look, there he goes. He's worked his way down the cliff *at an angle*, and that's why we missed him. Crashleigh, *it ain't the first time he's been down that way!*"

"Once would be enough for me," replied Crashleigh, with a shudder. "He must be a cat."

"A swift eye and a sure foot will take a good man down strange places," said Rigault. "Well, he's down, and he's out of sight now, girl and all. Hang it! it's hard to have lost her. Now let's go down and see if they've got hold of Smudge. I feel like hanging somebody, I do."

"Stop!" said Crashleigh. "Look there. The veiled fiend alone. He is going down to the end of the ravine. Now, Rigault, have you any pluck? If so, let us see what we can do. Get the rifles ready, quick! I'll go and tell the boys that he is coming. One to so many. We can't miss this time."

CHAPTER XI
THE FLIGHT OF SMUDGE—PURSUIT OF HIS OLD FRIENDS —AT THE SUMMIT OF THE RAVINE—RESCUE.

SMUDGE fled for his life, and as he bounded down the side of the mountain he felt like a man in a dream. It seemed to him that he scarcely touched the ground.

But fright, as a stimulant, very quickly evaporates; and fright, as a laxative, takes its place. Before the plain was reached poor Smudge felt his knees giving way.

Happily for him, he had at first distanced his pursuers; and, owing to the turns in the road, was well out of their sight.

But he could hear them coming on, and the terror of the hunted brute, in whose ears rang the bay of the advancing hounds, took possession of him.

He had no idea at first whither he was going, no definite destination. But as he neared the level ground he thought of the Veiled Captain.

It must be remembered that Smudge had not witnessed Lucia's rescue. As far as he knew, the Veiled Captain was in his haunt, the ravine, and to that he turned.

"It's my only chance of life," Smudge gasped, as he wheeled to the right and hurried over the broken ground.

Ere he had gone far he looked back, and saw the foremost of the Red Robins in pursuit.

He threw himself upon the ground, and from behind a rock watched the coming of the others.

One by one they appeared, and halted together. They were looking for him on every side, and were plainly puzzled.

They were also rather chary of coming lower down, and hung about for a long time, talking together, and moving slowly to and fro.

' I wish they would get back again," muttered Smudge.

He lay as close as he could, but every now and then he took off his hat and cautiously peeped out, to find there was no change in the situation.

The men hung about in a purposeless way until Larry Turrell appeared on the scene, rifle in hand.

"What!" he said, "have you lost him?"

"We haven't seen him since he started," replied one.

"But he can't be far away," said Turrell. "Scatter yourselves, and look about you. The dog is only lying in some hole.'

Smudge could not hear what was said, but he heard the noise made by the Red Robin chief, and another peep revealed the fact that there was a general move in search of him.

"All over now!" he gasped.

The Red Robins scattered as directed, and, in a few minutes, one of their number was coming straight towards the hiding-place of Smudge.

This was Trant, who bore some resemblance to the decidedly nervous servant of the Red Robin chief.

Now, of all the band, Smudge least feared this man.

He was coming along, holding his rifle carelessly, and in a way that gave a smart man the chance of snatching it and bolting.

Smudge was not smart, but he was desperate.

He lay quite close until Trant was within two feet of him, then up he sprang, knocked the rifle from him, and bolted towards the ravine.

It was barely a quarter of a mile off, but the ground was rough and hard to get over.

Smudge bucked along like a goat, and the Red Robins, shouting and yelling, came in a scattered semicircle on his trail.

Foremost was Turrell, who now and then took a pot-shot at Smudge, but failed to hit him.

At length the ravine was within hail, but Smudge was pretty well done. His legs bent under him, he had no breath left, and, within a few yards of safety, he sank behind a rock with a low wail of despair.

A yell of triumph sprang from the lips of Larry Turrell, to die away the next moment.

At the mouth of the ravine appeared the Veiled Captain.

He held his rifle carelessly poised, as if HE had no cause for fear, and his clarion voice rang out over the plain!

"Back, you curs! The man who advances another pace dies!"

They pulled up, the majority dropping behind the rocks to shelter themselves. Larry Turrell levelled his rifle and fired. He missed.

The Veiled Captain waved his hand contemptuously.

One of the rank and file of the band raised his rifle next, and pulled the trigger.

He had barely done so when the Veiled Captain brought his rifle to the present, and the next moment his would-be slayer lay stretched out dead.

The quickness of the shot, the sureness of the aim, terrified the Red Robins.

Whatever may be the lot of man, he clings to life, and Larry Turrell and his followers had the instinct of self-preservation very strong.

As the rifle of the Veiled Captain, a repeater, shifted round, they either dropped quite out of sight, or fled precipitately.

"Come here, Smudge," said the Veiled Captain; "you are safe now."

Smudge heard his voice, so soft and friendly, and with a cry of joy came out of his hiding-place and ran towards him.

The Veiled Captain pointed to the ravine.

"Go on," he said; "I will follow you directly."

Smudge, trembling with joy, did as he was told, and hurried on.

Ere he had gone far he ventured to look round, and saw the figure of his preserver like a statue at the mouth of the ravine.

Not a Red Robin was in sight.

He walked on, and in a little while came upon Lucia sitting on a mossy stone.

She looked pale, like one who had endured a great mental strain, but she recognised him with a smile.

"How came you here?" she asked.

Smudge, in a few trembling words, told her.

"I'll die for him—for this great unknown—this king of men," he said.

"Better live for him," replied Lucia.

"By what miracle did he get you down here?" asked Smudge, after a pause.

"By the miracle of skill and nerve," was her reply. "See! here he comes."

As the Veiled Captain came up, Smudge took off his hat, but the mysterious hero of Eagle Craig, with a motion of his hand, bade him replace it.

"I do not need servility," he said, "only obedience."

"I am a poor cowardly wretch," replied Smudge; "was born so, and shall die so, but I'll do my best to serve you."

"Do that," was the answer, "and you will in my eyes do as much as any man."

Turning to Lucia, he said, quietly:

"Have you rested sufficiently? If so, we will go on."

She rose up, and they went slowly down the ravine side by side, Smudge following.

When they spoke it was in an undertone, and what they said only reached Smudge's ears in a soft murmur.

He was not at all anxious to know what they said. His life was saved, and he was grateful. The poor weak-nerved, ill-treated follower of Larry Turrell felt a warmth in his heart he had not known for many a day.

It was a long road, but by-and-by they saw a man walking slowly and sadly towards them.

It was Hal, who, as soon as he caught sight of them, halted and stared as if he could not believe his eyes.

The Veiled Captain held up his hand and Hal ran towards them.

"Saved!" he cried.

" Lucia is here," was the simple answer; " take her back to the camp, and she can tell you all about it.   And this good fellow—you will learn from Lucia's lips why you should treat him well."

" How shall we ever repay you ? " exclaimed Hal.

" By never naming so simple a thing to me again," returned the Veiled Captain.

He was standing by the rough way that led up to the mountain-top, the way he had taken before to the lonely resting-place where he passed the night.

Hal knew his leader too well to say anything more, and with his face aglow with joy he put his arm round his sister, and led her away. Smudge, as before, following.

The Veiled Captain with a light step climbed up the rugged cliff-side and half-way up paused to look down.

From this place he could command a view of the plain.

In one spot there was a cluster of small figures, and in another a stretched-out form with a solitary man peering at him over a rock.

The quiet one was the man who had been shot, and Trant was now looking to see if any sign of life was left.

" Vain hope," said the Veiled Captain, grasping the meaning of this group: " when my rifle speaks it will never waste its breath. As for you," he added, turning to the larger group, " do what you may, hide or fly, none but the poor shivering fellow I have saved to-day shall be spared.   If aught was needed to clinch my resolution it has been given by your dastardly conduct to-day.

Then he resumed his way, and mounted leisurely to the Eagle's Nest, his watch-tower, and there alone he spent the rest of the day and the long dark night.

CHAPTER XII.

SAFE AWAY AT LAST—FOILED AT HAZARTON—TO THE DARK FOREST—THE SOLITARY FIGURE IN THE MORNING.

IN the dead of night the Red Robins brought down their horses, and made another effort to get away.

Larry Turrell made up his mind to risk returning to civilisation, or such civilisation as the country afforded.

Scattered about, many miles apart, there were small towns and settlements, the nearest of which was called Hazarton, and was thirty miles west of the Great Cone.

It was a settlement on the banks of a small river, where gold had been found in sufficient quantities to pay for the labour of searching for it, and the inhabitants, all told, were about two hundred.

Of these, about fifty were men, too small a body to offer resistance to the Red Robins—so Larry Turrell thought.

All night long they rode, and when the sun rose up in the morning, the cluster of wooden houses was well in view, and the Great Cone, with its rugged surroundings, just visible on the horizon.

On the outskirts of the town, a solitary horseman was seen riding towards them. When he got within two hundred yards he reined up, and examined the band for a few seconds, then turned round, and rode back to the town with all speed.

" Confound him!" muttered Larry Turrell, " what does that mean ?"

" It means," said Crashleigh, " that we have been expected and watched for."

" It can't be," hissed Turrell.

"It is so," replied Rigault grimly.

" Let us go on," said Turrell.

They rode forward, and ere long found that they were indeed expected.

Close to the town was a large stockade, into which the women and children were seen hurrying, escorted by armed men.

The stockade was built on a bit of rising ground, and commanded every approach to the town.

In the centre was a tower-like erection about fifteen feet high, built of solid timber which no bullet would penetrate. It was pierced on every side for the use of those within.

Larry Turrell took in the hopeless position at a glance.

"We can do nothing here," he said, "but face round and offer ourselves to be shot."

His men sat grim and silent in their saddles waiting for some suggestion from their leader. It did not come very readily.

At length he said:

"Let one of us go forward and buy some provisions."

They had brought all their moveable property with them —gold-dust, cooking utensils, and ammunition.

They had means to pay like honest men, and now they felt they would have to act up to that character for once in a way.

Rigault offered to go forward as a herald of peace.

Taking out his handkerchief he tied it to the muzzle of his rifle, and rode on.

Everybody within the stockade had disappeared, and he looked about him warily, expecting to see a puff of smoke and hear the whiz of a bullet, or perhaps feel it.

There was no sign of anybody within until he was only thirty yards away.

Then a dozen rifles popped over the stockade, and a stentorian voice cried out:

"Stop there!"

Rigault lost no time in reining up.

A grey head rose over the stockade, and a question was asked, "Who are you?"

"Honest men," replied Rigault, "who only want to purchase provisions and then go upon their way."

"We have nothing to sell," was the rejoinder.

"But we MUST have provisions," urged Rigault.

"You will get nothing here," was the curt reply, "unless is powder and lead."

" And is that your final answer ?

" The only one."

Rigault turned his horse round and rode back with the message.

" What's their position ?" asked Larry Turrell.

" One we can't get the better of," answered Rigault; "they could pick off every man of us without our getting a fair shot at one of them."

A bitter exclamation burst from the lips of the Red Robin leader.

" I'll bear this place in mind," he said, " and one day we'll come back to it."

" Where now ?" asked Crashleigh; "back again?"

" No," said Turrell, with an angry oath; "I've done with the Cone, whatever comes. We'll go north to the Dark Forest. It's full of game, and we can live there for a time."

" The Dark Forest !" cried some of the men in dismay.

" Yes, why not ?" said Turrell.

" It's never been searched into," said one of the men, "and they say that it's got a race of wild men that are worse than wild beasts in its depths."

" I've heard the story," said Turrell, "but I don't believe it. Wild men or not we had better go. Who follows ?"

" If one goes all must go," said Rigault.

They rode a little way from the town, and watered their horses at the river. Then they went higher up, found a ford, and crossed.

On this side of the river there was a small farmhouse, and the occupant of it was seen to mount his horse and ride away as they approached.

In a shed they found a solitary cow which they killed, and, having lighted a fire, satisfied their hunger with ill-cooked, half-raw meat.

The men looked haggard and worn, and on their faces there was the look of hopeless despair which poets attribute to the lost.

No sounds of laughter, no jest, not a smile; scarcely a word came from their lips.

In grim silence they partook of their rough meal, packed up what was left of the half-cooked meat, remounted their horses and rode on.

LUCIA'S HEART BEAT QUICKLY AS SHE SPED TO THE MOUTH OF THE TENT.

The Dark Forest was a long way off, and they did not reach it that day.

The night was spent in a dark and dismal bivouac on the plain.

Having pegged their horses, they gathered in a group and smoked a pipe or two of the small store of tobacco they had left.

Now and then one would speak and sometimes get an answer—sometimes not. Finally, one by one they went to sleep.

Larry Turrell was the last to close his eyes.

·It would be a difficult task to put his thoughts into words.

Ruffian as he was, there had been a time, and not so long ago, when he had been in a respectable position in life.

He was the son of honest people, farmers in the old country, but, as the saying goes, had been a little wild.

At his own request he was sent abroad to the Gold Coast, and there he had speedily developed what was bad in him, and sunk to his present level,

Turned out here, warned off there, he had taken up with his villainous life, gathered a band of ruffians worthy of himself together, and made the name of Red Robin a terror to all who heard it.

We know what he did at this Great Cone, and there is no need to dwell upon the other portions of his career.

His crimes well may, and must be guessed at. He had done his worst, and the time of retribution was coming on with giant strides.

As he lay there, upon the bare ground, with his eyes upon the vast firmament, brilliantly lighted with stars, he thought of his old home.

What would he have given to be there again!

But he knew it could never be.

His father and mother were dead now, and both had died brokenhearted, for the brute never so much as wrote a line to them after he left; and the old homestead was in the hands of strangers.

Never more would he sit by the old fireside.

At last he fell asleep, and such dreams as he had gave him no rest.

The dawn found the band on their way again, riding through a broken country, with here and there a small winding stream or a clump of trees, the land rocky and sterile, and useless to man.

A little before noon they saw a long black line in the horizon.

"That is the Dark Forest," Larry Turrell said.

Before they came to it they saw some deer grazing in the distance, and two men of the band, old hunters, went forward to stalk them. They succeeded in shooting two, and again there was a supply of food.

"We shall not starve here," said Turrell, triumphantly.

"No," said Rigault, "but is the life worth living, and suppose HE should find us here?"

"Let him come," answered Turrell, "and get at us in that forest if he can."

Well was that forest worthy of the name it bore.

To most of the men it was only known by reputation, but several of the band had in years gone by visited it in search of game.

They all gave a dismal account of it.

"A wood where one might look for the fiend himself," they said.

The trees were for the most part of giant size, with huge crowns that spread out dark and thick like a pall.

Some of them had never been heard of or named by civilized man.

As the Red Robins rode into the gloomy shade one man said it was like going into a tomb.

Larry Turrell cursed him for his idle talk, and all felt that somehow the simile was applicable.

They dismounted a little way in, and, having secured their horses, set to work making some form of shelter.

Many of the trees, though so huge, were of soft wood, and the skilful use of the axe soon laid several of them low.

In action the men found some rest from their perturbed, miserable state.

While some worked in erecting huts, others went in search of food. A handy spring was found, and there was abundant fodder for horses on the plain.

Several days passed, and they were undisturbed in their new haunt. Once more the star of hope began to gleam.

"We might do worse than this," said Rigault.

Of course they speculated on what the Veiled Captain might possibly be doing.

Perhaps he had not discovered their flight.

Or if he had, he might be seeking them in every direction, and after a long and vain quest, he might give up pursuit and leave them to themselves.

It was only a question of time and patience.

So a week passed.

Two long rough huts were built, far enough in the wood to be out of sight from the plain.

In one they stabled their horses, in the other they herded together.

Larry organised a daily duty for all.

The various modes of toiling were portioned out. A sentry was always kept on duty, day and night.

All took a turn at watching.

One night it was Larry himself, who went outside the wood and paced up and down.

The night was hazy, but not so dark as it is sometimes, for there was a new moon behind the clouds giving out a faint light.

All was still.

It was one of those windless nights, when all created things seemed to be at rest—not so much as the chirp of an insect fell upon the ear.

Once, it was about midnight, he thought he saw something like a herd of deer moving past ahead.

He also fancied he heard the sound of their hoofs, but he was not sure.

"Perhaps it is nothing but the night mists moving," he said.

It was a six hours' watch with him, and Rigault was to take his place at dawn. His lieutenant, faithful to his duty, was there just before sunrise.

The darkest hour is before the dawn, and the two stood together, waiting for the first flash of light.

It came, and died away quickly, then a few moments later the cold, grey, heralding light spread across the sky.

Rigault's eyes wandered over the plain. He suddenly grasped Larry Turrell's arm.

"Look there," he cried, in a tone of suppressed agony.

Larry Turrell looked to the right, the direction in which he pointed, and his heart seemed to leap into his throat.

About a mile, or a little more, upon the plain, not far from the forest, was a tent, and outside it a solitary figure moved slowly to and fro.

Once seen, that figure was one never to be forgotten.

It was the Veiled Captain.

For a few moments the two men stood dumb.

"He's got something to back him up," said Rigault, between his teeth, "or he dare not do it."

"He dares everything," replied Larry Turrell.

"Come back, quick!" said Rigault hurriedly. "I have an idea."

Larry Turrell was beginning, in a wild, passionate way, to make offensive remarks concerning his idea, when Rigault dragged him back into the shadow of the wood.

"What's the good of mouthing and shouting?" he said, "that won't help us."

"Nothing will help us," hissed Turrell.

"Listen to me," said Rigault; "after all, his being here may be a matter of chance."

"It is you, now, who talk stuff."

"Never mind, there's the chance of my being right."

"And that's the only chance of the business," said Turrell.

"Hear me, will you?" said Rigault angrily. "I say that I've an idea, and it's this. He's been looking for us, without a doubt; roaming here, prowling there, and now he's dropped on the spot where we are, but he hasn't found us out."

"That's your idea."

"Well, doesn't it seem so? Fancy the fellow pitching his tent where we can take a pot-shot at him. Where are his men?"

"Oh! don't run away with the idea that he's alone," said Turrell impatiently.

"He's either ahead or behind his men." replied Rigault

"and I say he IS alone. Let us go to Crashleigh, and hear what he says. But, first, I'll take a peep out and see what he's doing."

Rigault stepped forward a few paces, and stealthily peered out upon the plain.

"Just what I told you," he said exultingly. "He IS alone. He is going into his tent. Now, Larry, be bold for once. If we make a rush upon him, we can shoot him like a dog in a hole. I'll look up Crashleigh, and he'll make one with us."

"As you like," said Turrell, bracing himself up, "he's here, and we are not safe. Suppose we get all the men——"

"Bah!" interrupted Rigault. "A flock of sheep to worry a dog! No, we must do it quietly—creep up like wolves, spring upon him, and put an end to the whole business. Their veiled fiend slain, the rest will not stand an hour. Come, Larry, the wood will cover us until we are close upon him—one rush, and the victory is ours."

CHAPTER XIII.

LUCIA SHOWS HER LOVE—THE RED ROBINS' PANIC—CRASHLEIGH CALLED—THE WAY HIS OLD FRIENDS STOOD BY HIM.

RIGAULT might argue as he willed, but the fact remained.

The Veiled Captain had tracked them to their hiding-place in the Dark Forest.

Himself ever on the watch, sleeping little, and keen-eyed as the hawk, notwithstanding the veil he wore, and his men, as a matter of duty, always on the alert, what chance had the Red Robins to get away?

It is true that they had been unmolested for a week or more, but their terrible pursuer chose his own time to strike, consulting no man, not even Hal—the most trusted of his followers.

Boldly, without the wood, he had pitched his tent. Within the wood his men were camped.

The women and children had been left behind—Lucia excepted. She could not rest, she said, if she was not permitted to share the perils and hardships of the pursuit.

"I, too, have wrong and insult to avenge," she said.

So she was permitted to come, and that morning, just at the time Larry and Rigault were arranging an attack upon the Veiled Captain, she was walking with her brother up and down within the wood.

"I do not like it," she said; "he risks too much, Hal. He is too daring. Why should he offer himself as a mark for their rifles?"

"He has no fear of them," replied Hal, simply, "and believes that he will go unscathed through all."

"He may not."

"I think he will, Lucia. He is a terror to them, and their hands are palsied when he is near them. I think he may be trusted to look after his own safety. At least, we ought to obey his commands."

Hal walked away, and Lucia paced up and down awhile uneasily.

She had a woman's natural apprehensions for the safety of one who was very dear to her, and the outcome of her thoughts was that she resolved to disobey the Veiled Captain's commands, and put herself as a watcher over his safety

She walked back to where the main body of men were silently preparing their morning meal.

Accustomed to be dumb when necessary, they moved about making little more noise than spectres would have done, so as to give to the Red Robins no indication of their presence.

For Lucia they had constructed a rough shelter of boughs, and, silent as the rest, she stooped under it, and brought out a rifle of lighter make than usual.

It was her own, a present from the Veiled Captain.

Gliding along, she speedily reached the verge of the wood just behind where the tent was pitched.

Nobody was in sight—all was silent.

She crept up cautiously and peeped inside the open mouth of the tent.

Within, on a camp chair, reclined the Veiled Captain, apparently asleep.

"No wonder," murmured Lucia, "for two days and nights he has not closed his eyes."

Softly she stole up to him and listened to his long-drawn, regular breathing. Undoubtedly he slept.

"I know my duty now," murmured Lucia, with a glad smile.

By the entrance to the tent she took up her stand, remaining as still and silent as a watchful Indian listening for the footsteps of a foe.

Presently a crackling sound fell uper her ear.

She knew by experience that somebody was coming stealthily over the ground where decayed vegetation was lying, and her heart beat quickly.

It was no friend approaching, but a foe.

Cocking her rifle, she advanced a pace and peered out.

About fifty yards away she saw Larry Turrell, Rigault, and Crashleigh creeping towards the tent.

Like all women, Lucia was impetuous, and to act on the thought of the moment was natural to her.

Stepping into the open space, she took rapid aim at the trio and fired.

Crashleigh sprang up and put his hand to his cheek, but he did not appear to be seriously hurt.

As Larry Turrell and Rigault turned and fled in alarm, he turned too, and followed them.

At the same moment the Veiled Captain, aroused, rose quickly from his chair, and came up behind Lucia.

"What is it?" he asked.

"See there," cried Lucia, pointing to the flying men, "they were coming to kill you, and I—I——"

"Lucia," asked the Veiled Captain, "how came you here?"

"I am so anxious—so fearful," she replied, "but will you not punish them, they are getting away?"

"Let them go," said the Veiled Captain contemptuously. "In my own time I will call them to account. But, again, why are you here?"

He spoke kindly and gently, as he always did to her.

She looked up with a smile.

"You forgive me?" she asked.

"Forgive you," he said, "of course; and I am grateful for your devotion, but be not afraid. I saw those men coming in my dreams, and a moment later I should have been ready for them ; but I thank you all the same. Only remember this —I will not have you risking your life for me."

"I will obey you, if I can," she answered.

He held out his hand, and taking hers, gently pressed it.

"Go," he said, "and send Hal to me."

Let us follow the flying Red Robins.

Scared out of all proportion to the danger they incurred, they lost no time in getting with in the shelter of the wood, where they paused for breath, Crashleigh holding a handkerchief to his cheek.

"Confusion seize the wench," he cried, "but she is almost as good a shot as the veiled fiend himself."

"Who would have thought of the girl being there," growled Rigault.

"It was a fool's idea of yours," snarled Larry Turrell, "I knew it would not do."

"You know a lot," returned Rigault, "so perhaps you will tell us what we are to do now."

"Get away at once," replied Turrell.

"Where to ?"

"We must risk the forest—get through it, and out by the other side."

"And where is the other side ?" sneered Rigault.

"It's no use arguing," said Turrell ; "evidently we've got to go."

Crashleigh said so too, and they went back to the main body of the Red Robins.

There was no time to be lost.

The men were called together, and hurriedly told of the arrival of their foe.

A general panic ensued.

The break in upon their sense of security was so terribly sudden that they lost whatever courage they possessed, and for a while scarce listened to the commands of Larry Turrell.

But after a time they became quieter, and then he bade them pack their few provisions and bring out their horses.

Grimly they hastened to obey, asking each other if "they were doomed never to rest again."

Sorrowfully and bitterly they looked upon their labour Rude as was the shelter they had constructed outwardly, they had begun to think of the huts as "home."

There was one brief space of time when all the men, including their leaders, were either in their own hut or that made for the horses.

Some of the men in the latter place thought they heard a slight tapping outside, but paid little heed to it.

When they came forth, the first thing they saw was one of the dreaded messages from the Veiled Captain nailed to the rough logs that formed the walls of the hut.

CRASHLEIGH IS CALLED BY THE VEILED CAPTAIN. HIS TIME HAS COME.

The men gathered about it, and Crashleigh came up to read it with the rest.

When he saw his name all the life-blood left his face.

He turned round, and standing with his back to the hut, looked round at his old companions but not one returned his gaze.

They stood in groups looking gloomily upon the ground, Larry Turrell and Rigault apart from the rest.

"This sort of thing seems to me all brag," said Crashleigh, speaking huskily. "You will stand by me, comrades, I hope?"

"What's the use of it?" asked Rigault. "You had better stay behind."

"It seems to me," said Larry Turrell, "as I said before, that we've got more than man to deal with. That thing wasn't there a quarter of an hour ago. It's there now. Who put it there?"

"It's no use discussing that now," said Rigault, impatiently. "Let us get away."

He muttered a few words in an undertone, and Larry Turrell nodded assent.

They separated, and each said a few words to one of the men.

Crashleigh still leaned his back against the hut, looking

dismally about him, seeking in vain for some gleam of commiseration.

But there was none.

They only thought of themselves. He was as a leper, as one baned by all society, an outcast from the band.

Suddenly. Larry Turrell, Rigault, and the two men they had spoken to fell upon him.

He guessed their purpose, and struggled fiercely, but they threw him down; and having bound his hands and feet together, left him lying.

"It's just as well," said Larry Turrell to the men, "if the Veiled Captain wants him he's bound to have him, and any kicking against it may get some of you into trouble."

"Turrell, Rigault," said Crashleigh piteously, "don't leave an old pal like this. We've been friends together, and have shared good and bad luck for years. Now, for the love of old times, don't desert me."

"If there's any man here who wants to set you free let him do it."

No man came forward to cut his bonds.

One and all thought of self. Flight was their only chance of life.

"Curs all," said Crashleigh, between his teeth. "Go, but here, as I lie, to all purposes a dying man, take my curse with you. I can see, as doomed men have often seen, marks upon your faces not seen by ordinary men. The mark of the awful being who wears the veil is there. He has set his seal upon you."

"Don't heed him," said Turrell, "bring out the horses and away."

The horses were brought out with all speed, and the few goods and chattels they possessed slung upon the pommels of the saddles.

Then the men, in eager haste, leapt into their seats.

All this time Crashleigh never ceased to pray or revile.

He begged of them to take him with them, to shoot him as he lay, to do anything but leave him to the Veiled Captain, but they paid no heed to him.

Then he changed his note, and cursed them with all the fury of despair.

With Turrell and Rigault at their head, they rode away into the forest, and left him to his fate.

As they passed by—a living panorama—he called upon each in turn, but no answer was vouchsafed him.

The last man disappeared, and he was alone.

He ceased his cries, and when the sound of their horses

hoofs died away, a dreadful silence lay on all things around him.

The morning sun sent its rays into the forest in narrow shafts of light.

They gleamed to the right and left, and above him, but none fell upon him. In the shadow cast by the dense foliage he lay helpless, as his cowardly, selfish companions had left him.

To watch, to wait in silence for ANYTHING coming is trying. What must it have been to that doomed man waiting for *death?*

He had not long to wait, although it seemed hours to him.

With quiet footsteps a man appeared, rifle in hand, and took up his stand a few yards away.

Their eyes met, and Crashleigh uttered a sharp cry.

"Raustin!" he cried.

The man made no answer, nor did he stir after he had taken up his position.

In a few seconds another man appeared, then another until there was a semi-circle round Crashleigh.

The whole thing was so strange, so dramatic, so unlike real life, that the hope he was but dreaming began to dawn upon him.

But it was soon dispelled.

When the semi-circle was complete there came one quietly along who passed into the centre of the assemblage and stood before Crashleigh.

It was the Veiled Captain, and the doomed man could see the flash of his eyes behind the veil.

" Disarm, unbind, and raise him," was the command.

It was quickly obeyed, and, with scarce strength to stand, Crashleigh was put upon his feet face to face with his unknown foe, guarded by four men.

CHAPTER XIV.

THE CONDEMNATION AND FATE OF CRASHLEIGH—UP THROUGH THE FOREST—THE NIGHT BIVOUAC.

FOR a moment there was silence; then the Veiled Captain spoke in a clear resonant tone,

"John Crashleigh, you stand here charged with robbery, murder, and outrages which are here unspeakable. I will not enumerate your crimes, but I ask you to plead. Are you guilty or not guilty?"

Crashleigh looked about before replying. Like Espardo before him, he felt that denial was useless, and all he could do was to palliate his offences.

"I am no worse than the others," he said; "why pick me out?"

"Answer my question," said the Veiled Captain, sternly; "are you guilty or not guilty?"

"Not guilty, then," cried Crashleigh, desperately; "at least, I ought not to be tried by you——"

"Raustin, stand forth!" said the Veiled Captain.

"Not him," cried Crashleigh, "it is a mockery to call a man I do not know."

"Not know me!" said Raustin, stepping forward, "when we were neighbours for a year, and I trusted you as I would a brother, leaving you in charge of my home, my wife, and little ones, when I went away to the coast to see an old friend. How did I find my home when I returned?"

Crashleigh's head fell forward on his breast. He had no answer.

"Wrecked!" cried Raustin, raising his right hand, "my wife and child, where? Their blood has long cried out from the ground for vengeance on you. At first I thought that you had given up your life defending them, but others had seen you ride away with the spoil you robbed me of—oh, villain! villain!"

"Enough, Raustin," said the Veiled Captain kindly, "you see he stands condemned by his silence. Place him within yonder hut, and give him half an hour's grace. Meanwhile, dig his grave."

"That be my task," said Raustin, "not that I gloat over his death, but it is right that I should do it. Oh! angel wife and lovely boy of mine, avenged at last."

Crashleigh had to be helped to the hut, and there he was left alone for awhile.

He made no attempt to find a loophole for escape, as he knew in his heart there was none.

Presently the door opened, and the Veiled Captain came in.

"Crashleigh," he said, "with you, as with Espardo, I reveal myself before you die. Can you not guess who I am."

"I know the voice—that is all," Crashleigh answered

"Look upon my face."

The veil was drawn aside for a moment, and Crashleigh, with a gasping cry, fell upon his knees.

"You!" he cried.

"Yes," was the answer. "Say, is my condemnation of you just?"

Crashleigh fell forward on his face, grovelling on the ground.

"It is just," he moaned, "but hear me, be generous and forgive. You were always noble and good. Spare me!"

"And if I do," said the Veiled Captain, "what am I to say to Rauston? No, Crashleigh, there is no hope, so do not dream of it. Farewell."

As he turned away, Crashleigh tried to grasp his knees, but failed. His trembling hands had lost their power.

Wildly he crawled after his earthly judge, but could not overtake him, and as the Veiled Captain passed out, two men entered.

"Rise," they said; "be a man."

"I was one once," replied Crashleigh, "but all the nerve has been taken out of me. I have wondered who he was, but never dreamt that it was HE, of all living creatures. Can't you let me go? I have some gold in my belt that I've hidden away from my old friends. Come, it is yours. Give me a run for life——"

They lifted him up and bound his arms.

"It is useless to talk of that," said one man; "a mine of wealth would not tempt us to be untrue to our noble leader"

He said no more, but relapsed into sullen silence, which he maintained until they led him outside and planted him on the verge of a shallow grave dug by Rauston, who stood apart rifle in hand.

Then Crashleigh began to cry out again, but half-a-dozen men formed a line in front of him ; his eyes were bandaged, and Rauston gave the word to fire.

With an infinitesimal interval of time between the reports the rifles belched forth their fire, and Crashleigh, without a groan, fell back into the grave prepared for him.

Rauston stepped forward, and knelt beside him.

" He is dead," he said, after a brief examination.

Then they laid him out, in his last resting place, quickly covered him with the soil, and in silence strode away.

Meanwhile the Red Robins had gone on straight into the forest, or as straight as the obstacles they occasionally met with would permit.

Here and there they came upon the trunk of a monarch of the forest, which had yielded to time and fallen.

Or perchance a clump of thick prickly undergrowth barred the way, still, for the most part, the way was tolerably clear.

The huge trees stood wide apart, and gave them ample riding room for two, side by side, and occasionally more.

It was not until they had ridden some way that Larry Turrell thought of one thing needful.

They had no fodder for the horses, and the forest yielded little for their sustenance.

He mentioned it to Rigault, who coolly said the horses must wait, perhaps they would be clear of the forest on the morrow.

There was no sign of life among the trees.

Not even a bird flitted by, and no animal, little or big, crossed their path.

" This place should be called the Dead Forest," Rigault said.

A midday halt by a spring that bubbled from the earth, and lost itself in the rotten foliage around, led to the general discovery of the absence of food for their horses.

Then the men began to murmur, and some suggested going back.

" We can't go on far, anyway " they said.

But Larry Turrell reasoned with them.

"WHO WOULD NOT BE YOUR SLAVE?"

Their only chance was to go forward.

It might be, nay, he was pretty well sure that the forest was not of the extent people supposed it to be, and he had heard of a fertile, lovely country lying beyond it, inhabited by a peace loving race, who would easily be reduced to a sort of vassalage.

As for the yarns about wild men, he ridiculed them.

The horses drank at the spring, and nibbled some green fern growing about, which appeared to content them, and then they rode on again until the light began to wane.

A halt was now imperative, and another spring being sought for and found, the horses were tethered near it, so as to get the benefit of the green things growing about this favoured spot.

Then, at a short distance, the Red Robins lighted fires, and prepared to bivouac.

Hardly had they done so, when a rumbling sound was heard far away.

"A storm's coming," said Rigault.

In a little while, lightning was seen, a drop of rain came down, and then the storm raged.

It was muffled a little by the dense foliage that was overhead, and the rain could not penetrate in anything like force, although it ran in streams down the trunks of the trees.

The greatest danger and discomfort was from the incessant lightning.

One huge tree near the Red Robins was struck and split in twain, mighty branches were also rent, and came toppling down, and the men were in a constant state of watchfulness until the riot in the elements was over.

It lasted about half an hour, and then passed away.

Once more they made up their fires and gathered around them.

They only thought of themselves. He was as a leper, as one baned by all society, an outcast from the band.

Suddenly Larry Turrell, Rigault, and the two men they had spoken to fell upon him.

But the discomforts of the night were not yet over.

Strange horrible cries were heard around.

Some times they were far away, at other times quite near.

Specks of light, which some of the men said were the eyes of wild beasts, were seen in the darkness around.

Then suddenly one cried out that he saw a face, and pointed in the direction in which it appeared.

Ere long others saw a face, white, ghastly, and gibbering like some monkey

After this there were other faces appearing in every direction, now here—now there—by one, by twos, and threes.

It was horrible beyond description.

As for lying down to sleep with such surroundings nobody there so much as thought of it.

A suggestion from Rigault that a pot-shot should be taken at one of these strange visitors met with a remonstrance from Larry Turrell.

"You would bring them on us, perhaps, like a horde of wild cats. Let them be. We had better sleep half at a time."

But even this suggestion could not be carried out.

Those who tried to get Nature's sweet oblivion found themselves unable to do so.

Those dreadful faces kept them alert and watchful.

Again, the cries increased in force, and the men, shuddering, whispered to each other that it was like nothing they had ever heard before.

Later on there was more to terrify them.

Flashes of strange light, revealing uncouth figures capering among the trees, and, anon, rough bits of wood were hurled at them from the darkness.

Then Rigault's suggestion was carried out.

A couple of shots were fired at a gibbering face a few yards away, and, in answer, there came mocking laughter of the most blood-curdling description.

How they longed for the dawn !

If they had been better men they would have prayed for it

All things come in time, and, the night passing away, a faint light appeared overhead.

The faces disappeared shortly after, and when there was light enough to see, no living thing was in sight. They went round in a body, and could find no trace of footsteps, nothing to guide them as to the manner of men who had haunted them through the long night.

Wearily they returned to the expiring fires, and having made them up, lay down to rest.

No man offered any suggestion as to the nature of their visitation, but all mentally concurred in the wild-man idea.

The story Larry Turrell would have had them laugh at was then no myth.

Although terror-stricken, they gathered heart from the fact that they had not been attacked. There was also the hope that ere night came they would be clear of the Dark Forest.

After the first party had slept an hour, they were aroused, and the rest took their turn.

Larry Turrell was one of the last to lie down.

Worn out he slept, but had scarcely got well away in the land of dreams when he was awakened by a commotion around him.

Rising up upon his elbow he looked about him. A little distance away was Rigault with a group of excited men together.

"What in the name of all that is evil is the matter now?" he asked.

"The horses!" replied Rigault.

"Well! what's the matter with them?"

"Gone!"

Larry Turrell leaped to his feet, and stared wildly at his lieutenant.

"Gone where?" he asked, huskily.

"The Veiled Captain's got them!" was the answer given with assumed indifference.

Larry Turrell looked from one to the other, and saw in their faces that Rigault had spoken the truth.

The other men who had lain down with him were now awaking, and had this dismal intelligence imparted to them.

"We know it is the Veiled Fiend who has them," cried Rigault, "because he's left a memorandum behind him. It was nailed to a tree, and here it is."

Rigault took from his breast one of the well-known strips

of parchment, and on it in a clear bold hand were written
these words :—

"I have your horses, having need of them. Seek me now
if you desire payment."

The last paragraph was undoubtedly a sarcastic reflection
on their courage, and the Red Robins read it so.

There was no help for it. They must go forward on
foot, and if the way was long they would surely perish of
starvation.

"We must make the best of it," said Turrell, grimly.

"There is no best in it," answered Rigault, "it is all bad
for us. A curse upon the day we first saw you!"

"It's childish to talk in that way," returned Turrell. "Did
I make you what you are?"

"You made us worse than we were," was the reply.

To this there was a general assent, and a lot of wrangling
ensued, which ended in a sort of peace being patched up, and
on foot they went forward.

But the day was dull.

The light overhead was feeble, and no especial rays of sun
came through the trees to guide them. Nor had they a
compass to keep them in the straight track.

Perhaps there is no more difficult task than that of keeping a straight line without a guide to the direction which
ought to be taken.

Blindfold a man and put him on a plain and he will
inevitably, in trying to walk straight, go round in a circle.

So it is with a man in a wood who relies upon his own
eyes only—he will surely deviate from the straight path, as
Larry Turrell did.

While he thought he was going straight he bore to the left
and the others followed him.

They toiled on for hours until they suddenly came upon the
track of horses.

"A path at last," cried Turrell.

They took up the trail and hastened on, Rigault with his eyes
wandering here and there.

"Seems to me," he said, "that I've seen some of the trees
before."

As he spoke Turrell, with an exclamation, stopped.

Right in front of them was the spot once seen not to be forgotten—on the day where on the previous night they had tethered their horses.

Blankly they looked at each other, until a low groan escaped one of the men.

It was taken up and swelled into a general moan.

Larry Turrell leaned against a tree and passed the sleeve of his coat across his brow. Rigault stood near gloomily looking at him.

"Well!" he said, "what now?"

"We are done for now," replied Turrell, "for to have to wait here for to-morrow's sun to guide us, is more than I can do."

"It's an old blunder you have fallen into," said Rigault, gloomily biting his lips. "I wonder none of us thought of it. You've gone round like a ball swinging on a string and here we are."

CHAPTER XV.

SMUDGE GETS INTO TROUBLE—HE SHOWS HIMSELF IN A
   NEW LIGHT, AND THE VEILED CAPTAIN IN THE OLD
   ONE.

ANOTHER night in that terrible forest!

The Red Robins felt they could not bear it.

The memory of those fearful cries and gibbering faces which had made the dark hours so hideous appalled them even in the daylight, and they stood in gloomy silence waiting for some direction from their leader.

Rigault, with a contemptuous smile on his colourless face, looked at Larry Turrell, whose eyes were bent upon the ground.

"Come!" said the half-breed, Rigault; "are we to wait here all day?"

"We must try again," replied Turrell; "perhaps we shall go on better if we bear a little to the *right*."

"Something in that," grunted Rigault; "I am glad you've got half an idea left in you!"

Turrell's face flushed with anger, but he made no retort.

"Come on, lads!" he said, "we've got to get along some-how. While there's life there's hope."

"Little life and no hope!" growled one of the men.

They passed over the ground where they had so miserably bivouacked on the previous night, and, bearing a little to the right of their previous trail, resumed their way.

Ere they had gone far, Rigault, who was stalking silently along by the side of Turrell, suddenly sprang forward, and threw himself upon a clump of undergrowth.

His astonished friends had no time to enquire the reason of this strange movement ere a plaintive voice was heard.

"Oh, don't! please; I've not hurt you! I'm here by accident—I meant no harm."

"Smudge! by the piper that played before Moses!" exclaimed Turrell.

"I've got him!" said Rigault, with a serpent-like hiss. "Come out, you rat! and let us have a look at you."

He dragged out the old servant of Turrell, white with terror, but, for all that, not looking quite such a cur as he used to do.

"Get upon your feet," roared Larry Turrell.

Smudge without any assistance got up and looked at his old master squarely.

"Tie his hands," said Turrell, "and bring him along. When I've got to a quiet spot away from here, I'll talk to him."

"Hadn't you better let me loose?" said Smudge, with a sort of groan.

"Oh! yes, I'll let you loose when I've done with you," returned Turrell. "Now keep up. If you hang back I'll use the point of a knife as a spur."

"I'll go," said Smudge; "only mind what you do; you will be sorry for it afterwards."

"No doubt you're a valuable animal for the Veiled Devil to lose," said Turrell, sarcastically.

Bidding two men keep a hold on Smudge, and not lag in the rear, Turrell hurried on, and his men moved on not far behind him.

They all displayed a laudable anxiety not to be left in the rear, and as they walked their eyes wandered right and left.

They were in a state of constant apprehension.

In their haste they forgot how the day had advanced, and it was late in the afternoon when they halted to eat what scraps of food they had left from their store.

This time they seemed to have kept straight upon their way, for they returned to no familiar spot, and the trees around them were now of a different character.

They were such trees as we see in our forests at home. There was the oak, the beech, and the birch; also many others that they had seen elsewhere. The depressing influence of the mighty trunks they had left behind was no longer felt.

Larry Turrell and Rigault squatted on the ground, and Smudge, after his legs had been tied, was put down in front of them.

"You cur!" cried Turrell; "you traitor! It's you that's been running against us all the time—doing the Veiled Fiend's work, posting proclamations, and other games."

"You talk like a fool!" said Smudge, boldly.

"Hey! what's that?" exclaimed Turrell, raising his eyes.

"I've nothing to gain by being civil to you, and nothing to lose by being the other thing," said Smudge. "You will kill me, I dare say, but I'll try and not disgrace my master."

"You won't disgrace ME."

"You are not my master."

"We will see about that presently," said Turrell.

Smudge sat quite still, watching Turrell and Rigault with a curious look in his small eyes. It was a compound of fear, hatred, and courageous resolution.

"Where's your new master?" Turrell asked, abruptly.

"I don't know," replied Smudge.

"Do you think he's anywhere handy?"

"No! if he was I should not be left here."

"So you think he'd look after you?"

"He would look after a worm that was faithful to him," replied Smudge, "and I'm all that."

It was again growing dusk, but with new surroundings the Red Robins had lost some of their fears. They reckoned that they had put a good ten miles between them and the spot where they rested the night before, and possibly had got right away from their foe.

The fact that no attempt had been made to rescue Smudge also favoured this idea.

So as light waned they lighted fires, and Larry Turrell, when he had rested and smoked his pipe, again turned his attention to Smudge.

" You've been with the Veiled Fiend some days," he said.

" He is not a fiend," replied Smudge.

"Captain, then. I won't bandy with you for a word. Tell us what he is like."

" You know something of him," replied Smudge, "and before long will know more about him."

" Don't answer me in that way," said Turrell, savagely.

" I will not answer you at all," replied Smudge, " unless I've a mind to."

Rigault and Turrell exchanged glances—a murmur of surprise passed round among the men.

Was this the coward Smudge who used to quail before every angry word, and tremble at half a threat?

" I know I astonish you," he said, "but the Veiled Captain's got the magic power of giving some of his courage to others. He makes even a poor shaky wretch like me ashamed of being afraid."

" I'll see if I can't get a squeak out of you," said Turrell, fiercely. " My lads, get what bits of rope you've got together, and tie him to a tree."

Many of them had a yard or two of rope round their waists, carried there to be made use of as an extra halter, when they had their horses. Now they could spare it for other uses.

They took Smudge aside and bound him to a tree, hand and foot, giving him a sense of helplessness that would have made many a stout heart quail.

His face looked as if he was vividly alarmed, but the face is not always an exact index to what is in the mind and heart.

Larry Turrell took up a position in front of him, rifle in hand. Rigault also stood by, and the Red Robins scattered about, watching with interest the movements of their leader.

"Now, Smudge, what is the sort of man who is your leader? Does he show his face to his men? If so, who and what is he?"

"You had better go to him for all you want to know," replied Smudge.

"Answer me straight."

"I won't."

"Rigault," said Turrell, "I think we will trim his ears. You begin, but don't take too much off, as we shall all want a hand in the job."

Rigault drew a knife from his pocket, opened the blade, which was long and keen, and with some ostentation felt the edge.

Then he went up to Smudge, and laid the edge of the blade upon his ear.

"Will you answer my question, now?" said Turrell.

"Hurrah, for the Veiled Captain," faintly replied Smudge.

Then with a hiss of pleasure, for Rigault loved cruelty, he cut off a thin slice of the top of Smudge's ear.

That the poor wretch flinched was plain, and it was no dishonour, but he closely compressed his lips as if resolved not to speak again.

"Who wants the job of trimming the other ear?" asked Turrell, as Rigault closed his knife reluctantly and stepped back.

"The man who touches him again——dies."

That dreaded voice ——that dreaded form there again.

With startling suddenness, as if he sprung from the ground, the Veiled Captain, revolver in hand, stood between the Red Robins and their prey. The Red Robins fled wildly.

At the same moment a shout was heard in the wood and the tramp of advancing men was heard.

The Veiled Captain raised his weapon, took a rapid aim at Rigault, who clapped his hand to his ear.

"Advance, my men," rung out that clear voice, and suddenly a little host of men came on the scene

The Red Robins fired a few wild shots, and fled.

With wonderful rapidity the revolver of the Veiled Captain was fired, and three men fell. His own men did not fire a shot.

"Hal," he said, "see that they do not suffer,"—and Hal, stepping forward, examined the three Red Robins who had fallen. Each man was fairly and squarely hit between the shoulders, and life was extinct.

"A short pursuit, Hal!" said the Captain. "Scare the cowards, but shoot no more.

Then, as Hal and the men broke away like bloodhounds upon a trail, the Veiled Captain cut Smudge's bonds, and set him free.

Smudge sank to the earth and clasped the knees of the strange being who had saved his life.

"Forgive me, master!" he cried. "Oh, wonderful man! vho would not be your slave?"

"Rise, Smudge," said the Veiled Captain, gently; "you know how I object to this. How is it that you fell into the hands of those men?"

"I wanted to do something for you," replied Smudge, "and asked brave Hal to put me on scout duty. He did so, and I lost my way. I wandered miles, until I heard something moving in the wood. I thought it was your men, noble captain, and went on boldly enough until I saw it was the Red Robins. I hid under a bush, but Rigault, who has the eye of a hawk, saw me."

"I can understand the rest," said the Veiled Captain; "you are not the man for scout-work. It was a mistake, but no great harm has come to you. I commend you for your bravery."

"Oh, dear! MY bravery?"

"Yes, Smudge, you were brave. I saw and heard all. I would have rescued you before, but I left you for a test. You do not know much, but if you had betrayed the little you DO know, I would have left you to your fate. As it is, you are now fully enrolled in the Veiled Captain's band, in which there are only men who have been tried and found true as steel."

"I said I would die for you," said Smudge eagerly, "and I meant it. I didn't flinch, but it wasn't my courage, captain, that held me up; it was *yours*."

At this moment Hal came back, a little out of breath, with half-a-dozen men behind him.

"They are tearing through the forest," he said, "yelling for mercy."

"Like other cowards," said the Veiled Captain, "they shall die a thousand deaths ere I have done with them. Remove the fallen men. Lucia will soon be here. It is not a f sight for her to look upon."

CHAPTER XVI.

A STRANGE DISCOVERY—THE CITY OF THE LAKE—A NIGHT JOURNEY—THE BITTER CRY UPON THE WATERS.

IT was not long before Lucia appeared. She was accompanied by two men who had acted as a body-guard by the desire of the Veiled Captain.

Hal met his sister, and exchanged a few words with her, and then she came over to the strange leader, who took her hand in his, and pressed it gently.

"Safe here," he said, "but why not have taken my advice, and returned to the camp?"

"Because I could not rest," she said. "Stephen and Fenby have returned with the horses, and will remain there until they hear from you."

"They will hear again when they see me," replied the Veiled Captain. "When I go back to the Eagle's Craig my task will be done."

"Why not hasten the end?" Lucia asked.

"I cannot go from the path I have marked out," he answered. "If I do, I feel assured of partial failure."

"Are we near the end of this dreadful wood?" Lucia inquired.

"I think so," he replied, "but of that I know no more than you."

"Perhaps your foes may escape you, here!"

"They will not escape," he said simply.

His men, who numbered about thirty, had been busy replenishing the fires which the Red Robins had lighted, and they afterwards lit one apart from the rest, and by this the Veiled Captain sat down alone.

Lucia joined Hal and half-a-dozen more around the fire, among whom was Smudge.

True to the general character of these assemblages there was little noise. The men spoke in low tones that were not heard a few feet away, and the blazing branches crackled. Beyond this there was no sound in the forest.

Reclining at full length, and leaning on his elbow, the Veiled Captain lay gazing into the glowing fire.

" He is sadder than usual to-night," whispered Lucia.

"He was speaking to-day of those we have lost," replied Hal, "it was only a few words, but I knew that he would be sad to-night."

As Hal spoke the Veiled Captain rose up, and without a word was moving towards the dark depths of the forest alone, when Lucia sprang up and ran after him.

" Where will you go ? " she asked. " Why not remain with us ? There is no Eagle's Craig here."

"Let me do as I will, sweet Lucia," he answered, " it is only in solitude that I can still the troubled thoughts that will arise."

He took her hand and pressed it to his heart. Then with a motion of his head he bade her return to her brother, and glided away into the darkness.

Lucia resumed her seat by the camp fire, and now that the captain was gone the men talked with greater freedom. There were even some jests exchanged, and a little laughter, but it was still of a subdued nature.

Ere long Hal arose, and calling upon two or three others to help him break off some boughs, constructed a rude shelter for Lucia.

Wearied with a long day's walking she was glad to get to rest, and her example was speedily followed by the men.

They seemed to have no fear of their own safety, and to treat the possibility of fear with contempt.

On the bare ground they slept, and the fires soon fell into a heap of red-hot smouldering embers, still giving out warmth, but little light.

This, too, died away, and in the midst of profound darkness they slept on.

Hal lay by his sister's resting-place, and he saw nothing.

heard nothing until he was awakened by a hand pressing his breast.

Opening his eyes he saw the Veiled Captain.

"Come with me, Hal," he said. "Did I disturb your rest?"

There was just light enough to see each other, and Hal knew the dawn was breaking. Rising he followed his leader, who strode quickly and silently away.

In a little while Hal said:

"You have not slept."

"No," replied the Veiled Captain. "I am in one of my wakeful moods. I feel as if I shall never sleep again."

"They grow on you," said Hal, dolefully.

"It may be," replied the Veiled Captain, "but as yet I am not weakened. Oh, Hal! mine is a lot out of the common. I have a task to do, and it must be done. Having set my face to the plough, I must not look back. But this is idle talk. I made a discovery last night. By the light of the moon I came upon a strange and wondrous sight—a city of the dead, in the midst of a silent lake.

"Here—in this forest, captain?" exclaimed Hal.

"The end of the forest is here," was the answer. "See the trees break—before you lies a land unknown to civilised men."

The forest came abruptly to an end on the verge of a cliff that sloped down to a plain five hundred feet below.

On the right the descent was easier, and at the foot of the cliff there was the faint outline of a road.

Away, a mile inland, there was a lake, about three miles wide, and in the centre of it was a city built on arches and of stone.

Mapped out there were streets with miniature houses, and towers, square and strong, were dotted about. In the centre was a large building that was like a citadel of some old European city.

It was a city almost square and fully two miles in each direction, but from end to end there was no sign of life.

"What think you of that, Hal?" the Veiled Captain asked.

"I can think nothing," replied Hal, "I can only look and wonder."

"But see there—the main way that leads to it," said the Veiled Captain, pointing to a long narrow bridge with endless arches, that ran from the city to the mainland. "The only road—no boats, no anything for the use of an invader. Provisioned, a hundred men could defend it from two thousand."

"It is a great discovery," said Hal. "In such a place we may look for treasure."

"Or relics of the past that are better than gold," said the Veiled Captain. "But see—we are too late—others have discovered it—the Red Robins have found another nest."

He pointed as he spoke to a jutting part of the cliff fully three miles away. Down this a number of small black specks were cautiously moving.

"Let them go," said the Veiled Captain, "it will be but a trap for them. The means erected to keep the invaders from the city will also suffice to hold secure those within it. See there a herd of wild deer grazing close to Larry Turrell and his men. They see no danger in the approach of the unknown. Man is strange to them."

"A puff of smoke—two!" cried Hal; "and two of the beasts have fallen. The Red Robins will have a good breakfast."

"Go back to the men," said the Veiled Captain, "and bid them remain where they are until night. Then return to me."

Hal sped back with the tidings of the discovery made, and every man longed to come and look upon the strange sight on the plain.

But such was the discipline of the troop that no man stirred from the spot all day.

Lucia and Hal alone went back to the Veiled Captain.

In the afternoon Hal returned to say that the Red Robins had crossed the bridge, and taken up their abode in the Silent City.

"They are as rats in a trap," he said, "and our captain can kill or set free those whom he will."

It was not until the twilight hour that Hal and the men moved on. It was almost dark when the cliff was reached.

"HURRAH FOR THE VEILED OUT?" SMUDGE FAINTLY CRIED.

and the strange city of a bygone race could only dimly be seen below.

But all preparations had been made for their descent to the plain.

The Veiled Captain had chosen a spot where descent was comparatively easy, and, as the sun went down, leaving a glow on the craig he led the way, with Lucia close behind him, and Smudge, like a faithful watch-dog, following.

With the sure-footedness of the mountain goat the men followed their leader, clinging here, dropping there, but without slip or mishap safely reaching the plain below.

Then they gathered together, awaiting a short conference he was having with Hal.

One of the men, known as Old Brill, was finally summoned to their "palaver."

He was a man of sixty, and had been a traveller and wanderer all his life.

"He was not   tranger, as many knew, to the Dark Fores but he was usually a silent man and never bragged of his achievements.

"Brill," said the Veiled Captain, "have you ever been here before ?"

"No," replied the old man, "but I have heard of this place. When I had a run into the Dark Forest I met a man coming back. He told me of this City, but I didn't believe it. Some men are such liars, you know."

"But you see, Brill, he spoke the truth."

"Yes, Captain, and if I'd believed it I'd a come on and had a look at the place," was the simple reply.

"What did he say of it ?"

"Of the City, very little. He only looked at it from a distance, for he saw what he believed to be people moving about, and he didn't care to show alone."

"As he spoke the truth in one thing, so he may have done so in another. I, myself, saw, or fancied I saw, something moving about late this afternoon."

"I do not fear whatever there may be," the Veiled Captain continued, after a pause, "but it becomes me to go warily wherever I tread. I have no right to unnecessarily risk the lives of you men. I will go forward alone and reconnoitre."

"Captain," said Hal, earnestly, "I beseech you to let me go with you."

"Why?"

"Well, two are better than one."

"Sometimes, but two here will not serve. You can follow me slowly. Keep in a line with the Northern Star and you will be on my track. Not another word—you know me—I go alone."

And then, in a moment he was gone.

"He's right," said old Brill, "in scouting one man of pluck is enough. Two only hamper each other. But, I tell you, Hal, that I think we've got into a warm box if all that party told me is true."

"What did he tell you," asked Hal, uneasily

"Maybe it was lies," replied old Brill, easily; "anyhow, I didn't think it worth while bothering the Captain with it. He is not likely to be taken by surprise."

Lucia now drew up to the side of her brother and took his arm.

"Hal," she said, "you have let him go again alone."

"Let him," replied Hal, gruffly, "there's not much letting when he's bent on a thing. We've got to go on slowly."

"And here's my good dog to look after me," said Lucia, as Smudge came up.

Hal passed the word to the men, and they fell into a line behind him, two by two. Old Brill walked by Hal's side, and with scarce a sound the brave followers of the Veiled Captain went upon his trail.

They knew from experience that he was swift of foot, and already far ahead, and they got over the ground quickly.

It was rough here and there, and a prickly shrub was dotted about, which ere long made itself felt to those who carelessly trod too near it. Old Brill said the way they were dotted about reminded him of the cactus gardens of South America.

"Perhaps we are in a garden," suggested Hal.

"Well, it may be so," replied Old Brill, "but I won't say it is."

"Will you say it isn't?"

"No."

Hal softly laughed.

"You are a cautious old bird," he said, "always on the right side of the hedge."

The rough way soon ceased, and they came to the old road which Hal and the Captain had seen from the cliff.

It was not so smooth as it appeared up there, but it was better than the unprepared ground, being tolerably hard and even.

Here and there they came upon what seemed to be a pile of broken crockery by the roadside, which puzzled Hal not a little.

"What does it mean?" he asked. "Who on earth can have been shooting their rubbish here?"

"I can guess," said Old Brill, "but I can't say I'm right."

"Guess away."

"I think that this road was once all tiled, and that somebody took the trouble to break it up."

"It's long odds you are right," said Hal, "but, hark! what is that?"

They all stopped and listened.

From afar off, apparently in the middle of the lake, there came a long, wailing cry, piercing and shrill.

"What is it?" asked Hal, breathlessly.

"I won't even guess at that," returned Old Brill, "as I never heard the like afore."

"Hark! again!"

The cry was repeated, this time in a higher note, and the sound was followed by the shouting of men, and the trampling of feet upon a hard roadway.

CHAPTER XVII.

THE STRANGE CRY AGAIN—ON THE BRIDGE OF THE CITY OF THE LAKE—WHAT THE SIGHT REVEALED—WHAT WAY OF ESCAPE IS THERE FOR THE RED ROBINS?

"HURRY up, men," said Hal, "the captain may be in danger. Lucia, you keep to the rear, there may be work going on which is not fit for a woman to share in."

"Brother, why should I not share your peril?" Lucia asked.

"Because you would only hinder us, Lucia," he answered, "you know the captain's wishes in that respect."

Lucia argued no more but fell back with Smudge, who was her watch-dog now.

The men, needing no incentive, hurried forward in the wake of Hal and Old Brill.

They were kept to the road and in a few minutes came to the foot of the bridge that led to the strange city of the lake —in the faint light they could see it was massive and broad.

Here they halted for a moment, and as soon as all was still, Hal listened for any sound that might guide him to his next movement.

But save for the murmur of the wind all was still.

"Where's the captain gone?" Hal softly asked,

"Looks as if he'd got into trouble," replied Old Brill uneasily; "he's found this place, you may reckon. We'll go on."

As he spoke, the strange cry was heard again.

They were now quite near it. It did not seem to be more than a hundred yards away, and was *up in the air.*

It was most unearthly.

"Heaven save us!" gasped Old Brill, "what can it be?"

"Whatever it is," said Hal firmly, "it must not turn us from the path of duty."

"And that lies before us," said Old Brill.

There was no commotion among the men. Whatever they may have felt, like well-disciplined soldiers they gave no expression to their feelings.

As Hal and Old Brill moved forward they followed, silently.

Lucia and Smudge came last, and if the former had a fear in her heart, it was for the brave and mysterious leader of the band.

As for Smudge, he hardly knew himself, so little did he feel the terror of the hour.

He was like a man braced up by some strong stimulant, and, with scarce a quiver in his once too-sensitive nerves, he walked behind his charge with eye and ear on the alert to discover and protect her from danger.

Suddenly the whole band stopped.

There was no noise and unseemly bustle, but as if they formed the portions of one corporate body, the men came to a standstill.

Then a faint whisper, it could scarcely be called a sound, travelled down the line, and reached Lucia.

"The Captain !"

Yes, he was there. As the men were moving on, he stepped out from the shadow of the bridge, his upraised arm just visible in the gloom.

"Hal !"

In a low clear tone he spoke, and Hal answered him by stepping forward a pace.

" We can go no further until there is light. The Red Robins are here."

"What noise was that we heard, captain ? "

" You know as much as I do. It was sufficient to scare the scoundrels. They seem to me to have fled in all directions."

He spoke quite calmly, as if the terrible cry had in no way affected him. Hal was not ashamed to admit that it had both troubled and scared him.

"It is something I cannot understand," said the Veiled Captain, "but I am not childish enough to believe there is anything unnatural in it. I have been across the bridge to what appears to be the gates of the city. It is there that you and I and Brill can take our stand for the night. The rest had better return to the shore."

" And Lucia ? "

" It will be better for her not to be here."

The command was passed, and the men, without a word softly retraced their steps. Lucia lingered for a moment and the Veiled Captain, interpreting her hesitation, went to her side.

"Lucia," he said, "a little distance from the foot of the bridge you will find shelter for the night. Go, rest your self."

"And you ? " she asked.

" I guard the only road of escape for my foes," he replied.

" Again no sleep."

" Again and again, if need be. Good-night, do not linger here."

The strange wailing cry was heard again, overhead, and not far away.

" How awful ! " said Lucia, shuddering ; " it sounds like a wail for the dead ! "

"It is neither a wail for the dead nor the living," replied the Veiled Captain. "Daylight will explain it to us. Besides, what have we to fear?   Good night."

They parted, and Lucia glided away with Smudge at her heels.   The Veiled Captain returned to Hal and Old Brill.

Then, and during the night, when they spoke to each other they maintained the quiet tone referred to. It had been their way of speaking when in the ravine at the foot of Eagle Craig, and practice had made them perfect in speaking low, and yet distinctly, to anyone near.

"We have fallen on one of the long-hidden secrets of the earth," said the Veiled Captain.   "As far as I can see this city was the home of a people who has utterly disappeared.

He walked slowly on, and they followed him to what appeared to be a massive archway, with quaint weird figures carved upon the upper parts.

Under the shadow of it they paused.

"Here we wait for dawn," he said.

Old Brill and Hal dropped quietly to the ground, and lay at full length with their heads upon their arms, ready, like old campaigners, to make the best of everything and to get rest in the best form they could.

The Veiled Captain, with a scarcely audible footstep, paced slowly to and fro.

As the night passed, the quietude increased. The wind dropped, and literally no sound broke the stillness.

Nothing was heard of the Red Robins, nor anything moving to be seen.   Nor was the strange cry heard again.

Dawn at last; a faint light in the sky, reflected in the lake, and then the roseate flush that accompanies the rising sun.

The sky was clear, every dark cloud had disappeared, and high in the heaven was a pretty mottling of white cloud.

Neither Hal nor Old Brill had slept.

As the light advanced they rose up, and with their leader took a look about them.

It was the strangest scene they had ever looked upon.

The City, built of massive stone, was of an order of architecture they had never heard of or conceived.

The gateway under which they stood was covered above

with fantastic figures carved in the solid stone. Serpents, dragons, men and women of a curious half negro, half mystical type of features formed the leading figures, but flowers, fruit, and quaint ornaments abounded.

The city looked more vast than it had appeared to be from the summit of the cliff.

Before the amazed beholders lay a view of broad streets, squares, terraces and shapely buildings of stone, all like the archway, richly carved, and in some places ornamented with gold.

There was one tower on the far right that appeared to be built of the metal which is the purest and most valuable on earth.

"Well, Captain," said Hal, "what do you make of it?"

"Nothing," said the Veiled Captain, "as yet."

"I've heard of places like this," said Old Brill, "but put it down to lies. But it just shows us that the world wasn't made yesterday."

On one side of the archway there was an opening about wide enough to admit a man.

It seemed as if it led to a staircase, but on inspection no staircase could be found.

It was simply a shaft that went right up to the top of the tower.

"Curious place for a chimney," said Hal.

"It is no chimney," replied the Veiled Captain, "for no fires have ever been lighted here. But I think I can understand it. Now is not the time to investigate these things. We have other business on hand, Hal. From this place shall no Red Robin, save one, go forth alive."

"Bravely spoken, Captain," said Hal, "But why spare one?"

"For Larry Turrell," replied the Veiled Captain, "I have an especial and a fitting doom. The rest shall be dealt with as ordinary felons and murderers."

They passed out from the shaft-like opening, and Old Brill, by direction of their leader and Hal, walked back to the bridge.

The Veiled Captain alone closely scanned the city again.

It was as a place of the dead.

He judged that the face was turned in his direction, and he stepped into the open to show himself. The moment he did so it disappeared.

"I was right," he said, with a soft laugh, "it is well that they should know that I am here."

Then he called to Hal, and gave instructions for the men. A hunting party was sent out for meat, and rude shelter formed for the night for Lucia. The rest were to camp in the wood, and be ever ready to advance.

No arrangement was made to guard the bridge by any additional body of men, at which Hal wondered. He ventured to refer to it.

"Hal," said the Veiled Captain, with a soft laugh, "if nobody were near the bridge would be well guarded. You know me. It is in no boasting spirit I speak, but as a simple matter of fact. If they know I am *here*, they will try to find some means of escape, by the lake, or the air for aught I know, but they will not venture this way. An infant with a toy gun might guard this bridge."

And Hal felt in his heart that what his leader said was true.

Whatever road they might seek for safety it would be some other than the only visible outlet from the City of the Lake

CHAPTER XVIII.

IN THE DESERTED PALACE—RIGAULT SEES THE VEILED CAPTAIN—WAS IT A DREAM?—THE AWAKENING TO ITS REALITY.

THE discovery of the City of the Lake had been as wonderful to the Red Robins as it had been to the Veiled Captain and his band.

Larry Turrell, like Old Brill, had heard of such places, and treated the stories told him as legends. They were, indeed, no more than legends to the narrators, who could only speak of what they had heard from others.

The existence of the City of the Lake had never been believed in, but now the Red Robins had it before their eyes.

As previously related, they secured a supply of deer-meat, and with it they crossed the bridge in the afternoon, unconscious of being watched by their restless and unswerving foe.

On such men the beauty and strangeness of the place was, in a measure, lost.

They cared nothing for the architecture, or its history, nor that of its lost people; but they saw in it a good hiding-place, and possibly the depository of vast treasure.

"People who built a place like this," said Larry Turrell, "had other things beside stone to make them happy."

The sight of the Golden Tower inspired them with joy, and there was only one drop of bitterness in their cup, and that was a pretty big one, the fear that even here the Veiled Captain might trace them out.

We know that it was done, but they knew nothing of it during the first hours of their sojourn in the City of the Lake.

Acting on his old plan, Larry Turrell divided his men into two parties; one he took with him into the city to explore, the other remained under the command of Rigault by the archway under which the Veiled Captain passed the night.

They remained there, lying close, and, under the influence of fear rather than discipline, making very little noise, speaking in undertones when they spoke at all.

Darkness set in, and they knew nothing of the approach of the Veiled Captain. To them there had been no trace of his presence.

It was while they were whispering together, the hope of having got clear away from him forming their theme, that the piercing cry before described was heard.

On them it had a terrible effect, for it was right over their heads.

Every man sprang to his feet and stood aghast.

"What's that?" asked Rigault, as quietly as he could.

Nobody could answer him, and in a few seconds the awtul sound was repeated. Then, acting together like a herd of frightened deer, they ran in the direction of their comrades

This was the sound of scuffling feet heard by Hal and his friends.

In the gloom more than one of the Red Robins ran against some projecting ornament of the buildings, but, although some were sorely bruised, none actually disabled themselves.

Fortunately the road or street ran through to the square, where they found Larry Turrell and the rest of the men alarmed by the strange cries and the following commotion.

The flying Red Robins had a narrow escape of being fired into by their comrade, but Rigault, recognising the tall form of Turrell in the gloom, called out to explain who they were.

"What now, who is it yonder?" cried Turrell.

"We've got to some place where there's a ghost," replied Rigault, with affected lightness; "didn't you hear the howling?"

"We heard it," said Larry, "it's some trick of that veiled fiend's."

"Not that!" said Rigault. "He's not within miles of us. It was right up overhead."

"Well, come in here," said Larry Turrell, "we've found a rare place to skulk in. Veiled Captain or not he can't harm us to-night."

He led the way to a side of the square and entered a fine doorway, at the top of which there were small gleams of light.

"Precious stones of some sort," said Larry Turrell, "but we can't tell what they are until we get them down. Walk straight on—you won't fall."

A hard polished stone floor echoed to the sound of their footsteps, but the way was completely dark until Larry Turrell pushed a curtain aside and revealed a huge hall with a fire burning in the centre on the floor.

"Enter comrades," he said, "and feast on trapper fare where kings have fed."

They passed on, and gazed wonderingly around them. The

light of the burning wood only imperfectly revealed the magnitude and beauty of the place; but they could see that it was a hall of rare beauty, with mighty work in the way of stone and marble carving, while sparks of light dotted about betrayed the presence of precious stones.

"And can't be so very old either," said Rigault, "or that curtain would have rotted."

"That curtain," replied Turrell, "was woven in *threads of gold*. It won't rot for another day or two."

"We needn't go plundering any more," said Rigault cheerily.

"No," returned Turrell, "say that we get away from here, I'm satisfied that we shall be all rich men. Oh! that I'd fallen on this place ten years ago. I wouldn't now be living the life of a hunted wolf."

"It's no use howling over what you've done," said Rigault, "there may be better luck in store. We've got a chance. While there's life there's hope, you know."

"Yes," said Turrell, but his look showed that he had very little hope.

There, in the hall once trod by now forgotten kings, the Red Robins passed the night. They slept on—the just and unjust sleep alike when tired out—and it was not until the light of day had come that Larry Turrell awoke.

The sun shone through small openings in the hall that served for windows. They were glazed with thin sheets of horn stained different colours, and the effect was weird and beautiful in the extreme.

The hall or chamber was fully two hundred feet long by a hundred broad, and to describe the marvellous beauty of the workmanship would occupy many pages.

All that was quaint in design seemed to have been gathered there.

Rich ornaments, flowers, trees, beasts, birds, men, women, children, with jewels for eyes, seemed to be jumbled together upon the walls, but were in reality all arranged in wonderfully harmonious design.

Larry Turrell had looked upon the scene the day before, but with the renewed daylight it had a fresh fascination for him.

He lay on his back with his eyes roving from figure to figure until a footstep aroused him from his dream of wonderment.

It was Rigault, who came in by the curtained entrance.

He swaggered and endeavoured to look calm as usual, but Larry Turrell could see that something had troubled him.

"HE is here," he said.

"Yes," replied Rigault, laconically. "I peeped out now and saw him standing by the archway on the bridge. You know what that means. We are shut in HERE."

"Furies seize him!" cried Turrell in a paroxysm of passion.

"Ay! that is all very well," replied Rigault! "but the furies won't, and he will seize us unless we make a bold bid for liberty."

"In what way?"

"Make a rush for it—fight our way out."

"I'll think of it."

"Yes," sneered Rigault, "you will think of it, and think of it, and that is all you will do."

"And what will you do?" asked Turrell.

"I!" said Rigault, drily, "nothing. I am not leader. I await orders."

"Well, stop this wrangling!" muttered Turrell.

The men were now waking up, and as they arose, shaking themselves like beasts who had slept in their lair, Turrell told them the Veiled Captain had taken possession of the way by which they had entered the city.

"But of course it is not the only way out," he said, with assumed lightness, "places like this were not built without some means of escape in case of siege."

"You mean that as a soother, merely," said Rigault, in an undertone, "but for all that there may be something in it."

The palace, part of which they now occupied, stood at the top end of the square, commanding a view, down a straight broad road, to the archway.

The exterior of the palace, strange to say, was plainer than most of the buildings around, but for all that there was no meagreness in it.

Whoever built the place lacked neither materials, nor labour.

Larry Turrell went out with Rigault to see his foe, and no Veiled Captain was there.

Nor was there anyone in sight.

"Rigault," said Larry, "you've been dreaming."

"I was wide awake enough when I saw him," replied Rigault, curtly.

"But may you not have been mistaken? We've all had Veiled Captain on the brain, and it's a stiffish way to the bridge. You may have conjured up that accursed figure."

"I may have done so," returned Rigault, "but I don't think I did."

"Anyway, if he was there a little time ago he will come again."

It was arranged that they should set a watch at the entrance to the palace without showing themselves. If by noon the Veiled Captain did not reappear, nor any of his band show, then they might venture out.

Rigault soon began to have doubts about his vision.

After all he had only caught a hasty glimpse of the dreaded figure, and the moment he saw it he had retreated. Possibly it might have been fancy only.

Hour after hour passed, and the Veiled Captain was not seen again.

From the palace entrance the Red Robins could not see beyond the archway, as the bridge bore off at an angle to the left, and the houses at the bottom end of the square hid it from view, but there was no sound or sight of living beings for hours, and the hunted villains regained confidence.

Rigault was willing to admit that he had only glanced hastily at the figure, and himself set the example of showing a disbelief in what he had seen by strolling out into the square.

They were soon all out moving about, and still upon the watch, but there was no appearance of their dreaded enemy.

"Some of us ought to go outside and look round," said Rigault.

Who "some of us" were to be did not at first appear to be very clear. Nobody was at all in a hurry to play the part of scout.

Eventually the old thing was resorted to. Lots were drawn

for two men to take this duty, and fate decreed that two of the ordinary men named Greyling and Globb should go.

They started off and were watched by their comrades as they stepped warily down the broad roadway. On they went to the archway without pausing or looking back.

"The way is clear," cried Rigault, exultingly.

As he spoke the men passed under the archway, and at the same moment the Veiled Captain came out of the narrow, shaft-like opening, and grasped them by the collar.

Their amazed captain saw them drop their rifles as if terror had deprived them of all strength, and fall upon their knees.

A groan passed round the Red Robins, but no man spoke until their two comrades had been dragged further down from their view.

Then cries for mercy were borne upon the still air to the ears of their old comrades. They could even hear the word "mercy!" as it burst from their quivering lips.

"We cannot escape him," said Larry Turrell, turning away.

"For all that," said Rigault, "*I* do not give up all hope. There may be a secret way from this man-trap. Let us scatter about and seek it. To-night, with good or bad luck, let us re-assemble here."

Nobody stirred one step, as we have seen, to rescue the captured Red Robins. In the iron grasp of the Veiled Captain they were helpless. If they had not been, their terror would have made them so.

Without uttering a word he dragged them down to the bridge, with its parapet broken away here and there by Time, and, at the same moment, Hal, Old Brill, and two or three others came out of the wood to meet him.

They ran along a part of the shore and up the bridge, marvelling in their hearts at the strength of their young leader.

As they drew near he flung his captives away from him, so that they fell at the feet of the others.

"Take them away," he said, "and prepare for their trial if they think they need one."

"Mercy! mighty leader," gasped Greyling. "I am not fit to die."

"Nor fit to live," was the answer. "Take them away, Hal. I will see what has become of the rest."

He turned back alone, and Hal, with the aid of Old Brill, pinioned the arms of the captives.

They made no resistance, they seemed to be past it.

A dull hopeless look was in their eyes, and, as they were led from the bridge, their legs dragged rather than walked over the ground.

They were taken across the roadway into the wood, to a spot where the Veiled Captain's men had gathered around a broken marble monument of strange fantastic form, through which gushed a spring of water.

It was a picturesque scene, the men standing about in groups, with quiet, dignified mien, exhibiting no triumph over the capture of their foes, but grave and implacable as Justice herself.

The Red Robins looked around them in the dull, hopeless way of men who have no hope, but suddenly Globb gave his arms a wrench, and he was free.

His bonds had been carelessly knotted, and the yielding of the rope suddenly awoke him to a feeling that there was yet a chance for his life.

He was a swift runner, and he bounded back towards the city at a rate that outpaced Hal and some dozen others that started in pursuit.

He reached the wood, and, seeing the bridge apparently clear, bounded upon it.

But the Veiled Captain was at his post. Alone he was keeping guard upon the way to freedom, and as the Red Robin came bounding along the dreaded figure came forth and barred his way.

HIGH IN THE AIR HE HELD HIM.

"Man or fiend," cried the wretched man, hoarsely, "is there no escape from you?"

"None," replied the Veiled Captain, as he sprang upon him.

"Who are you?" cried the Red Robin.

The Veiled Captain whispered a word in his ear, and the doomed man cried out:

"It's a lie—it can't be!"

"Back there!" cried the Veiled Captain to Hal and the others who were coming up. "Leave this man to me."

He turned to the Red Robin and pinned him against the side of the bridge. The Veiled Captain had his back to his men.

"See here!" he said, whisking the veil aside. "Do I lie? Have you forgotten me?"

"You are not mortal; you cannot be!" was all the wretched man had to say.

He seemed to have lost all his strength, and made no further effort for his freedom.

The magnetic influence of the Veiled Captain's spirit deprived him, as a mesmerist does his victim, of all muscular power.

He felt himself raised like a 'child in the air, carried a short distance, and then tossed into the air.

He fell into the cold water of the lake, heard the splash he made, and went down into its depths without making one effort to save his life.

The water closed over him, eddying and whirling, and when it grew smoother a few bubbles came to the surface, but that was all.

Like a plummet the Red Robin went to the bottom to be seen no more.

CHAPTER XIX.

THE SECRET OF THE STRANGE CRIES—SMUDGE HAS HIS NEW-FOUND COURAGE TESTED—TWO MORE OF THE DOOMED.

THE fate of the other captive Red Robin was soon after decided.

He, like the others who had paid the penalty of their crimes before, had an accuser whose charge he could not deny.

The trial, the sentence, and the burial were speedily over.

In a nameless grave he was left in a wood untrodden for many a day by foot of man, there to moulder away.

That afternoon the Veiled Captain slept in the wood, watched over by Lucia, who hovered near.

Hall and Old Brill kept the bridge, and the other men all kept ready in case of their being needed.

Grave, quiet men, all.

Engaged in a stern work, which, apart from their desire to punish those who had wronged them, they felt to be their duty.

A people in a crude state must have some sort of law or it will soon cease to exist.

There is sure to arise one who will play the part of law-giver, and this the Veiled Captain had done.

And now the end was drawing on.

The band of ruffians who had made existence a burden to honest settlers were being decimated. By ones, by twos, by threes, they were being melted away.

Two of their officers were gone—two left.

And they were all shut up in the city of the lake.

A calm still rested on the place. All the day there had not been a breath of wind.

But when the night came on again, a breeze sprang up and Hal and Old Brill heard strange cries and moanings in the air.

"What can it mean?" asked Old Brill.

They stepped out upon the bridge and listened.

The sounds came from the summit of the tall arch way, now rising, now falling, but always horrible and discordant to the ear.

"I've heard many sounds," said Old Brill shuddering, "but never anything like this."

"If the captain isn't afraid of them," said Hal, "why should we be?"

"I don't believe in ghosts," rejoined Old Brill thoughtfully, "and never did. But what is it?"

"Nothing, absolutely nothing," replied the quiet voice of his leader.

The Veiled Captain had come upon them like a shadow, and was content to find them at their posts.

"Call that nothing?" asked Hal, as a wild screech uprose, swelled to a piercing sound, and died away.

"No," said the Veiled Captain. "Did you never hear of the wonders of the gardens of the Celestials—how they constructed niches and caverns, so that when the wind blew they gave out all sorts of sound, some musical, some otherwise?"

"I've heard of such things," said Old Brill, "but never believed them."

"Nevertheless the stories are true," returned the Veiled Captain. "The wind blew last night."

"Yes, it did."

"And you heard these sounds?"

"Yes."

"There has been no wind to day, and you did not hear them."

"No."

"Now, can you not see what is the meaning of that shaft which Hal thought was a chimney? Yes, Hal, when the wind blows there is something constructed above to give out sounds, intended to frighten foes, or it may be part of a fetish worship. It is strange, but there is nothing to fear. Now mark—the wind is rising—how the sounds rise and fall with it."

"Even now I know what it is," said Hal, "it gives me

a horrible sensation. What inventive fiends they must have been to have constructed such a thing."

"I go on duty now," said the Veiled Captain, " and Smudge shall be my companion. Send him to me."

"Smudge!" exclaimed Hal.

"Yes, Smudge," was the reply, "I have devoted myself to the task of giving him a *heart*. One of the processes is to make him familiar with things that inspire terror. Towards dawn we enter the city. Be here with all the men to guard this way."

He turned from him and they went their way, marvelling at what they called the freaks of their leader.

Take Smudge into the city—into the thick of the Red Robins!

It was running a risk, when secrecy was so much needed.

An exclamation, a false step on the part of a nervous man might lead to disastrous results.

But they knew that they had only to hear and obey.

No man on earth ever felt prouder than Smudge did, when he heard of the honour to be bestowed upon him.

"I am ready," he said, "my life is his."

Shouldering his rifle, he strode on to the bridge and joined his leader there.

And through the night they watched together.

Smudge unenlightened about the strange sounds in the air, heard them, and, if in his heart he felt fear, he did not show it in his body.

Erect, he kept to his post—pacing to and fro—muttering no word of complaint, showing no sign of terror.

During the night there was no sound in the city save one, when he thought he heard distant footsteps, but they soon died away.

Just before dawn there was a faint noise at the other end of the bridge, and the Veiled Captain's band, now headed by Old Brill and Hal advanced

A few words of command were given in an under-tone, and then the Veiled Captain touched Smudge on the arm.

"Come with me," he said.

Without the least semblance of hesitation, Smudge shouldered his rifle, and followed his leader.

He had already picked up the quiet step of the band, and, with scarce a sound, they went up the broad way to the square.

The light of the stars guided them, and it sufficed.

The square was reached, and they went slowly onward, the Veiled Captain stopping here and there to listen.

Presently he stopped, and with a sign of his hand bade Smudge be very still.

They were now at the entrance to the strange palace before described.

From the inside there came the faint murmuring of voices.

After listening awhile, the Veiled Captain entered through the open doorway.

Smudge followed.

They could now hear the speakers more plainly, and they apppeared to be two in number, and about thirty or forty feet away.

"It is strange," one was saying, "that none of the others have returned."

"Well, all we can do is to stay here and wait for daylight."

"Ay, that's so. Listen, didn't you hear something?"

It was Smudge, who had stumbled against some projecting piece of stone.

The Veiled Captain grasped his arm, and held him tight.

So they stood still, while the men who were just within the vast chamber before described, with the curtain raised, listened with all their ears.

"It was nothing," one said.

"It is horrible to live in this way," replied the

other, "trembling as we do at the flutter of a butter-fly's wing. Let us lie down and see if we can get some sleep."

The noise of men settling down was heard, but apparently the repose they sought did not come, for presently one spoke again.

"Are you asleep, Ben?"

"Hang it, no—never more wide awake. It's getting light, however, and that's some comfort."

The dawn had come, and light came stealing in.

It crept through the open door or gateway of the palace, gradually lighting up the passage and the two still figures there.

It was a great ordeal for a man to go through to keep so motionless, but Smudge went through it bravely.

He had the example of and his devotion to his leader to aid him in his task.

Rapidly came the light of day, and, when a glimpse of the vast chamber ahead could be got. The Veiled Captain motioned for Smudge to be ready.

"Now!" he said, in that soft whisper of his.

Like an avenging shadow, he swept down to the curtained doorway with Smudge at his heels.

There was light in the hall, and the two Red Robins, lying at full length upon the flags, simultaneously saw the dreaded form.

With a wild cry they leapt to their feet.

"Yield yourselves!" thundered the Veiled Captain.

But they turned in terror, and fled to the far end of the hall.

Swifly the Veiled Captain and Smudge followed.

At the upper end there was an opening, dark and dismal to look at, leading to a flight of steps.

Down this the Red Robins plunged.

After them went the swift pursuers.

Down nearly two score of winding steps they went, escaping a fall in a manner little short of the miraculous.

Below was a vault, lighted through various openings,

small shafts it seemed, a most dismal place.

It was like a resting-place of the ancient dead.

Although a vault it was marvellously dry, and a cool air rushed through from various directions.

In square holes in the wall were grinning skulls; to the right and left, slender graceful columns supporting the roof.

The Red Robins had lost ground, and their pursuers were upon them.

The Veiled Captain seized one by the throat, and dashed him against the wall.

Smudge, with a strength he did not think he was possessed of, threw the other to the ground.

"Yield, knaves!" cried the Veiled Captain.

They made no answer.

Like hunted beasts fairly caught and cowed, they offered no resistance.

"Secure your man," cried the Veiled Captain.

Smudge pressed the Red Robin's hands across his chest, held them with one hand, and took a piece of slender strong cord from his pocket.

He had been taught the trick of securing a prisoner quickly, and two turns of the rope with a slip-knot had him fast.

Then for the first time the man he had captured recognised him.

"Smudge!" he said.

"Yes, Tyler," was the reply, "it's Smudge; but not the Smudge you used to kick and cuff whenever the humour seized you."

The Veiled Captain had also secured his prisoner, who was regarding him with awe.

"Rigault is right," he said, "you *are* a fiend. You've got a power of taking the pluck out of us. As a man I'm more than your equal; and I never before lacked courage, but now——"

He could say no more. Tears of mortification sprang into his eyes, and his head sank upon his breast.

The other man was even more mortified.

"Taken prisoner by Smudge!" he said. "Here, take me away and let the end come. Do not let any of my old comrades witness my degradation."

"Whether they do or not," replied the Veiled Captain calmly, "is for me decide. If you would escape further humiliation come quietly with me."

In doubt and wonder—doubt as to the possibility of his being there with Smudge alone, wonder at the crushing power of his presence—they allowed themselves to be led up the steps like dogs on the chain.

Through the great hall they went, the Veiled Captain taking no visible notice of its splendour, and so out into the full light of day.

CHAPTER XX.

WITHIN A GREAT MAZE — THE SCENE IN THE MORNING—RIGAULT IN SEARCH OF A CLUE.

THE Red Robins had not been able to carry out their original idea of meeting in the square, with the exception of the two who were captured by the Veiled Captain and Smudge. The rest had been fairly lost.

Surely, of all strange places in this world, the City of the Lake was the strangest.

The interior was a maze.

Many of our readers have had experience of mazes, such the one at Hampton Court, and will well understand how easy it is to get in, and how hard to get out.

So it was with the centre of the City of the Lake with the addition of the maze of streets being ten times more difficult than any maze known in modern times.

Larry Turrell and Rigault, for instance, went together, and, in the search for a subterranean way of escape, penetrated into many wonderful places.

They went through streets and courts, into narrow and broad ways, and were finally lost.

When the day was almost past and they sought to return, then they found the difficulty they were in.

Hither and thither they turned to find themselves in streets that came abruptly to an end.

They picked up some of the band, and with them wandered here and there in their fruitless endeavours to get back to the place they started from.

Seven in all did they pick up, and the rest they never saw again in this world.

They were lost, hopelessly lost, and no comrade of theirs ever set eyes upon them again.

Hunger troubled the nine men who wandered together, but, weary and heartsore, they huddled together in a corner of a street when darkness came on.

There they passed the night.

And when the morning came they rose up, nine grim, silent, despairing men.

It was broad daylight, but early as yet, and with set teeth they renewed their efforts to escape.

One turn, two turns, brought them —could it be ?— yes, to the great square.

Within easy hail of their previous haunt they had passed the long, dark hours.

"This is an accursed place," said Rigault, " built by some magician"'

"The Veiled Fiend, perhaps," said Larry Turrell.

"You speak of him, and behold," said one of the men.

He pointed across the square towards the road that led to the bridge, and there saw the Veiled Captain and Smudge with the two men they had captured.

They were standing still, and the Veiled Captain was seen beckoning somebody to approach.

The Red Robins were close to their previous haunt, and lost no time in getting under cover.

From the doorway of the ancient palace they looked forth upon a scene that added fresh terror to their lives.

Hal and old Brill appeared, heading the other followers of the Veiled Captain, all marching with the regularity of well-disciplined soldiers, but with no sound that reached the ears of the Red Robins.

The cat-like footstep practised, and made perfect by them, could not be heard far away.

I nsilence they opened out and formed a semicircle round the prisoners, and their captors who stood with bowed heads like broken men.

Then out from the ranks there stepped two men who confronted their prisoners, and said a few words which reached the ears of the Red Robins in the form of a faint murmur.

The prisoners seemed to be asked for a reply, but they just lifted their heads and made a movement that indicated they had none to give.

Then they were left to the Veiled Captain—his men suddenly facing about and turning their backs on their leader.

The prisoners were touched in turn upon the arm and they looked up.

A movement of the hand and the Veil was drawn aside for a moment.

Larry Turrell saw his captive followers stagger back a pace, and a cry from their lips was borne shrilly on the air.

The rest of the tragic scene was speedily over.

The followers of the Veiled Captain faced about again, and half-a-dozen stepped from the ranks.

Side by side stood the doomed men. Behind them a stone wall.

A movement from Hal and the rifles were levelled.

The report—it sounded like one shot—followed, and the Red Robins lay huddled on the ground.

They were lifted up, placed within the shadow of an angle of the wall, out of sight, and then the avengers, in that strangely quiet manner, marched away.

For awhile the Red Robins stood still without uttering a word. The silence was broken by Rigault.

" Well, Larry," he said, in his constrained would-be jaunty manner, "what do you make of that?"

"Let us go into the hall and talk it over," was Turrell's reply.

In the hall the first thing they did was to search for such poor scraps of food which might be left.

They found a few pieces of deer-meat, but it was very little for nine men.

When they had eaten all, they half-filled their pipes, economising their last scrap of tobacco, and, lighting up, smoked awhile in silence.

"If we knew who was fighting against us, it would be something," said Rigault. "Can't you think of somebody who is likely to play this game upon us?"

"No,' replied Turrell.

"No," echoed the others.

"Think," said Rigault, "call back to memory all you have wronged."

"They need no calling back," replied Turrell, with a moan. "I am haunted day and night now. I am a child, and I don't mind confessing it. I feel sometimes as if I should be glad when it is all over."

"While there is life there is hope," said Rigault.

"Little life," returned Larry Turrell, "and no hope."

The seven men, ruffians of the coarser type, looked at him with lowering eyes.

In common with men who have done evil, reaping its fruit, they associated their misfortunes with the criminality or neglect of others.

On Larry Turrell they fixed the blame,

But they only dare mutter it among themselves at first, until a few words reached his ears. His eyes flashed up with the old fire.

"What do you say, you dogs?" he asked.

"We blame you for all," replied one of the men.

"How do you make that out?" asked Turrell. "I was not aware, Dan Grimes, that there was anything of the saint about you."

"For all that," replied Grimes, "we are white compared to you."

"Don't talk rubbish," interposed Rigault. "We are all pretty well tarred with the same brush."

"But you forget one thing which we don't," said

Grimes, "didn't the veiled man, or whatever he may be, say that Turrell was to be left to the last? It was posted up. We all read or heard of it. And why? Because he wants him to suffer most."

"I see what you are aiming at," said Turrell, "but the game of giving up won't do. Our enemy does not want any assistance. He comes and takes us when he pleases."

"Anyway," said Grimes, "we want a chance of our lives."

"How?"

"We would like to take up quarters by ourselves."

"Go, and be hanged to you," said Turrell fiercely, "if you had not been such a white-livered lot of curs we need not be in the fix we are."

Grimes rose up and the other six men followed his example.

Turning to Rigault, Grimes said:

"If you had been our leader we might have had more heart, but Turrell is only a blusterer—won't you come with us?"

"No," replied Rigualt, "I don't shirk my duty—I stand by him to the last—I keep my path."

Grimes shrugged his shoulders, and, followed by the other six, departed.

"We are diminished now," said Turrell, "there is little left of the once terrible Red Robins."

"I let them go," replied Rigault, "because our only chance of safety now lies in the smallness of numbers. I have long seen that the men hampered us, they are better gone."

"I wonder where the others are—those we lost yesterday?" said Turrell thoughtfully.

"Wandering in that maze," returned Rigault, "the big man-trap set, I should say, for any foe that might invade the city. If we only had the secret of it, we might lure the Veiled Fiend and his men into it, and leave them there."

"That's not a bad thought," said Turrell, "but we want the key; you are a better educated man than I

am, Rigault--can't you suggest some place to look for
it?"

"The ancients," said Rigualt—"I allude to those
who lived thousands of years ago—made all records
on stone—their weights, their measures, their history
were all graven on marble or stone that would defy
the work of time."

"Was that so," said Turrell, "they must have had
little to write."

"Even letters were written on clay and burned
into bricks," continued Rigault; "you need not go further back than to Babylon for that."

"Isn't that far enough?"

"This place is older than Babylon, perhaps. Anyway, Larry, I'll undertake to say that a plan of the
maze is to be found somewhere."

"But where?"

"Most likely here. This seems to have been a
kingly residence, and such works were kept in the
Royal Vaults—if I may use the word. We have not
had a look below yonder. Suppose we do it now?"

"I'm willing," said Turrell. "Anything but lying
here and thinking."

The way down to the vaults has been described.

It had been observed by Larry Turrell on the
previous day, but no attempt at exploration had been
made.

Together the two deserted Red Robin leaders descended the steps to the vaults below.

Larry Turrell's eyes fell upon the grinning skulls in
the wall.

"It's a tomb," he said, "come out of it. I can't
stand that sort of thing."

"Don't be in a hurry," said Rigault, coolly. "These
are not real skulls. Bones as well as flesh would have
been dust long ago."

He walked up to one of the openings and tapped
upon the skull with his forefinger.

"As I guessed," he said, "cut out of stone and
polished. What splendid work. This is a sham

tomb, Larry. I guess we shall find what we want here." ☺

The vault at first did not appear to be of very great dimensions, but it was so constructed as to be deceptive.

The columns were arranged so as to hide, from a hasty view, a passage leading to another underground chamber.

This appeared to be a facsimile of the others, and a third one was discovered.

This was different.

On every side there was nothing but polished marble, with openings in the upper part to let in the light.

They were smaller than in the other vaults, and the light therefore much fainter.

But after a few minutes, Rigault, who had keen eyes, could see with tolerable distinctness.

He began to examine the walls, and a cry of joy burst from his lips.

"What is it?" asked Larry.

"We are on the right track," Rigault answered, "we shall find the plan of the maze here."

The inscriptions on the wall he first examined were unintelligible to him.

Birds, beasts, men, women, and curiously-shaped scrolls were mingled together—finely traced on the surface of the marble so as not to be readily discerned.

Slowly and patiently Rigault worked his way round the chamber, examining every inch of the marble.

He was about two thirds round when another cry escaped him.

"I've got it," he cried.

Larry went over to his side, and, staring at the wall, saw nothing but a lot of lines twisting in and out each other.

"It looks like childish scribbling," he said.

"Very careful scribbling," returned Rigault.

He put his finger in a straight line, and bade Turrell look at it.

"Do you see nothing different in it to this?" touching a curved line.

"It seems to be a little deeper cut?" replied Turrell.

"Just so, and therein lies the secret," said Rigault. "Keep to the deeper lines, and we shall find out the maze. And see here—this spear—and here is another, and another. They point to the way to go. Alternate east and north is the way in—alternate north and east is the way out."

"It's all Dutch to me," said Turrell, shaking his head. "I can't make head or tail of it."

"I do," said Rigault, "you leave all to me. Now, if we only had some provisions——"

"But we haven't, Rigault, and I feel as if I could eat a horse."

"There is one thing about this city," said Rigault, as he slowly retraced his steps. "Not a single bird seems to live here, or even fly over it."

"It's the fearful sounds we hear that's driving them away."

"I daresay you are right, Turrell. I wonder if——"

"If what? Speak out."

"The place is really haunted."

"We are, if the place is not," said Turrell grimly.

They returned to the hall, where, after carefully examining their rifles, they went cautiously to the outer archway to see if their foes were about.

No human being was in sight, but close to the door was a coarsely-woven rustic basket filled with something.

Attached to the outside was a piece of parchment, on which was written:

"The Veiled Captain does not care to war with starving foes. Eat."

The two men looked at each other in utter amazement.

"This beats all," Turrell said.

"I can't say anything to it," replied Rigault.

"Perhaps it is a trap—the food, if food it is, may be poisoned."

"No," said Turrell, "he is not so merciful."

He took up the basket, and, opening it, found some deer-meat and half-a-dozen birds, apparently fine pigeons, ready cooked.

There was also some wild fruit, a species of apple.

They sat down where they were and fell upon the food thus strangely provided for them.

Hunger is a sharp thorn, or a whip it may be, so, as other men in their place would have done, they ate first and thought of the consequences afterwards.

CHAPTER XXI.

LUCIA AND THE CAPTAIN—SMUDGE HAS WORK TO DO—THE LONE TEMPLE BY THE RIVER.

IT was high noon, and the Veiled Captain lay upon the sward by the spring in the wood.

By his side sat Lucia, busy with her needle, repairing a tear in her dress.

A short distance away a number of the men had gathered in a group, partaking of the midday meal.

Of provisions there was no apparent lack, for in the distance were two men engaged in cutting up a deer suspended, with another, from the lower branch of a tree.

And gathered in big rough-made rush-baskets there was a variety of wild fruit, and several sorts of edible fungi which the experienced eyes of the Veiled Captain's men had enabled them to select from the injurious.

It was a peaceful scene, and, with the exception of the Veiled Hero, such as one may often find in new countries, where the pioneer is master of wood and plain.

The men, as usual, were softly speaking when they spoke at all. The Veiled Captain was quietly looking at Lucia through his luminous veil, and she was silent too.

Thus they remained for awhile, until Lucia had finished her task and dropped the hem of the garment she had been engaged upon.

Then the Veiled Captain spoke :

"You have fears, Lucia," he said, " which I feel to be groundless. There is nothing in dreams."

Lucia looked at him mournfully, with a suspicion of tears in her bright eyes.

"In ordinary dreams," she said, "I know it is so, but there are special visions of warning now-a-days, as there used to be in the old times."·

"And you have had a vision ? "

"No, a dream."

"Well, what was it ? "

" Three nights in succession it has come to me," said Lucia, "not as a dream only, but as a vivid picture burnt into my brain as the potters burn the design into their ware. I feel that this dream is part of myself, and will be a lasting memory while I live."

"Let me hear what this terrible dream was like," said the Veiled Captain.

"It is your habit to treat my fears with lightness," Lucia said, " because you think they make me unhappy, but I cannot shake off what I feel, even at a word from you. In my dream I saw you and all here shut up in a vast hall, where the light of day came through one blood-red window above.

" One ray only entered the hall," continued Lucia, "and it fell upon YOU."

" That was something in my favour, Lucia," he said.

" You still jest——"

"Lucia, I have ceased to jest."

"I beg your pardon, I mean you still speak lightly for my sake, but the dream was too real—I saw you and the others slowly waste away. until all the horrors of starvation, were stamped upon you—the sunken cheeks, the bloodless lips, the wasted frame— oh! it was horrible. Finally I beheld you all lie down, die, and moulder away."

"Lucia," said the Veiled Captain, "all this is very terrible from a woman's point of view, but, believe me, no dream, or a hundred dreams, even if they were my own, could turn me aside from my course."

"No," said Lucia, "and you will die and leave broken hearts behind you."

She rose up in the petulant manner of a woman thwarted in her will and walked quickly away. The Veiled Captain half rose, as if to stop her, but with a half-suppressed sigh sank back again.

"What have I to do with dreams—who will know me if I fail in my venture—failure!—the thought that in the end the villain may triumph—for the triumph will be Larry Turrell's even if he alone should survive—but no—it will never be—I too have had my dream— months ago and THAT will come true if no other does."

He was roused from his meditations by a footstep, and, looking up, beheld Smudge before him.

"Well?" he said.

"I have done as you wished, noble captain," replied Smudge, "the second lot of food was placed in the centre of the square."

"And none saw you?"

"There was nobody in sight.'

"You went alone?"

"It was your orders, captain, that I should do so, and I obeyed."

"You have done well, and you will be a truly brave man ere you die," said the Veiled Captain.

Smudge's cheeks flushed and his eyes lighted up with pleasure. The praises he received were very sweet to him, coming from such lips.

"There is other news, captain," he said, after a pause.

"What is it?" his leader asked.

"The Red Robins are broken up," replied Smudge,

"a portion is in the interior of the city, and seven men live in one of the houses of the square. Larry Turrell and Rigault are alone in the great hall we visited."

"Larry and Rigault can wait," said the Veiled Captain. "The only thing to be done with regard to them is to see that they do not pass our guard and get away. Of the seven men we will take three to-morrow morning."

"Early, captain?"

"At dawn. I shall want you, Hal, and Brill. Be ready an hour before sunrise."

A wave of the hand dismissed Smudge, who, bowing low, left his leader. The Veiled Captain rose up and slowly sauntered away.

Lucia had been watching him from a distance, and with a quick movement, she stepped out so that she was right in his path.

With a courteous movement of his hand he bade her stand aside.

"One of my sad hours is approaching," he said "and then it is better for me to be alone."

"Oh that you would let me be a comfort to you!" she pleaded.

"Lucia," he said, "whatever I may say in the future to you—there can be no moving me—if the bare utterance of the words 'I love you' are of value, pray take them from my lips with the assurance that they are honestly spoken—but there I stop."

"Your will is law," she said, and with a sob and sigh mingled, she stood aside so that he could pass.

He walked on out of the range of the camp, bearing slightly to the left until he came to a narrow stream running through the wood.

It was one of the tributaries to the lake and on its banks there was a small temple, plain and square, and standing erect and strong, save the porch, which had been thrown down.

Lying on the ground and more than half buried in

the thick coarse grass that grew around, were three hideous idols, each with a jewel representing a solitary eye in the centre of the forehead.

Passing them by with scarce a glance, he entered the temple and looked around him with the half-curious glance of one who has been there before and only partially examined it.

There was little in it to please the eye.

Plain, square, and massive were the walls, with round openings here and there to let in the light.

On the walls of polished marble there was a number of hieroglyphics and outlines of animals delicately traced on the surface, all evidently with a meaning, but far from being clear at first to the Veiled Captain.

"This must be the place Hal spoke of," he said, "and it was the upper end that gave out the hollow sound."

He walked to the end and struck his heel upon the hard stone floor on which lay a heap of dust.

A faint booming sound was the response below.

"That is not an ordinary vault beneath me," he said.

He went out, and, having pulled off the lower branch of a species of fir-tree, returned with it to the temple.

Making a broom of it, he swept aside some of the dust in the centre, and, kneeling down, carefully examined the floor.

At first he could only see very faint lines where the stones had been fitted together with marvellous exactness, but on one particular stone there was some tracery which he fancied matched that upon the wall.

A quick comparison assured him that this was the fact, but why it should be so, or of what use it could be to him or others, was a complete puzzle.

But that there was some meaning in it he was as certain as a man who has only his reason to guide him can be.

He worked his way all over the stone until he came to a small circle in the tracery. It was about three inches in diameter, and it seemed to him that there the cutting was deeper than usual.

He put his hand upon it, and felt a slight current of air.

It was no more than would have come through a pin-hole in a board, but it was THERE.

He pressed upon it with all his might, and it began to sink slowly.

"I shall get at some secret here," he said.

As he spoke the circular piece of stone suddenly shot out of sight, and the slab on which he was kneeling turned on end upon a pivot in its centre.

He saw a yawning gulf beneath, and strove to save himself from falling.

First he threw himself back, and then he clutched at the edge of the opening,

In vain !

There was nothing to get a fair hold of, and down he went.

The instant that he disappeared the slab righted itself, the bolt of stone shot back into its place, and all was as before.

A few minutes later Lucia appeared at the entrance to the temple and peered in.

Seeing it was empty, she slowly entered and looked round.

" Not here," she said, " and yet I saw him pass in. I have not moved my eyes from the doorway since. Where is he ? "

She stared around her in wonderment, as well she might.

Slowly her face paled, and she shuddered.

" Can it be," she muttered, " that after all he is not of this world ? Have we been following an avenging spirit ? "

" No !" she added, quickly, "he is mortal, but not to be numbered among common men. He has passed out and gone back to the camp. I will seek him there."

She sought him there, and, of course, found him not. Nor was he on the bridge with a guard, nor did he, as the weary hours went by, return.

In gloomy council did Hal, Lucia, old Brill, and Smudge gather together.

"Some accident has befallen him," said Hal. "That temple may be a man-trap. The whole place seems to be a vast bit of mechanism in stone."

"I shall not be sorry to leave it behind me," said old Brill, "I had a dream last night——"

"What was it?" asked Lucia, quickly.

"Oh! I don't believe in such things," said old Brill, quickly, "but it wasn't a pleasant dream, and it has kind o' stuck to me. I saw the whole lot of us starving-—"

"In a vast hall?" interposed Lucia.

"Yes, that was it," replied old Brill. "You've guessed it."

"I dreamt the same thing myself," said Lucia.

"Oh, hang dreams!" said Hal. "There is nothing in them. We've got a reality to deal with—the captain's disappearance."

"He will be here by dawn," said Smudge, confidently, "for he has called upon three Red Robins. The notice is prepared. It is to be posted ere the night comes."

"That is my task," said Hal. "I can go and return like a shadow. But, say, what is to be done about our missing captain?"

"Nothing," said old Brill. "He will return."

"If he does not," said Smudge, "his wishes ought to be carried out. We must secure three of his foes."

"Easier said than done without his help," muttered Hal.

"You can but do your best," returned Lucia.

CHAPTER XXII.

THE NIGHT PASSES AND THE VEILED CAPTAIN DOES NOT RETURN—CAPTURE OF, THE THREE RED ROBINS.

SLOWLV passed the day, and night came on.   The Veiled Captain was still away.

Immovable, the big slab rested in the temple, and no sound from beneath broke the stillness of another quiet eve.

It was known now to all the band that their leader had suddenly and, to them, unaccountably disappeared.

There was not so much in the length of the time he had been away, as in his going without a word to Hal or Lucia, a thing he had never done before.

All he had said to Lucia was that one of his sorrowful fits was coming on and, as usual, he wished to be alone for awhile.

But the length of his absence was too great to be associated with his ordinary attacks of sadness.

Still there was no panic.

Every man was on the alert, and ready to do his duty.

Hal, now in command, was as implicitly obeyed as the Veiled Captain himself.

Meanwhile, the seven men who had separated themselves from Larry Turrel and Rigault, lay hidden in a house on the right side of the square and close to what may be termed the bridge road.

It was two days since they had parted from their leader, and they had not set eyes on him since.

To them as to him there came a gift of food, and they had partaken of it with something of the feeling of being preserved like wild beasts for slaughter.

The house they were in now was nothing like the palace in which they formerly were.   It was solidly built, but there was little or no ornament in it, and no jewels serving as eyes for sculptured figures.

They talked of little else but of schemes to get away, all of which were abandoned almost as soon as conceived.

If by any means they could have made a raft, they might have had a chance at night; but, in all their wanderings in that strange city, they had found no sign of timber.

It was all built of stone.

On the night when the Veiled Captain was missing they determined to see if a close watch was still set upon the bridge, and were going out in a body when a stern voice at the door drove them back.

"Three of you will be called for in the morning," said the voice. "Draw lots, who it shall be. If you do not obey, ALL will be taken."

So inspired with terror were they, that they ran like frightened sheep back into the room, and remained there listening for awhile.

At length the moon rose up, and, its rays coming through the holes that served there as elsewhere in the city for windows, lighted up the place sufficiently for them to see each other.

"Three are called," said one suddenly, "and we are told to draw lots."

"Better obey," said another, "it gives four of us a chance."

"A poor one," muttered a third.

Then ensued a silence, to be broken, by and by, by one more resolute than the rest.

"We can but die. Let us refuse to obey this veiled fiend, and fight for it."

"Agreed," said a second.

"Agreed," cried a third.

Then the four remaining men with the quick instinct of cowardly self-preservation saw their chance of escape.

"Agreed," they cried together, each in his heart resolving to back out of the fighting.

Not a word was exchanged between the four, but they seemed to understand each other, and, without any apparent design, the seven men broke up into two groups.

Though no plans were discussed, nor a whisper passed on the subject, the four knew exactly what would be done when the hour for action came.

To what a pass had continuous terror reduced these once daring men.

It was the CERTAINTY that death awaited them when summoned, that made their hearts like wax.

Only the very bravest of men can face inevitable destruction.

With a clear conscience a martyr can walk boldly to the stake, but the Red Robins were men who had every reason to fear the consequences of their sins.

Therefore at the prospect of death they became as children.

We will not dwell upon the anxious hours they passed before the dawn came. It was at hand when a voice was heard, with footsteps without.

The trio, true to their resolve to fight, sprang to their feet with loaded rifles. The other four held back, and suddenly raised their weapons and covered their own friends.

"Hands up," they cried, "you are wanted and must go."

The astounded men had no time to remonstrate, or even to grasp the real nature of their position.

Such a depth of treachery in friends they had never even dreamt of, although they might have thought it possible had they reflected on Crashleigh's fate.

But, absorbed in their own anxieties, they dwelt but little on the past.

The next moment half-a-dozen men entered the room, Hal and Smudge foremost. The four traitors fled by a side doorway.

Resistance on the part of the three men was useless, and, their arms being secured, they were led away.

Not a word was spoken to them, nor did they say anything until they turned out of the square into a narrow bye-way, with a flight of steps leading to an upper part of the street.

Then one of the captives said, " I don't see *him.* Where is he ?"

"Our captain will be with you ere long," replied Hal, gruffly.

By the steps stood Lucia, armed with the light rifle the Veiled Captain had given her.

Her face looked pale, and her eyes were troubled, for there had been no tidings of their leader, no sign of him through the watches of the night.

"You can rest there," said Hal to the men. "You will not be troubled to travel much further."

They understood but too well that they had arrived at their place of execution, and, in sullen despair, they flung themselves down by the wall at the foot of the stairs.

The men who accompanied Hal and Smudge kept a watch over them while a consultation was held with Lucia.

"The appointed hour for their execution has come," Hal said ; " ought we to delay ? "

"He ought to be here," returned Lucia, " but I fear we shall see him no more."

"He will come back to us," said Smudge, "I have no fear of it."

"You, once the coward," said Hal, "put heart into us now. We will hope on, but what has come to him is a bitter mystery. These men must have an hour's grace—no more."

"Go to the camp and see if any of the scouts have tidings of him," said Lucia; " a certainty will be better than this terrible doubt."

"I can keep guard over these men," said Smudge.

It was a congenial task to him.

In the old days he had borne many a cuff and kick from these men, as he had from the rest of the Red Robin band. Now was his hour, and he, as many others would have done, made the most of it.

Hal and the other men went away, the latter remaining on guard at the bottom of the street while Hal hurried over the long bridge to the shore.

Lucia remained with Smudge, and the two kept a close watch upon the prisoners.

Their restless eyes flashed with the bitterness they felt. Smudge saw it, and had a difficulty in repressing a chuckle.

"You little thought of this day," he said, "when you used to treat me like a dog. But it shows that even a worm *can* turn, as the old proverb says."

"I'd like to have you alone to deal with," growled one of the men.

"I should not fear it NOW, Delf," replied Smudge, addressing the man by name, "I've had a heart put into me. Bah! to think that I was ever afraid of you! It makes me ill."

"Smudge," said Lucia, quietly.

He turned to her with an apologetic look in his face.

"I know it is wrong," he said, "but I have suffered. However, they are doomed men and I will say no more."

Nor did he address one of them again.

They reviled him, feeling free to do so as the one being they dreaded so much was not there.

Somehow they got an inkling that there was something in their favour in his absence, and as the minutes fled they got bolder.

Possibly, after all, their lives might be spared.

The return of Hal soon dispelled this illusion.

Lucia, hearing his footstep, looked up quickly, hoping that he was the bearer of good tidings.

But a glance sufficed to show that he brought with him nothing to cheer her.

Loosening the lower bonds of the Red Robins, which had been put on to prevent their flight, he bade them stand up.

"You have five minutes to live," he said, "no more. If you have anything to say against the justice of your doom, say it now."

"We want to know why we are to be slaughtered

like cattle?" asked he who had been addressed by Smudge by the name of Delf.

"And who is the man who has pursued us so remorselessly?" demanded another.

"Ask yourselves if you do not deserve your doom," said Hal. "Think of your past, and tell me, if you can, of one instance when you in your anger spared man, woman, or child."

"We spared *you*," said Delf.

"Because I, with others, yielded to you," replied Hal. "I thought that the Red Robins, as others did, were all-powerful in our country, but another has taught me that you could be broken up like glass. Enough! I have done with you."

"At least tell us who is our greatest foe," said Delf.

"No, I cannot do that,' replied Hal, "that is his office alone. We are sworn never to reveal what we know of him until he gives the word."

This seemed to be adding to the torture endured by the prisoners.

All along a burning curiosity had been felt by the band to know who the mysterious avenger was. Delf and his companions felt it would be still harder to die with that curiosity unsatisfied.

"Perhaps we shall see him at the last moment," they said. Then Delf, intercepting a glance exchanged between Lucia and Hal, jumped at the truth.

"You have lost your captain," he cried, "ha! ha! Larry Turrell's finished him; now, lads, a struggle for life and liberty.'

Like a man given the strength of giants to renew a contest, Delf burst his bonds and sprang upon Hal.

The other men were not so successful in their efforts, and Smudge promptly knocked one down.

Lucia covered the other with her rifle, and he was still.

Even five minutes' grace at the end of existence is something.

Hal could not get at any of his weapons, and, as his rifle had fallen out of his grasp when Delf made his onslaught, it was a hand-to-hand struggle between them.

The Red Robin fought for his life, but he had a cool opponent, supple of limb, inured to hardship, and a practised wrestler.

It was only a matter of moments, after all, for barely had a minute elapsed when Hal threw his man, with terrific force, upon the stone roadway,

Panting, bruised, and almost blind with impotent fury, he lay upon the ground, and allowed his arms to be rebound without a struggle.

"You are all fiends inspired by a fiend," he said.

"Good words to come from *your* lips," replied Hal scoffingly.

Having resecured his man, he rose up and uttered a peculiar cry.

It was soon answered by the tramp of men, and half a dozen of the Veiled Captain's band appeared.

"Place them against the wall," said Hal to Smudge. "Lucia, this is no scene for you; leave us."

Lucia was turning away, and Smudge was placing the men against the wall, when a quiet voice was heard from the summit of the steps.

"Stay a moment—I am here."

A cry of joy burst from the lips of Lucia and the rest.

It was the Veiled Captain.

SMUDGE AND LUCIA ON THE LOOK-OUT,

CHAPTER XXIII.

THE RED ROBINS MORE THAN SATISFIED—WHERE THE VEILED CAPTAIN HAD BEEN—A SUBTERRANEAN CITY.

THERE was no other demonstration.

It was not the time for congratulation or enquiries, and it was, for the moment, enough that the Veiled Captain had returned.

Slowly he descended the steps, like one weary with a long journey, and on the level he halted.

Under the veil his eyes could be faintly seen as they rested on the Red Robins.

They were satisfied, and more than satisfied now.

"You have done well," said the Veiled Captain, turning towards Hal and Smudge; "though absent for awhile, I knew you would do your duty. What has been done?"

"Nothing but taking them, and bringing them here," Hal replied.

Turning to the Red Robins and drawing a little nearer to them, the Veiled Captain asked if they had anything to say.

"Only tell us who you are," replied Delf. "I would ask for mercy, but I know I should not get it."

"Mercy," said the Veiled Captain, "would be thrown away upon you. You would only renew your old lives. In addition, justice demands that you should die."

The heads of the men sank down upon their breasts, and they said no more.

The Veiled Captain held up his hand, and his own followers turned their backs to him.

Then he raised his veil and gave the Red Robins a glimpse of his face.

"You know me," he said, as he let fall the gauzy covering again.

They stared at him in a dazed, frightened way, and then at each other.

Delf alone spoke, and the words came from his lips in a broken manner.

"It——can't——be. Why, you——died before our eyes——you——you are——not mortal."

"I am," cried the Veiled Captain. "Stand erect and do one thing to the credit of your worthless lives. Die like men."

But erect they could not stand.

Leaning against the wall they stood, with knees bent and hands quivering, three images of amazement and terror.

"Hal, do your duty."

Lucia was gone by that time, and, as the Veiled Captain stood aside, his men advanced and presented their rifles at the doomed men.

"Aim carefully, my men," said the Veiled Captain. "Do not put even these to needless pain."

Hal took a handkerchief from his breast, and held it up.

One——two——

The handkerchief fell, the rifles belched forth their fire, and the three Red Robins fell forward in a heap.

Immovable the Veiled Captain stood while Hal examined the fallen men.

"The aim was true," he said.

The Veiled Captain, with a motion of his hand, signified his approval and walked away.

He went first down to the square, and looked round him. All was quiet there.

Then he turned to the bridge and saw Lucia standing halfway down towards the stone archway in its centre.

He walked slowly towards her, and when he reached her side they strolled on together, not speaking for awhile.

"You have been in great peril," she said, at length.

"I have been in some danger," he replied, "but it is over. Lucia, for the first time since I formed my band and set out on path of justice, I am worn out. I will rest under the arch while you get me some food and drink."

"Forgive me," she said, "but you have been so strange, so different from others in these matters."

"It is true," said the Veiled Captain. "But I have had a terrible time. Had it not been for the resolute purpose I have in view I must have died."

CHAPTER XXIV

YET ANOTHER CITY.

"TELL me," said Lucia, "where you have been."

"I have been in an underground city," replied the Veiled Captain.

"Can it be possible?"

"It is true. Under this strange pile of stone there are streets and byeways designed for some purpose that is not clear to me. It is feebly lighted up by orifices cut through the ornamental walls. But let me begin at the beginning."

He sat down on the broken stone coping of the bridge, and she took a seat beside him.

Pointing in the direction of the temple, he asked her if she had seen it.

"Yes," she replied, "twice. Once with Hal, and yesterday, when I followed you and lost you there."

"I lost myself there," replied he, grimly.

And then he told her of the stone that moved and dropped him into the dark depths below.

"I fell," he went on, "upon a sort of sliding place of smooth stone, down which I shot with amazing velocity. Fortunately I went feet first, and I stopped short at the bottom, shaken, but comparatively unininred

BROUGHT TO THEIR BEARINGS.

"At first," he went on, "I was in utter darkness, and I began to grope my way by a stone wall, cold and clammy to the touch.

"It was covered with ornamental work, from which, as I slowly went along, I dislodged many a creeping thing, colder and more clammy than the walls."

"Ugh," exclaimed Lucia, with a shudder.

"It was a little trying—not to my nerves, but to my sense of cleanliness," continued the Veiled Captain, "and the utter darkness added to the horror of it. By and by I began to see a dim light ahead, and hope dawned in my heart.

"I judged I was working towards the Lake City, but was not sure. In any case, daylight was what I had been trying for, and ere long I was near it.

"To me it seemed quite brilliant, after the utter darkness, but I know now that it was poor and feeble. It came filtering down through many holes above, and showed me a strange scene.

"I was in a street—the counterpart of the one above, I believe. There were houses on either side, not so lofty, but still plainly built for the habitation of man. The roadway was paved, and strewn about on every side were strange arms weapons of bronze and steel, silver, and even gold. On every side a quantity of pungent dust, fine as flour, that rose with every step I took, and floated cloud-like in the air.

"Lucia," said the Veiled Captain, "it was a dreadful sight, this underground city of a forgotten age. What meant those scattered arms, that pungent dust. The arms were the weapons of men who had fought in those gloomy streets—the pungent dust, all that remained of the fallen."

He stopped as if overcome for the moment by the memory of that great and awful discovery.

Lucia sat still, breathless and absorbed in his moving story.

"Awe-stricken, yet entranced with this wonderful discovery," the Veiled Captain resumed, "I wandered slowly on, and presently mustered courage to enter one of the houses. There I found an answer to the empty palaces above.

"At one time—Heaven only knows when—the Lake City must have been besieged—its inhabitants then removed below, taking all their goods and chattels with them.

"It must have been the work of days, weeks, or even months, for in the old times cities were besieged sometimes for years. Below in this city they intended to dwell until they could escape by the temple in the wood.

"In this they were foiled. The foe entered the city, penetrated their hiding place, and in the underground city a great battle was fought. Possibly none on either side came forth alive, and so the place became a thing of the past."

"And are the streets as wide?" asked Lucia.

"The same," replied the Veiled Captain, "but with strong pillars, twenty feet thick, in the centre to support the streets above."

"The wealth of gold and jewellery below is almost boundless," he continued. "It is more than we can ever hope to take away; but, in any case, all who have followed me can return rich when our work is done."

"Is the way out easy, or is it hidden?" asked Lucia.

"Hidden," replied the Veiled Captain. "I sought it in vain while daylight lasted, and then when darkness came I could only lie still and wait for dawn."

"Sleep at first would not come to my eyes, and strange sounds filled my ears. There was a rushing noise, as if a shadowy host was being borne on the wind. That was hardest to bear, alone, as I was, down in that vast labyrinth. Oh! Lucia, I thought I had a bold heart until last night, but the solitude of that dismal place proved to me that it was like that of other men."

"Some would have died," Lucia said.

"It may be so," he replied; "but I lived on. I

slept, and when I awoke a faint light was creeping in, I resumed my search for a means of escape, and presently found it in one of the houses. There, in an upper chamber, I came upon a strangely constructed trap-door of stone. A turn of a polished marble lever lowered it, and I found myself not far from you.

"Your voices fell upon my ear—oh, how sweetly! I hastened towards you, and the rest you know."

"It is wonderful. It is like the story of a dream," Lucia said.

"One day we may look upon it as little more," he answered. "For the present there is a dread reality about it that is beginning to pall upon me. I must be active and bring about the end. Go to Hal and say I would speak to him and Brill—I shall be in the camp."

He rose up and walked away with a slow step, a sure sign that he was weary.

Lucia, with shuddering thoughts of the strange city beneath the lake, hastened back to meet her brother, who, with Smudge and the men who had acted in the recent tragedy, were approaching the archway.

"Hal," she said, "I have good news. Our leader has declared that the time has come to finish his work."

"Good news, indeed," said Hal, and the faces of the men lighted up with pleasure.

The message of the Veiled Captain was then given to Hal, and, leaving Smudge as commander of the City Guard, he hastened to the camp.

On the way he picked up with Old Brill, who, with a backwoodsman's expertness was lopping off some branches for firewood, and together they sought the Captain.

He was not to be seen, and one of the men said he had gone into the wood to break his fast. So they sat down to await his return, and presently he came.

The conference between them was soon over, and Hal and Old Brill returned to the outpost of the city The Veiled Captain walked away to find a quiet corner to rest in.

Lucia was then with Smudge, whom she had been regaling with the story of the Veiled Captain's great discovery, and she had to hark back and tell it all over again to the new comers.

"To my belief," said Smudge, "this place was not built with natural hands."

"It was built with the help of wise heads," replied Hal, gruffly. "It is too solid to be supernatural. For all that, I shall be glad to turn my back upon it."

"And I shall part with it easy," muttered Old Brill. "It's not natural in the light of our experience."

Then they talked of the coming end.

There were several Red Robins beside the two leaders, Larry Turrell and Rigault, still within the city.

How would the Veiled Captain proceed so as to land them all with one haul.

"There's a power o' streets about this place," said old Brill. "It will be like hunting rabbits in a warren."

"We must starve them out," said Smudge.

"No," answered Hal, "that the captain will never do. He'll make short and sharp work of it when he begins, unless——"

Hal stopped and looked about him with a strange expression of face.

"You remember that dream of yours, Lucia," he said.

"Can I ever forget it," she answered.

"I suppose," said Hal, "that it must have made a great impression upon me. I dreamt the same thing last night. Not that there was anything in it, but——"

He stopped again and looked at the others in turn, as if hoping they would say something to help him out.

They were all silent.

"Dreams can't mean anything," he said.

"They have meant something before to-day," replied Old Brill, "but whether they do or not—or whether there is anything in our dreams or not—we have to obey orders and take what follows."

"Hear, hear," said Smudge quite cheerily, and the manner in which he shouldered his rifle as if to go on immediate duty caused the others to smile.

"Hear, and obey," said Hal ; "yes, that is our motto. A man can die but once, and he can die no better way than in doing his duty. Hurrah! for the Veiled Captain."

CHAPTER XXV.

THE RED ROBINS AMALGAMATE AGAIN—RIGAULT'S PLANS—A COUNCIL INTERRUPTED.

"I HAVE now the whole plan complete," said Rigault, as he rubbed out some marks he had made on the floor of the great hall.

"I hope you have," growled Larry Turrell, who was lying at full length upon his back close by.

"By being economical with the provisions provided by our mysterious foe," said Rigault, "we have enough to serve us for a week, and to-day we had better enter the maze, and remain there for a time."

"You are *sure* you will be able to get out again?" asked Turrell. "Remember what it was the last time, and half a score of men we left behind are there still."

"The puzzle of it is very simple, now that I know it," said Rigault.

"Like all other puzzles," said Turrell.

He rose up and shook himself like a water-dog, then stretched his arms and yawned.

"I'm getting tired of it," he said, "and sometimes wish it was all over."

"You will be singing another song shortly, perhaps Even now. Hush!"

There was the sound of footsteps without, and the two men stood with ears upon the stretch.

Larry Turrell grasped his rifle with the clutch of a desperate man.

The curtain was thrown aside, and there stood in the doorway, not foes, but the four men who had recently so shamefully deserted their comrades.

Let us honour them with an especial record of their names.

Terence, Brady, Gorton, and Marner.

They were the four who had returned to their leader as dogs return to a master.

"Well! what now?" asked Turrell, scowling.

"We have come back," said Terence, "determined to stand by you to the end."

"Hoping that I shall stand by you!"

"Well, that's so, Captain."

Larry Turrell looked at Rigault who was leaning on his rifle closely watching them.

"There were seven of you," he said. "Where are the other three?"

"Dead," was the answer.

"That was the firing we heard yesterday morning."

"It was so; they were shot by a flight of steps at the lower end of the square."

"How were they taken?"

"They were summoned and were called for at a time appointed," said Brady. "We intended to fight, but the other side were too strong for us"

"You intended to fight!" sneered Rigault. "Bah! it makes me ill to hear you."

Turning to Turrell, he said something in an undertone. Turrell nodded his head in assent.

"Shall I speak to them, or will you?" Rigault was heard to say.

"You," was the answer.

"Hark! you men," said Rigault, facing them with sternly knitted brows, "you can remain here if you will promise to be obedient, and, at a pinch, show a spark of courage. Bear in mind one thing—you can but die once, and whether it's now or by-and-by is only a matter of a few years of miserable existence.'

"Yes, it is miserable," said Gorton.

"We are now," said Rigault, "about to make a bold bid for liberty and revenge. Never mind what my plans are—you have only to obey. Come with me?"

Rigault was virtually the leader now Turrell had abdicated. With the rest he followed Rigault from the old palace.

The square was empty; nor was there any foe in sight in any direction Rigault walked down to the bridge, and looked in the direction of the old archway to see if the watch was still kept.

There, also, nobody was in view.

"I must get an inkling where they are!" Rigault muttered.

"Come up the steps," suggested Terence; "from the top you can see all over the city, and along the shore."

They turned down the street, and presently came to the spot where their comrades had been shot. On the marble pavement there were stains bearing dismal record of that event.

In the old days such a sight would have troubled them little, but now they averted their eyes, and, shuddering, began to ascend the steps.

"I'm hanged if we are not children," muttered Rigault. "To this pass has the Veiled Fiend brought us."

He was leading the way, and was two-thirds up the flight, when a cry from Turrell, who was immediately behind him, fell upon his ears.

"There he is!"

Rigault started violently, and, raising his eyes beheld the Veiled Captain standing quietly on the summit of the steps.

There was a statuesque grace and stillness in the figure that was more impressive than any violently threatening attitude would have been.

Now was the time to test the preaching of Rigault.

He could put his theoretical boldness into practice. Did he do so?

No.

As if acted upon by one impulse, the whole six Red Robins turned and fled, followed by the mocking laughter of their Veiled Foe.

It was not until they reached the square that they stopped.

Rigault was the first to pull up, and, to cover his own cowardice, he began to revile the others.

"Is this your boasted courage and obedience?" he asked. "Why did you not stand and face him? He was one, and we were six."

It was the old story with them,

The terror inspired by the sight of that strange figure always unmanned them. His movements were so secret, his appearance so startling in its suddenness.

"He makes *babes* of us," groaned Rigault. "A curse upon him! If he would only remove that veil and let us see who he is, we might meet him as man to man."

"What face is it that is hidden behind the veil?" asked Turrell. "I have dreamt of it scores of times, and it has always been something very terrible. Now Rigault, you are leader, what now?"

"Let us await him here," replied Rigault. "Here in the open until HE comes; then I will carry out my plan. It will be all the easier, as the first part is flight. I intended it to be a sham one, but we may stake our lives it will be real enough."

"No doubt," said Terence, with a grim smile. "It's a peep at him and a run for life."

It was high noon then, and a blazing sun was in the sky.

Its hot rays fell upon the stone streets and made them hot to the touch. To bide under its influence was to court sunstroke.

So Rigault led the way to a shady part of the square and threw himself down.

The others followed his example, and the six huddled together like the Lazaroni of Naples.

An hour or more passed and they scarcely exchanged a word.

Occasionally one would make a remark, and sometimes would get a word or a growl by way of reply, but for the most part no heed was paid by the others.

The stillness of all things was profound.

Not a cloud marred the blue sky, and the sun shone with a brilliancy that was blinding, even as a reflection from the white walls of the houses, and the heat was intense.

Not even in the shade could these men escape from the overpowering influence of the time.

The inevitable thirst began to assail them.

Larry Turrell was the first to rise and creep under the shadow of the houses to the ancient palace—water, the only drink available, was there.

It was not the drink the Red Robin chief most desired, but it was "better than nothing," as he muttered to himself.

Terence was speedily on his trail and Gorton next.

These three had just passed into the great hall when the voice of Rigault was heard.

"Come out there, the enemy is on us!"

They ran out with their thirst unquenched and beheld a sight that made them shiver with terror.

Hal at the head of a score men, or more, was advancing along the bridge, and as he reached the narrow way that led to the flight of steps, the Veiled Captain came out and joined them.

There was no greeting—not a word apparently was exchanged.

He took his place at their head, and the whole body came marching across the square with that awful, quiet, ghost-like step peculiar to the Veiled Captain and his men.

"He means to finish us this time," cried Larry Turrell, hoarsely.

"Follow me," said Rigault, "if there is strength in your coward limbs to do it."

CHAPTER XXVI.

THE RETREAT INTO THE MAZE—LURED WITHIN
THE TRAP.

THE desperate courage of Rigault, if courage it could be called, gave strength to the other five, and they followed him at a run, as he made for a street which may be called the opening of the maze.

It was the street in which he and Turrell had passed the night when they were lost in the labyrinth, not dreaming that they had by accident escaped from it.

"Not too fast," said Rigault ; "let them keep us in sight so that they may follow us. Look back Turrell ! Are they coming ?"

"Yes ; steadily and quietly," Turrell answered.

"Good," said Rigault, between his teeth. "It shall go hard if none of these rats die in the trap."

He turned into streets to the right and left, making a great show of flying quickly, but at no time getting quite out of the sight of his foes.

On they came, steadily.

No sound was heard save the faintest swish, swish, which might have equally been the sound of their footsteps, or the rattle of their clothes.

They marched steadily, but swiftly, so that Rigault had no need to make too much of a sham of his flight.

He had studied the plan of the maze, and so far it was clear in his mind.

Going in and out must be alike performed without any mistake.

An error would throw him into confusion.

To turn to the right once when he ought to have turned to the left, would lead him into a part of the maze from which he could not easily escape.

Knowing this he kept on muttering to himself

"Right, left; right, left," as he turned, and the number of turnings he tried also to keep in his head.

At length he began to increase his pace, and in an undertone he called on the others to "hurry up."

They broke into a smart run, and Rigault, leading the way, urged them to increase their speed.

"We've got to outrun them," he said; "are we doing it?"

"No," said Turrell, after a hasty glance backward. "They are as close as ever."

"Running?"

"No, walking."

Rigault, with a bitter exclamation, looked behind him, and saw his remorseless pursuers not more than thirty yards in the rear.

There were no signs that they had increased their pace, or that they were at all conscious that he was making an effort to get away from them.

Without a sound, beyond that strange swish, swish, we have spoken of, the Veiled Captain and his men came upon the track of the Red Robins.

It was dreadfully uncanny, and it made the flesh of Rigault creep.

"They are not human!" he suddenly cried.

Then a wild despairing terror laid hold of him, and he bounded forward like a man who really flees for his life.

It was earnest running now, and the same spirit of terror laid hold of his friends.

In and out the streets they ran, one or the other looking back occasionally and gasping out, "they are still coming—and nearer."

Suddenly the pursuers broke the dreadful silence of their march.

As if with one voice a cry burst from them, so shrill, so fierce, so vengeful that Larry Turrell, fairly leaped in the air and uttered a scream of mortal fear.

Then he fell heavily upon the ground, to lie only for a moment.

Up he sprang, as the hunted deer springs after a stumble, and with an effort reached Rigault.

"I'm done," he gasped. "I can't go any further. Stop!"

He had grasped his companion by the arm, and Rigault, with a fierce exclamation, tried to shake him off.

"Let go! will you?" he cried.

"We've got to keep together," answered Turrell.

He threw his arm round Rigault, and the two fell to the ground.

The other four staggered together against the wall of a house, and panting, turned their terrified eyes down the street.

What was it they saw?

Nothing.

The street was clear. The Veiled Captain and his men had vanished.

Rigault in his fury had turned on Turrell, and got him by the throat on the ground.

Both had dropped their rifles, and a hand-to-hand struggle was imminent, when the voice of Terence was heard.

"Easy all!" he cried, "they've gone."

Rigault, still holding Turrell down, turned his face down the street and saw what Terence said was true.

Slowly his grasp upon the throat of Turrell relaxed, and he rose to his feet.

"Where are they gone to?" he asked.

Nobody gave him an answer. The whole thing was too bewildering.

Larry Turrell, with an evil look upon his face, got up from the ground, and, recovering his rifle, turned to Rigault, and said:

"You are mighty free with your hands, I reckon."

"And you with yours," replied Rigault fiercely, "pawing and clawing at me like a frightened woman."

"We can't throw stones at each other on that score," said Turrell with a short laugh, "now then you've got your way. The plan of getting them into the maze has answered. Perhaps you will now lead us out of it again."

"Wait till I've got my breath again," Rigault answered.

He stood leaning on his rifle panting with his recent exertions, and the others, in grim silence, waited for him to make a movement.

In a few minutes he began to move slowly on the backward route.

The streets were narrow now, and the houses all built alike.

The turnings were at regular intervals. There was nothing to guide a wayfarer but a knowledge of the plan of the maze.

Rigault took a turning to the right, then one to the left, then another to the right and came to——a blank wall.

It was of smooth marble and fully twenty feet high. There were no projections or ornamental work, and without a ladder it was impossible to scale it.

"I've taken the wrong turning," he muttered, "the last one ought to have been to the left and not to the right."

He went back, altered his route, and proceeded again.

Left—right—left—right—left—right, and so on through half-a-dozen streets, and then——another blank wall.

The very appearance of the polished marble was chilling, and in the contemplation of it, the heat of the day was forgotten by the Red Robins.

Not a word was said as Rigault wheeled again and tried another route.

Four turnings, and then another of those dreadful walls.

At the sight of it he stopped and clasped his head with his hands.

"Confound you!" cried Turrell, "why don't you out with it? You've lost your way."

"Don't howl yet," answered Rigault. "Give me time to think."

They gave him time to think because they could do nothing else. He stood still for several minutes, and then looking up, he said:

"I think I have it now. We must get back to the place we started from just now."

Easy to talk about—hard to do.

There was nothing, absolutely nothing, to guide them.

Houses all alike, streets of the same width, turnings at the same distance apart.

Everything to bewilder, and nothing to help.

They twisted and turned under the guidance of Rigault, seeking in vain the place they started from. Perhaps they did come across it, but they could not be certain.

There was nothing to help them out of the maze.

Coming to another blank wall, Rigault leaned against it, and uttered a low moan.

"It's useless to humbug you any more," he said, "I'm clear out. We've got to work our way, and take our chance of getting free of the maze as we did before."

CHAPTER XXVII.
LUCIA'S DEVOTION—TERENCE'S REVELATION—WILL THE DREAM COME TRUE?

LOST in the maze.

Yes! the Red Robins, thanks to the blunderings of Rigault, were lost within the marvellous arrangement of the streets of the City of the Lake.

And how did it fare with the Veiled Captain?

Bent upon bringing his carreer, as an avenger, to an end, he had followed his foes, accompanied by his swift and silent footed men.

Suddenly, as we know, they had all vanished.

It happened in this way.

The Veiled Captain came to a street which had the appearance of being a short cut; by means of which he could head the Red Robins, and into this he turned.

A little way up there was another turning, and further—yet another.

And then the polished blank wall.

As this was his first experience of these barriers he softly called a halt, and the men drew up a grim and silent group.

Then he and Hal held a whispered conference together.

"For the first time," said the Veiled Captain, "my instincts have erred and I have led you wrong."

"Our foes by this time are now well away," replied Hal, "but they cannot escape. The gates of the city are guarded."

"Well! let the men rest," said the Veiled Captain, "they have done well. Their efforts have been prodigious."

"They have walked as other men run," returned Hal, "and the silent step makes the toil greater, but see, they are scarcely breathed. They have their hearts in their work."

"Let them refresh themselves," said the Veiled Captain, "and I will look around."

"Noble Captain," said Hal, "do not let one error be the forerunner of another. You may fall into an ambush of our enemies. This may be a day of ill omen."

"Hal! these are idle fears."

"Well, Captain, I am, I admit, somewhat superstitious. I cannot shake off all faith in dreams."

The Veiled Captain stood for a moment leaning on his rifle silent.

"Hal," he said at length, "I will not deride your belief and call it folly. There may be grounds for superstitious fears, but I cannot share them. Await here for awhile and I will speedily return to you."

He tossed his rifle upon his shoulder and strode away with scarce a sound accompanying his swift footsteps.

He returned by the way he came and reached the spot where he had last seen the Red Robins.

But he would not have known it but for a button which had been torn from Rigault's coat in the struggle with Larry Turrell.

It lay close to the wall of a house and had escaped the eyes of its owner.

But the sharp eyes of the Veiled Captain saw it through the silken covering of his face.

"It was here we left them," he said, "now to find their trail."

He looked around him, but could find no trail of them.

In the hard solid street there was no dust to speak of, save in the corners and against the walls.

There was nothing to leave a trace of footsteps.

"But I have them safe," he murmured. "Smudge guards the gate, and Lucia——"

He stopped.

Close by he heard a soft footfall and the rustle of a dress. Turning, he beheld Lucia herself behind him.

"I could not help it," she said, "cast me away from you if you will, but I was bound to follow you to share your lot."

"How can I blame you?" he said, "for it is your devotion that leads you to disobey me. But why are you so anxious now?"

"I have had dreams—you know of them," said Lucia, "and I feel here—touching her bosom—that a dark hour is drawing nigh. Whatever there is in the way of suffering and peril, I must share it with you."

"You are a brave girl," he said in the low musical tone he spoke in when moved. "Come, let us seek Hal and I will leave him with you while I——"

"Risk your life as you have done a hundred times before," Lucia interposed. "You may one day give the triumph to your enemies."

"I do not fear them. They are broken."

"The cornered rat will turn and fight, and is some-times a dangerous foe."

"True, Lucia, but the end is generally the same—he dies."

They were returning again to Hal, and the Veiled Captain, after taking two turns, paused.

"The terrible sameness of these streets or bye-ways is somewhat puzzling," he said. "I am not sure that I am going right, and yet this, I think, is the route. Lucia, how did you follow us so close?"

"I did not lose sight of the men all the way, until a little while ago. I lost you all at one of the turnings. It was chance that brought us finally to-gether."

"There is little chance in life. What is it the immortal Shakespeare says?—

　　　'There is a divinity that shapes our ends
　　　　Rough hew them how we will.'

So it is, Lucia. We may plot and plan and go here and there, do this and that, but the end is the same. We have a lot to fulfil and we must do it."

"Hark!" said Lucia. "I hear a cry."

A shout of surprise and terror was heard on the the left. A moment later it was repeated.

"Keep close by me, Lucia," said the Veiled Captain as he moved on rapidly in the direction of the sounds.

The next turning brought him to one of those terrible blank walls, and hastening back, he sped on to the next.

Again and again those cries were heard.

Two more turnings and he came into view of Terence in the hands of Hal.

His hands were bound, and he was uttering piteous cries for mercy.

"Peace," cried Hal, "our leader is here."

And as the veiled figure strode up, Terence ceased his cries. The very blood was frozen in his veins.

"It is all over with me now," he muttered hoarsely.

"As we stood here," said Hal, "he came prowling round the corner, and I pounced upon him as a dog upon a rat."

"I'll not ask for mercy," said Terence, in dry cracked tones, "because I know that it won't be shown me. I only ask you not to torture me long. After all it will be merciful to kill me. It is better to die at once than inch by inch."

"What do you mean by that?" asked Hal.

"The others will starve," Terence said.

"Starve!" echoed Lucia and Hal together.

Their dreams flashed vividly upon them on hearing that dreaded word.

"Yes," said Terence, "starve. They will never get out of the maze again."

"What maze?" asked Hal.

The Veiled Captain stood erect and undisturbed, not uttering a word, but listening closely to what was said.

"Don't you know where you are?" asked Terence with a sudden light in his eyes.

"We are in the heart of the city."

A strange laugh broke from the lips of the Red Robin.

"It is good—you are in it too—the maze where we were nearly all lost before," said Terence. "A few of us were saved because we did not penetrate so far.—How! we know not. It was chance. But well within it, as Rigault says, and a man is as good as lost. It is a most accursed place."

"You are speaking idly," said Hal sternly.

"I am not," Terence answered. "Rigault lured you here. He had found the plan and studied it. He brought you here to starve, but now he will die too. We shall all die. Ha—ha—it is a rare jest."

And Terence, in a wild semi-maniacal manner, threw up his arms and shouted until the street rang again.

"Silence," cried the Veiled Captain sternly, and at the sound of his voice Terence's mad mirth collapsed.

"Whatever is to be our fate," said the Veiled Captain, "yours is sure, Terence. You have been a notorious member of the band known as the Red Robins. Although not a leader you have never been backward in doing your share of cruel work. Prepare to *die*."

So solemnly were the last words uttered, that Terence sould not fail to feel their full force and significance.

"Prepare to die."

"Not to-morrow, or a week hence, but NOW."

When the moment comes the bravest may honestly quail.

Terence was not one of the bravest of men, but he had a certain elasticity of spirit that kept him up until the LAST.

But when he SAW the end near it opened his eyes, and he suddenly broke down.

"Give me an hour," he said imploringly: "I want to think a bit. I've got to feel sorry for what I've done before I die."

"I have no time to dally here if what you say about the city is true," replied the Veiled Captain.

"It was not true. I was jesting," said Terence, eagerly.

"Do not die with a lie upon your lips," was the solemn answer.

"You will not spare me for an hour?"

"No."

"Then starve and rot here," said Terence, violently. "Who are you to take men's lives in this way?"

"Come here," said the Veiled Captain, seizing him

THE VEILED CAPTAIN. 187

by the collar and dragging him aside. "Here! do you see me?" dragging his veil aside. "Have you forgotten me?"

"It can't be YOU," said Terence in a hushed voice, "you are DEAD. It's not true; it's all a dream, this horrible place; our long flight. Capture and death of man after man. Yes, it is all a dream!"

Then, as the Veiled Captain signalled to Hal, Terence broke out in another direction.

"No, it is true, my time has come, I've earned it. It is just. But to die by the judgment of the DEAD; it is horrible. No——."

Hal led him to the blank wall at the end of the street, and placed him with his back against it.

Then, taking out his handkerchief, he quickly bound it over his eyes.

"Stand!" he cried.

Out from the body of men stepped four with their rifles at the ready.

Hal drew aside and raised his hand.

"It cannot be," cried Terence, hoarsely. "It's all a dream. A man can't be tried and condemned by the DEAD. I——."

Hal's hand dropped, and the sharp report of the rifles filled the street with echoes.

Lucia, who had been drawn aside by the Veiled Captain, had her back to the scene.

She stood pale and erect, with her companion by her side.

Not a word was uttered.

There was a movement behind them, and a heavy tramping of feet as of men carrying some heavy weight.

The dead man was being laid aside, under one of the dark doorways near.

Then the men followed up behind their leader, a sign that their work was done.

A moment more and the Veiled Captain was gliding from the spot with his silent followers behind him.

CHAPTER XXVIII.

IN THE CENTRE OF THE MAZE—RIGAULT'S DARING —THE VEILED CAPTAIN ON THE ALERT—RIGAULT CAPTIVE.

THE day was almost gone, and the first shadows of evening fell upon the forms of the five remaining Red Robins, crouching beside a huge monument, in the centre of a small square.

Rigault had told them that it was the centre of the maze, and before and around them lay many ways of exit, all false save one.

And which was the one to take?

Terence had been lost through his own folly.

He had chosen to start alone, to find a way of escape, and had promptly, as we have seen, fallen into the hands of his enemies.

But with his fate the Red Robins were not concerned.

It was their own prospects of escaping from the mesh they were in that troubled them.

After the first burst of anger they had ceased to revile Rigault. Through him—if at all—were they to find their way back.

He was then kneeling on the ground and with the stump of a leaden pencil endeavouring to sketch out a map of the maze.

"I had it all so pat in my mind," he said, pausing and looking up, "but it's gone—clear gone."

"Take time, be steady," said Larry Turrell, "nothing can be done in haste."

"There is not much time to waste," Brady remarked, "night will soon be here."

"Eternal night perhaps," muttered Garton,

"Oh! hang your drivelling rubbish," said Rigault, savagely, "let me see—here was the deep line—to the left—no—to the right—no—ah! it's all gone."

"It is an accursed place," said Turrell, "why see here—we may take one way and walk for an hour to find a blank road in the end—and then another and another—the cunning or the devil has been employed in building it."

"The cunning of ten thousand devils," said Rigault, "or what is much the same—the same number of Chinamen—or men of the same race. You have never been in China?'

"No," said Turrell.

"It is a puzzling land and the land of puzzles," said Rigault, "their ingenuity is boundless in making up very hard nuts to crack—possibly they may be the descendants of the very people who built this man trap."

He turned to his work again and the others standing around, in a slightly stooping position, watched him with keen interest.

He drew lines one way—looked at them and then rubbed them out—then lines another way, and served them the same.

All his efforts to recall the plan of the maze were fruitless.

"No wonder they had it cut in stone," he said, "the very builder might forget the clue."

"And yet it seemed so simple," said Turrell, "left, right—left, right——."

"Yes," returned Rigault, "but *which* is the left to take?"

"Around us are a score of outlets. Nineteen are wrong, and each one has a score misleading ways. The whole place is a number of mazes within a maze. We may return a hundred times to the same spot, and unless we have some distinguishing mark, may never know it. Curse it."

He dashed down his pencil and rose to his feet.

"We've got to take our chance," he said, "and there's an end of it."

He raised his eyes and looked gloomily about him.

Above the house tops around arose many towers and domes.

But they were no guide.

On every side the arrangement was the same. A square tower here, a dome there, all placed with mathematical precision.

Nothing to guide them, nothing to help them, they

could only trust to chance.

The sun went down and a grey tint lay on all things around. In the east the evening star was gleaming in the sky.

"That is our direction," said Rigault, "but to take one of the streets on that side would only lead us astray. Of that I am sure."

"What can we do?" asked Turrell."

"Nothing to-night," said Rigault. "Let us try and get some sleep. Next to food that is the best thing for worn out men."

He set the example by throwing himself down close to the base of the monument and the others sullenly followed.

They talked for awhile, but as the darkness fell a silence came over them.

Occasionally a restless movement or a whispered word would show that they were still awake, but as the hours advanced they dropped off one by one, and slept.

Rigault opened his eyes after what he at first considered a few moments' rest, but early daylight had come again, and Larry Turrell was already awake.

He was sitting up with a listening look upon his face, and he held up his finger for Rigault to be cautious.

Rigault raised his eyebrows by way of enquiry.

Larry Turrell replied with a motion of his hand towards the other side of the monument.

Rigault bent his head in that direction and listened.

On the other side was the murmuring of voices

With the greatest caution Rigault got upon his feet, and stooping, whispered in Turrell's ear:—

"It's the enemy—it must be—and he doesn't know we are here."

"But he will know," said Turrell softly, shivering.'

"If we take him unawares, we may shoot him down," said Rigault, with a look of desperation in his eyes, "be bold for once, and follow me."

The monument was composed of a series of

platforms for a base, with a column and some fantastic figures in the centre."

By exercising the greatest care it was possible to creep up and get a shot at an unsuspecting person on the other side.

That it was the Veiled Captain Rigault had no doubt.

And he was right.

On the other side of the monument were Hal, Lucia and their leader engaged in close conversation.

But a few minutes before they had entered the square, and the men as yet had not come into it.

They stood within one of the streets in a group, in sight, and silently awaiting orders.

The Veiled Captain was no more than mortal.

His eyes, keen though they were, could not penetrate through many feet of polished stone, and he knew not that the men he sought for were so near.

But he was as usual on the alert.

His tongue was engaged in conversation, but he had eyes and ears for everything around.

A slight scraping sound attracted his attention.

He motioned to Hal to be ready and watchful, and glanced towards his other men.

Not one of them was looking towards him.

The majority leant upon their rifles, weary with the hours of toil, but not as yet suffering much from hunger, having brought a small supply of food with them.

The Veiled Captain continued to talk.

"Our foes are lost to us," he said, "and we have nothing to do but to return."

Hal raised his eyebrows in surprise, but a motion from his leader keeps him silent.

"Nothing to do but to retreat," continued the Veiled Captain, raising his voice a little, "and wait for them—sooner or later"—he raised his eyes, turned round a little without a sound and quietly handed his rifle to Hal.

"Nothing to do but—but——" he went on, and just

then a head slowly appeared over the edge of the marble above him.

Like a flash of light his hand shot up and he had Rigault by the throat.

A gasping cry broke from the ruffian's lips.

It was answered by a yell from Larry Turrell.

These notes of alarm were followed by cries from the other Red Robins as they awoke and leaped to their feet.

The Veiled Captain dragged Rigault over with his right hand, seized his rifle with his left, and dashed the boldest of the Red Robins to the ground.

Half stunned by the shock and wholly overcome with surprise, Rigault made no effort to resist.

He yielded up his rifle without an effort.

Then came a crowning indignation to the fallen ruffian.

Lucia, with the quickness of an expert, secured his hands with a piece of slight strong rope.

Bound by a woman.

Captured without making half a fight for his life.

His fury, his helpless mortification were so deep that he, the strong Rigault, fainted.

A mist swam before his eyes and he became insensible.

Meanwhile the attention of the Veiled Captain's men had been called to what was going on.

In a body they darted into the square, and, headed by Hal, went in pursuit of the Red Robins, now in full flight.

Larry Turrell as usual was well in front now that retreating was the order of the day.

Close behind him were Garton and Warner.

Brady, a heavier man than either of the latter two, lagged.

At him the swift-footed Hal rushed with a velocity and force that carried both to the ground.

They rolled over two or three times before they stopped, but Hal had him fast by the arms, and Brady was captured.

"OUR FOES ARE LOST TO US," THE VEILED CAPTAIN SAID.

By this time the other Red Robins and the men in pursuit had reached the street, and the former disappeared.

The latter halted, being under orders not to go out of the sight of their leader.

Brady was speedily secured, and led back to the Veiled Captain, who was awaiting their coming with his prisoner.

Rigault being a strong man, did not long remain in a swoon.

He was recovering as Hal came back with his prisoner.

"Who's that?" he asked, hoarsely, "is it Turrell?"

Nobody answered, and the next moment he saw who it was, and a deep curse escaped him.

"All the rest might have got away," he said, "but I wanted him to die with me, if it came to that."

"It will come to it in due time," replied the Veiled Captain, "and you will die together."

CHAPTER XXIX.

NOT TO DIE YET—BRADY'S DOOM.

RIGAULT turned his dark eyes upon the Veiled Captain wonderingly, and a question rose to his lips, but he did not utter it.

Not to die yet?

To be kept until Turrell was captured.

Well, that was something.

While there is life there is hope, and again the Red Robin gathered a little heart.

With Brady there was no delaying. He was not to be kept in reserve for any especial penalty.

He had been a common ruffian, and as a common ruffian he had to die.

Swift and sure was the end of him.

A few queries, answered by an appeal for mercy, and then he was led out to die.

Rigault saw the action of the veil being drawn aside and heard the prisoner's cry of alarm.

He uttered a name, too, but what it was Rigault

failed to catch.

No glimpse of the face was given to him, and his curiosity was raised to the highest pitch.

Who was this dreaded being—this swift and sure avenger?

Even when in the midst of the dreadful maze he had the power or instinct to unearth his foes.

From speculation on this point he turned his attention to his doomed follower.

He saw Brady left alone, and the men chosen to be his executioners stand out,

He watched Hal's upraised arm, and noted its fall, so swiftly followed by the report of three unerring rifles.

All was over:

On the west side of the square lay a huddled form, all that was left of Brady.

"But why not me?" Rigault asked himself. Then it flashed upon him that he had really been saved to be savagely tortured, and his blood ran cold.

The fears engendered by this thought were heightened by hearing the Veiled Captain give the command to watch him close.

"If he attempts to escape," was the order, "knock him down, but do not shoot without order from me."

"I wonder if he knows the maze," muttered Rigault.

But on this point no information was vouchsafed him.

The Veiled Captain and Lucia walked on, and Hal and the men surrounding the prisoner followed.

The route taken was that chosen by the flying Red Robins.

Matters were now serious all round.

Captured and captors alike had reached a dark hour in their lives.

They had no food, nothing to drink, for although the city was built upon the lake, the means whereby the original inhabitants used to procure water were not visible.

One thing there was about the houses different to those without the maze.

In the latter the doorways were open—within they were all closed and fast.

Door after door did the Veiled Captain try, and they were as firm as a rock.

So close did they fit that there was no crevice visible, and like everything else in this wondrous city, they were made of marble or stone.

"If we could only gain the summit of one of these buildings," said the Veiled Captain to Lucia, "we might be able to make out our way."

"We may do it by and bye," she replied, with an assumed cheerfulness she was far from feeling.

On their way they went, turning this way and that, to find, as before, the disappointments of the maze.

It was wearying, disheartening, crushing.

Not once did they sight any of the Red Robins, but by one blank wall they heard two of them speaking *on the other side of it.*

There was something tantalising in this, and Hal uttered an impatient exclamation.

It was the only sound heard.

Rigault grimly smiled, but he valued the little time left for him to live too well to act upon the impulse that tempted him to speak.

If anything were wanting to prove the extraordinary arrangement of the maze it was afforded that day.

No calculation could keep the plan in mind. It was impossible to say whether they had been in such a place before until the Veiled Captain hit upon a device.

"Let us tear our handkerchiefs into strips and drop pieces in every street we come to," he said.

It was done, and after a long tramp they came upon some of these pieces.

Then came a momentous question.

Which street did the pieces of rag represent?

It only made confusion worse. It confounded, dismayed them.

At last, just when they least expected it, they came upon the small square again.

Of this there could be no mistake, there were the evidences of their recent visit in the stains on the spot where the last Red Robins had fallen.

Not a man complained.

Although hunger was assailing all, and thirst was asserting its intolerable sway, not a voice was lifted in complaint or anger.

Lucia bore up bravely, but it was plain that she was suffering deeply.

The Veiled Captain called a halt, and in his usual cheeriness addressed his followers.

"Men," he said, "I cannot deny that we are in trouble. We have become involved in the most extraordinary maze ever constucted to confuse those within it.

"Were it less solid than it is we might break through it, but the barriers are too great to be thrown down by such means as we have at hand."

He paused, and looked slowly around him.

His men, with white faces, stood leaning on their rifles wearily.

"It may be," said the Veiled Captain, "that our end is here, but I cannot believe it. With courage, and a further display of your noble endurance, we shall get free from this vortex of stone."

"Perhaps," said Rigault, "but you would not be so sanguine as you are if you had seen what I have in a plan of this infernal trap."

"And having seen it," said the Veiled Captain, "how is it you do not remember it?"

"How do you know I have forgotten it?" asked Rigault cunningly; "give me a chance for my life. Let me try to lead you for once, and if I succeed give me my freedom."

"Men," cried the Veiled Captain, "what is your answer to this?"

Then came sudden life and movement into the hitherto silent group.

Up went the right hand of every man.

"He is to die," they said.

"The time and place of your own choosing, noble captain," added Hal.

"I choose it now, in case we are to perish here," said the Veiled Captain, "he is to live on until but three of us remain. The duty of the last of us will be to deal out his fitting doom."

"It shall be done," they cried, and they raised their right arms again.

Rigault's cheeks assumed a leaden hue.

His last hope was gone.

"Only one thing I wish for now," he said, "and that is you may get hold of Turrell. Half-hearted as he is, he was the biggest ruffian of us all. Here, speaking as a dying man, I solemnly declare that it was useless to preach mercy when he was by."

"And have YOU ever preached it?" asked the Veiled Captain.

"But once or twice," answered Rigault. "It is useless to try to deceive you. Next to Turrell I was the instigator of the deeds done by the Red Robins."

"That is stale news," said Hal.

Rigault turned to him and went on:

"YOU I know, and more than one man here. I can understand your desire for vengeance. But do not grasp who and what your leader is. I know his voice when he speaks, it is familiar to me, but I cannot call back when I heard it before."

"You will know in time, as the others have,' replied the Veiled Captain.

"Tell me now" pleaded Rigault, "are you of this world?"

"A fool's question," was the answer, "especially from a man who always professed not to believe in any other."

"I talked as I thought in the old days," said Rigault bowing his head. "I speak as I *feel*, now."

"Men," said the Veiled Captain, turning again to his followers, "here we must rest and pass another night. If the worst comes, I know you will accept your fate like men. If it pleases you to revile me, do so, I will not blame you."

Then they cried out, and there leaped into their eyes a fire and enthusiasm very wonderful in hungering men.

Half-starved, or "clemmed," as they say in Lancashire, the men prepared to pass the coming night in that open place.

No duty was neglected.

Some piled their arms, and others, told off for duty, took the prisoner under their charge and prepared to watch over him until relieved.

Lucia, Hal, and the Veiled Captain slept a little apart from the rest.

CHAPTER XXX.

MORE SUFFERING—THE VEILED CAPTAIN MISSING—SCENE ON THE HOUSETOP.

" HAL," said the leader, " are you losing heart ? "

" No," replied Hal.

" Or you, Lucia ? "

" I think only of you," she said.

" Sweeter than music are such words to me," said the Veiled Captain, " they comfort me in this hour of deep distress. For myself I care little. I had such faith in the success of my mission that I never thought of failure——"

" And now ? " asked Lucia.

" I am hopeful still," he answered. " But it is hard to see those around me suffer—and know that I have brought them to it. Better by far that the Red Robins had gone scot free——"

" Do not say that," interposed Hal, " we shall die in a good cause. The band of thieves and murderers have been broken up—only a few remain—their power for evil is lost—the land will be free of them. We are as men who have fought for the freedom of their country and perished in the hour of victory."

" Well said, Hal," cried Lucia, " let there be no more murmuring—not a word—I am a woman but I can die. If the morrow brings us further woes—so be it—if death is to come by starvation—it is well—for

Comes he slow or comes he fast.
It is but Death that comes at last.

"A thousand years would not suffice to repay such devotion," said the Veiled Captain. "Lucia, if we are spared I will try to make you some return. Hal! friend—comrade—brother. We shall escape from here Be of good heart!"

Hal smiled lightly, and their hands meeting, they stood with them clasped together for a minute or more.

Then Hal went back to the men and offered them words of good cheer,

"The Captain has no fear," he said, "and why should we quail? Through all, he has ever been right, and now he assuredly will not fail us."

They listened, and if not so confident as Hal they at least expressed no dissent.

Rigault heard what was said, and marked the demeanour of the men.

It amazed him, and, although filled with the thoughts of his own trouble, he could not forbear offering them the tribute of admiration.

"I understand now," he said, "the success which has up to now attended you. It is not the Captain and his men, but one man only. You are one man, one heart, one voice, while we were as so many broken straws being blown before the wind of vengeance.

Hunger and thirst.

Ah! these were the two great foes of the hour.

The day had been warm and the night was close and sultry. The sky was copper coloured as the sun went down.

The men, looking at it, said they had never seen such a sky, and they asked each other if it was not their affected vision that made it like a glowing dome.

And then there was the stillness—complete—profound.

When none were speaking, it was frequently the case, not a sound was to be heard.

It was strangely impressive—terrible—overpowering

" It is like the coming of the end of all things," one man said, and, despite their courage, a shudder ran through the men.

To ease the pangs they suffered some chewed bits of leather cuts from their boots, while others held a leaden bullet between their teeth, turning and biting it until it had lost its original shape.

Oh ! for a draught of cooling water !

They thought of that more than of food.

But there was no water at hand—only the copper-coloured sky—the coming night, and, it might be, death.

In the morning when Hal, who had slept the latter part of the night, awoke, he found the Veiled Captain was not there.

He had gone alone into the maze again, and left a message with the men whose turn it was to watch over Rigault, the prisoner.

" I shall return shortly after break of day," he said.

Break of day was there, and he was still away.

Under any other circumstances Hal would not have been uneasy, but he was in a depressed state of mind through hunger and fatigue, and, therefore, disposed to look at things on the gloomy side.

" We have lost him now," he said to Lucia, who had risen and joined him.

" Why did he go?" Lucia asked.

" How can I tell ? " he replied.   You know his way He chooses his own path. There is sure to be some reason for his action."

" What can we do ? "

" Await his return—that is all.'

In a little while all the men were awake, and they moved about in a sad and silent, but not despairing way.

Hunger and thirst could not fail to tell upon them.

Their brave faces were wan, and the hands that grasped their rifles palpably showed a falling off of power.

Rigault, with his arms bound, sat up, looking round on the Veiled Captain's men, scanning them closely and recalling one here and there as a memory of the past.

But none gave him a clue to the identity of the Veiled Captain.

Even in his hunger and thirst agony he felt his curiosity overpowering all else.

He asked one of the men to give him something to assuage his thirst, and he was given a piece of leather, which he chewed with the eagerness of those who suffer as he did.

Some relief was gained by it, and when Hal came round his way, he asked if he might speak to him.

"Yes." replied Hal.

"Where's your captain ?" he inquired.

"You will know by-and-bye," was the answer.

"I want to speak to him," said Rigault, "to ask him to put me out of my misery."

"You can spare your breath," said Hal; "all your pleadings will not turn him from his course."

"Tell me who he is then," said Rigault.

"I have never said I knew," Hal returned.

"But you do know."

"Perhaps.

A shout, feeble in its way, but still a shout, interrupted the conversation.

One of the band was standing on the lower platform of the central monument, pointing to a tall house in the distance.

On the summit of it was a man, standing on the parapet.

"That's not the Captain," Hal said.

Every eye was on him.

It was seen that he was cautiously moving to and fro, and occasionally peering down as if he feared to see someone in the street.

"He is pursued," Hal said.

"I know him," said Rigault, "It is Garton.

Another shout, this time from several.

A second figure was on the summit of the house.

There was no mistaking that lithe upright form.   It

was the Veiled Captain.

He held his rifle in his hand, ready for use, and Garton had his, which he fired in a wild random manner and dropped.

Then ensued a thrilling scene.

The Veiled Captain drew back his veil for a moment and Garton stood still upon the parapet, as if held by a spell.

Then in an instant the weapon of the Veiled Captain was raised and fired, and Garton fell.

The men in the Square saw him throw his arms up wildly, and fall backwards into the street below.

Lucia alone did not see the fall.

As soon as she knew the nature of the scene, she turned her back upon it, and stood with her hands before her face.

The Veiled Captain was too far off for Rigault to make out his features.

But for all that his face seemed to him to be familiar.

In vain he ransacked his memory to discover who it was.

He could not recall any face likely to be beneath that veil.

"Who is it?" he asked himself, and in the tokens of unsatisfied curiosity he forgot for awhile his other sufferings.

The Veiled Captain stood for a few moments with the light of the early morning sun upon him. Then he disappeared.

After this the dreary watching and waiting were resumed.

Lucia sat down on a shady side of the monument, for the day was already getting warm, and the sun, copper-coloured and half veiled in a strange haze in the horizon, assumed a most unnatural appearance.

It was swollen to five times its usual size.

Nor did it diminish its magnitude for the next hour, then it seemed to suddenly emerge from the mist and assume its natural appearance.

It was blinding them.

The hot rays came slanting upon the square and there was a general movement in search of shade.

Ah! how that dream haunted Lucia.

In her heart she feared the worst.

It was impossible for her, or those around her, to endure such tortures of want and heat, and live.

It is bad enough to endure hunger and thirst at at sea.

But there the sufferer has at least the cool shifting water under him, and, perchance, a cooling breeze to fan his brow.

Here, in the strange city of the lake, it was like being in a furnace.

The dreadful stillness of everything around added to the appalling nature of the hour.

But no man complained.

Rigault sat with his head bowed upon his knees.

Now was the hour for him to reflect.

And what a past he had to look back upon.

The future he dare not think of.

At last a deep despairing groan burst from his lips, He looked up.

"Will no man shoot me?" he asked. "Have mercy on me as a man would have upon a wounded dog."

But no man stirred.

They had their orders and would obey them, even though obedience brought them tenfold torture.

They were true to their trust, faithful to the mysterious being they had followed thus far.

Half the morning was gone, and the Veiled Captain had not returned.

Hal was lying at full length, and Lucia was sitting by his side, on the very spot where Larry Turrell and his companions had passed the night previously referred to.

"This suspense," she said, "is maddening, Hal. Let us seek him."

"Lucia," he answered, "we must bear it. Remember the oath we took."

"I have no need to remember it," she replied, "for you

know I only think of him. He is lost, and will die—ALONE."

Hal did not answer her.

He cut a fresh fragment of leather from a piece he had in his pocket, and put it into his mouth, biting it hard to still his mental and bodily agony.

"It was no idle dream," he said, suddenly, "but a warning."

"If we had obeyed it," said Lucia, "we could never have known that it was so."

There was so much force in this logic that he had no rejoinder to give her, and was once more silent.

Higher rose the sun.

As it drew near its meridian, the heat became oppressive, almost suffocating.

None there had ever felt aught like it.

"Is it real?" Hal asked himself, "or do we feel it so because we are weak and suffering?"

It was a question more than one man asked himself that dreadful morning.

As the sun got higher, the shade grew less. For a space of time there would be no shade worth speaking of within the square.

What were they to do when the sun was at its meridian?

How could they hope to endure its heat and accompanying thirst.

"Better die," said one man, speaking half aloud.

"We have the means of ending it all," said another touching his rifle significantly.

Hal saw the spirit of despair that was rising, and rousing himself, he did his best to drive it down.

Rising, he walked around, exhorting them to bear up, the words coming from his parched lips in dry, cracked tones.

"Remember your duty," he said, "and do nothing to disgrace your hitherto noble bearing. Only fools and cowards take their own lives."

They bore up, cheered a little by his words, and now there came a welcome, but awe inspiring relief.

No visible haze was around them, but the sun began to turn again to the strange copper hue and to grow dim.

It looked as if the great orb of day was losing its light.

A flock of birds suddenly appeared in the sky, flying in wild erratic manner, shooting forward and wheeling around uttering strange cries.

"What is this?" asked one of the men. "Is it the end of the world?"

The birds came right over their heads, and then some of them began to fall from fright or fatigue, or it might be both.

There were birds of various sorts.

Buzzards, eagles, crows, pigeons, and prairie hens.

The first that fell into the square was a buzzard, and immediately a dozen men had pounced upon it.

CHAPTER XXXI.

THE STRANGE RELIEF—RETURN OF THE VEILED CAPTAIN—MARNER'S LAST MOMENTS.

THEY tore it to pieces in their sudden frenzy, and ate the coarse flesh dripping with the life blood of the bird, and ere they had well touched their strange and to some perchance repulsive feast, other birds began to fall.

The air was almost dark with the vast flock between the city and the sun,

It seemed as if all the birds of the earth had been gathered together to fly away from some great source of terror.

It rained birds.

They came heavily and in great variety, for the most part killed by their fall, and among them were many that were good eating, which had been made familiar to the men during their wandering lives.

There was enough for all and to spare.

Hal picked up a species of dove and with his knife

removed the skin and cut it up.

Part of it he offered to Lucia, but she turned away.

"I cannot—*yet*," she answered.

Nobody else demurred, and with ravenous haste the men assuaged their hunger and thirst.

Nor was the prisoner forgotten.

It was no part of their duty to starve him and they gave him food.

Meanwhile the vast flock of birds had gone on its way screaming and falling in numbers upon the housetops and streets of the strange city.

And again the copper-coloured sun was looking down upon this strange, unearthly scene.

"Lucia," said Hal, "you must not die."

"I shall not die," Lucia replied. "I can bear up awhile, Hal. I am a woman and cannot save my life as these men and you have done—in men it is nothing —but with me it would be different."

Hal was half distracted.

He could see that Lucia was sinking. Her sufferings were overcoming her.

What could he do to save her?

Then a thought flashed upon him.

The men were all around, each had his rifle, but could not some be spared.

Their foes had diminished, only two were left beside Rigault.

Half-a-dozen rifles against his sister's life. What was it?

Did not the Veiled Captain value her far beyond that?

Yes! he valued her even as his own life. He had ever been tender and solicitous of her welfare.

It was against his wishes that she was there that day.

Without further hesitation Hal proceeded to carry out his scheme.

First he laid it before the men and they all agreed that it was a great thought—a wonderful one— though a matter of small detail.

HE THREW HIS ARMS UP WHEN HE FELL INTO THE STREET BELOW.

In two minutes half-a-dozen rifles were soon broken up and the men were splitting the stocks with their long keen knives.

They had the means of getting a light and soon a small fire was burning.

Of three oth er rifles they made a tripod and suspended two birds from it, roasting them rapidly and roughly.

All the moisture exuded during the process was caught in one of the drinking cups of metal they carried, and it was given to Lucia to drink.

It sufficed to take the keen edge off her thirst.

Then she ate.

It was rough, coarse food, perhaps, but the element of savagery was taken away from it. The hungry, starving Lucia *could eat*.

The men—s aved themselves from immediate destruction—shouted with joy.

They forgot everything else except that they were SAVED.

The copper-coloured sun burned in the sky, the stones below cast off an overpowering heat, but they had gained new life, and could bear it.

In the midst of their joy, they were reminded by Hal that their captain was still away, and that subdued them.

But their returned depression was not destined to last.

In a little while their captain was seen approaching.

But not alone.

He carried his rifle slung at his back, and he had a prisoner in his grasp.

Rigault recognised his old companion, Marner.

A bitter oath escaped his lips.

"One man free now," he muttered, "and that Turrell—will the fox escape?"

The bare thought of that made him furious. He was once more strong and could give vent to the bitterness he felt.

"You will let Turrell go," he said, "and then vow

work will only be half done."

"You ought to rejoice," replied Hal, "because he is your friend."

"Friend!" echoed Rigault, "I hate him as I have always done, with my whole heart. Kill him, torture him, and so long as you let me see *that*, I care not what you do with me."

"A nice lot to work together," muttered Hal.

He turned from Rigault and looked towards his leader, whom he now perceived to be walking very slowly.

His prisoner seemed also worn and weary.

Hal understood it and ran forward to his leader's assistance.

It was timely help he gave him, for the Veiled Captain was sinking with fatigue.

No rest that night and a series of adventures in the maze had broken down for the time his wonderful enduring powers.

As Hal drew near he pushed the prisoner forward and sank down upon the flags.

"Let me be," he said, "do nothing, I shall be better by-and-bye. I have found out the secret of the maze."

Lucia was now by his side.

She knelt down and whispered a few words in his ears

He took her hand and pressed it.

"Food," she said, "I have it. Will you not eat it here?"

"Not yet," he replied, "I have an oath to keep. It is not the time yet for me to be as other men."

But Lucia was not to be put away from her purpose.

She hurried back to the place where her own food had been prepared. Some of it was still left.

This she placed on one side of the monument, and asked Hal to remove the men.

This was done, and Lucia, returning to the Veiled Captain, assisted him to rise.

She led him to the spot where she had placed the

food, and, with a few tender whispered words, left him.

He was now so exhausted that he could scarcely help himself to the welcome nourishment, but, having got one piece between his lips, the rest was easy.

In a little while he was erect again, with his strength wonderfully renewed, a marvellous exhibition of the recuperative powers of the coarsest food.

The men were busy sorting out the edible birds, of which there were at least a hundred, and tying them in twos and threes to their belts.

Hal was not far away awaiting orders from his leader, and a word called him to his side.

"I must tell you my adventures in brief," he said. "I found my way into one of the houses, the door being gone. In it I found two men. I bound this one, and followed the other to the roof. His fate you know. I could see you from there, and perceived that you were all looking towards me.

"Yes," said Hal, "we saw you. It was a strange sight."

"That man," returned the Veiled Captain, pointing at his last prisoner, "was as much as I could hope to bring back with me. Had I found Turrell, I would have slain this one and brought Turrell with me."

"You know nothing of him then," said Hal, "except that he is here?"

"That is all," said the Veiled Captain; "but he is safe. He cannot get away, while I can come and go from the maze at will."

"You have found out the road from it?"

"Yes, but not by the way we came," was the answer. "Enough now. Let Marner be tried, if he needs a trial, and pay the penalty. It will be better for us not to linger here."

CHAPTER XXXII.

MARNER'S END—THE VEILED CAPTAIN'S ANTICIPA-TIONS—THE LAST SEARCH FOR TURRELL.

"NOT even HERE," thought Hal, as he walked away

"will he pause. Dying a few minutes ago, he is now himself again. It is marvellous."

Marner was being held in safe custody, weary and wan with suffering, but not ready to die.

When Hal went up to him, he immediately began to ask that his life might be spared for "a little time." He stood in need of repentance.

It was once more the old story.

He acted and spoke so much like many of his comrades who had gone before him, that it seemed as if one of them had come back to repeat a familiar story.

"You waste your breath," Hal told him. "Your hour has come—you will now be shot according to the law of our Captain. Have you anything to urge against your just sentence?"

"Nothing," replied Marner, "it would be useless I know—I say—nothing."

Then Hal returned to his leader, and the Veiled Captain went up to the prisoner.

"You are doomed to die," he said, "and have nothing to urge against your sentence."

"I did not say that," replied Warner, hoarsely, "I only said it would be useless to do so."

"Look at me now," said the Veiled Captain, speaking low but with a sternness that made itself felt by the prisoner, "now!"

His men had turned away, and he drew his veil aside just for a moment only.

But it was enough.

Marner uttered no cry, he was past that, but his head sunk upon his breast, and a groan escaped him.

"I do not understand how YOU are here," he said; "are you of this world?"

"Yes."

"Then how were you———"

"Enough," interposed the Veiled Captain stepping back, "you know me—say no more."

He turned from him and signalled Hal to proceed.

Rigault had a view of what was going on, and it moved him keenly.

He saw the veil drawn, and marked the look on Marner's face.

But neither one nor the other revealed what he longed to know.

The men, with their rifles, stepped out from the ranks, and Hal took up his stand to give the signal.

Then a thought came to Rigault.

Raising himself up he shouted out the name of his companion in crime.

"Marner!"

The doomed man heard the familiar voice and turned towards him.

"Who is he?" cried Rigault. "You can speak safely. It won't do you any harm to tell, and no good to keep his secret."

Marner opened his lips to reply, but Hal gave the signal.

The rifles sent out their message of death, and Marner with the name of the Veiled Captain on his lips, fell without uttering it.

"Curses on you all," cried Rigault furiously.

Nobody heeded him.

The dead man was picked up and laid aside, and Hal returned to his leader.

"Your sentence has been carried out," he said.

"It only now remains to capture Turrell," was the reply, "bring up the men and let us hasten from here. Believe me we have not a moment to spare."

"We have food now," replied Hal.

"Oh, yes; but I was not alluding to that."

"And you know your way from the maze?"

"Yes; but even that will not save us unless we hasten. Do you see the sun?"

"I do," replied Hal, "and an uncanny sight it is."

"Did you not mark the flight of the birds? But why do I ask you that? What do these signs portend?"

Hal looked at the veiled face wonderingly.

A feeling of awe was gathering in his heart.

"A tremendous commotion in Nature is pending,"

said the Veiled Captain, solemnly. "The warning is given! The birds have heeded it, and we must do so too. There is wreck and ruin in *the air!*"

As he spoke a low, rumbling sound was heard, and the ground beneath their feet seemed to rise a little and subside again.

"It is coming," said the Veiled Captain. "Hasten; but do not alarm the men. Say no more than is necessary."

There was no need to say anything to the men.

Instinctively they understood that heaving of the ground, and now they knew what the heated atmosphere and lurid sun portended.

Rigault knew too, and leaped hastily to his feet.

"An earthquake coming—and *here!*" he yelled. "Hurrah! We shall all be buried alive together. Hurrah!"

He began to dance and caper about like a madman, but was suddenly called to himself by Hal.

"Fall in there," he cried, "we are not buried yet and if it comes to that I will see that you don't escape."

As he spoke he laid hold of Rigault's coat collar and dragged him forward.

The men fell in, and the whole band, headed by the Veiled Captain, marched across the square.

Another shock was felt, and several of the men fell forward on their hands and knees, Hal among them.

He let go of Rigault as he stumbled, and the Red Robin, uttering a wild shout, broke away, and, bound as he was about the arms, ran for his life.

CHAPTER XXXIII.

THE FLIGHT—LUCIA MISSING—THE VEILED CAPTAIN'S SEARCH.

RIGAULT ran swiftly, but there was one swifter of foot speedily on his trail.

The Veiled Captain sprang after him, and ere he was clear of the square that iron grasp was on his collar and he was thrown.

"I yield," he gasped.

"I will take care of you now," the Veiled Captain cried. "Forward, men."

Of all things on earth calculated to inspire terror in man there is nothing that is equal to the commotion of nature known as an earthquake.

The bare idea of a power able to rock the mighty earth, to upheave its surface, is appalling.

It is then that even the strongest of men feels what a helpless creature he is.

Whatever comes to the earth he must cling to it.

To him the terror of the time is greater than can be known by the birds of the air and the fishes in the sea.

But as a matter of fact all creation feels it.

We have described how the birds of all descriptions first gathered together, and then flew screaming on their way—numbers falling from fatigue or fright.

It is no fancy picture.

Great travellers have truthfully told of more wonderful and more terrible things.

What were the feelings of the Veiled Captain and his band?

It is not easy to describe them, for no man spoke nor expressed it, save in hasty flight.

The Veiled Captain at all events kept a cool head, wonderful under the circumstances.

Again was the rocking or shifting of the city felt.

It seemed to glide a little way forward and then back again, like some model on a table moved by human agency.

"Be calm, men," cried the Veiled Captain.

They did not answer him; they could not, for at that moment the whole city rose up slowly and subsided with a sudden shock.

Behind them a crash of falling masonry was heard.

The huge monument in the square was down.

But the buildings immediately around them still stood erect.

Turning here and there the Veiled Captain rapidly

hurried on.

At every corner he passed he stopped to examine it, just for a brief part of a moment.

Hal, in a dim, confused way saw that fragments had been chipped out of the masonry.

In a brief space of time, although it seemed an hour to the hurrying men, they came to a building in which the door, so closely sealed in every other case, was absent.

"In here," the Veiled Captain said.

He stood aside still holding Rigault, and the white-faced men streamed in.

He ran his eye along them.

Hal and a man named Berrell brought up the rear.

"But where is Lucia?" cried the Veiled Captain.

She was not there.

In the strange terror and confusion of the flight she had fallen out from the body unnoticed.

It could not have been so but for the fact of the Veiled Captain being engaged with Rigault.

It was a great misfortune, but Lucia could not be left behind.

"Hal," said the Veiled Captain, "take charge of this ruffian. Let him not escape, I beg of you."

"If he does," replied Hal, "may my life be forfeited.'

"The lives of all are threatened," said Rigault, grimly.

Hal laid hold of him, and the Veiled Captain sped away on the backward route.

Like a faithful dog Berrell followed at his heels.

Another rock.

The houses on each side swayed visibly, and a few fragments of marble came topling down from the parapets above.

One piece struck the Veiled Captain on the shoulder, but heedless of it he sped on.

Another upheaval followed by a strange sound as if some gigantic beast was roaring below.

On—on rushed the Veiled Captain.

At each corner he paused as before to find the

marks he had made on his first visit, but he lost no time.

Berrell's eyes were standing out of his head with the horror of the hovr.

But with set lips he kept close to his leader.

He would have died a thousand deaths rather than desert him.

He would have died as many more for Lucia's sake, like the other men.

So on by the backward road right to the square again —and no Lucia.

"Where is she?" moaned Berrell.

"I understand," said the Veiled Captain, quietly, "she fell out from fear and fatigue, as was natural, because she is a woman, bolder and braver than most of her sex, but still a woman. Then recovering, she took up our trail, as she thought, and *lost her way*."

Lost her way—*here!*" gasped Berrell, his pinched, terrified face bearing a remarkable resemblance to that of Smudge in the old days.

"We must not stay here bewailing," said the Veiled Captain, "but bestir ourselves to find her—Lucia—Lucia!"

He turned back, and, as he came to a corner, he paused and called aloud to her by name.

One, two, three "turnings," and there was no answer.

Again came that dreadful motion of the earth.

Berrell staggered and fell upon his hands and knees.

But in an instant he was up again.

"Forgive me, captain," he said.

"I would forgive a man who is supposed to be much braver than you are," was the reply. "Lucia—Lucia!"

No reply.

The agony of the Veiled Captain was revealed by a sudden clasping of his hands, so tightly that the blood was driven from the tips of his fingers.

"We must go on," he said.

Two turnings more and the name of Lucia cried aloud, and no answer yet.

And now the whole city began to tremble again.

It was not so violent as the rocking, but it was continuous.

It was difficult to keep erect, for the sensation was horrible—it jarred them from head to heel.

Drawing out a knife the Veiled Captain opened it, and signalled to Berrel to follow him.

Then he turned aside from the regular route, and, as he reached the corners, notched them with his knife.

It was but a small nick he was able to make in his haste, but it served.

Suddenly he came upon an entire change of scene.

It was a part of the maze in a semi-ruined state.

It looked as if it had been battered down.

But the Veiled Captain had no time to inspect for there before him lay Lucia on the ground.

He sprang forward and raised her in his arms.

As he nestled her cheek close to his veil he could feel that the warm life blood was still flowing there.

"Back," he cried, hoarsely. "Heaven has guided us to her. Hasten."

The earth still trembled, but the motion was once more subsiding.

But the air was growing darker.

Berrell looked up and saw that the sun was completely hidden by a cloud that covered a third of the sky, and was as black as a pall.

He uttered a shout of terror, and staggered against the nearest wall.

"On for your life," cried the Veiled Captain.

The wretched man—oh! how much like the Smudge of the past did he look now, so potent is fear in changing the face—nerved himself and staggered on behind his leader.

The Veiled Captain was again cool and collected

He had found Lucia and hoped to save her.

The darkness deepened.

Sight was of little use in detecting the small marks chipped out of the marble wall at the corners.

The sense of touch had to be employed, and Berrell was the only one free to use it.

With wise and courageous bearing the Veiled Captain encouraged him, so that they finally came in sight of the spot where Hal had been left with his prisoner.

He was still standing there, holding him firmly in his grasp.

All the rest of the men were inside.

Hal, as he saw his sister, took off his cap and uttered a loud hurrah.

The cry was taken up by the men within.

" He must be more than mortal," thought Rigault, looking at the Veiled Captain and his burden. " Who else, of all men, would have risked their lives to seek her ? Who else could have found her ? "

Lucia opened her eyes, and for a moment looked about her wildly.

It was dim twilight now, and she could only faintly see her friends, but she saw the veiled face close to hers, and a faint, glad cry escaped her lips.

" Saved ! and by YOU," she murmered.

" Can you stand, dearest ? " he asked.

Her answer was to disengage herself from his arms. Then she said :—

" I was weak and foolish. I fell behind and lost sight of you—then when I found I had wandered from the route, I lost all heart, and terror deprived me of my senses."

" All is well now, dearest," said the Veiled Captain, " Hal, I can take the prisoner now."

He had grasped him by the coat collar, and was moving into the building, when a loud rumbling was heard and the crash of masonry filled the air.

" Get in there, quick ! " cried the Veiled Captain

" That place will be our tomb," gasped Rigault.

By way of answer he was dragged in. Hal and Berrell followed, and then as if a large extinguisher had been put over the whole city complete darkness fell upon them.

CHAPTER XXXIV.

IN A LIVING TOMB—DESCENT INTO THE UNDERGROUND CITY—CUT OFF FROM THE SHORE.

THE ground rocked, the din was deafening.

It was like the roar of a hundred pieces of artillery, and the hissing of commingled fire and water.

A living tomb!

Were the words of Rigault prophetic?

It was possible they might be, and every man felt in his heart that his last hour had come.

Suddenly the artillerylike roar ceased, and the rocking and heaving came to an end.

But the darkness remained.

And with it there were intervals of silence, with the crash of falling masonry between, that were apalling.

A living tomb.

The great shock of the earthquake was over, but they were shut in.

The lower chamber in which they were assembled had escaped, but the upper part of the house was down.

Its huge stones blocked up the door, with no crack or crevice to let daylight through.

Whether there was daylight without or not they could not tell.

During a silence the voice of the Veiled Captain was heard.

"Hal!"

"Here, Captain!"

"Come to me and take charge of Rigault—there is a way out from here—I must find it."

Hal groped his way through the men to where his leader stood, and Rigault was passed into his hands.

"Stand back men," said the Veiled Captain, "and get as close as you can to the wall. Do not move again until I tell you."

The men worked their way back, and when the shuffling ceased, their leader was heard softly moving about the floor.

Suddenly a click was heard, and something heavily fell.

"Captain," said Hal, "we have some matches; will you have a light?"

"I thought of that," was the answer, "but we must be careful with them. We have some way to travel in pitchy darkness for aught I know."

Then he was heard moving, and one of the men felt a hand laid upon his arm.

"Come with me," his leader said.

The man felt himself drawn forward, pressed into a sitting position, and then shot down an inclined plain.

There is no need to make any mystery of where the men were going.

The Veiled Captain had discovered a means of getting into the underground city exactly like that by which he had before involuntarily travelled when in the temple on shore.

One by one he led his men to the opening, and assisted them in their descent.

Hal and Rigault went together, and finally came Lucia and the Veiled Captain.

Below it did not seem to be quite so dark.

Although no object could be seen, there was just the faintest possible tinge of light which showed that the Cimmerian darkness no longer existed.

"We can spare a match now, Hal," said the Veiled Captain.

One was lighted and its little flame was sufficient to throw a light on all the faces around.

It was a strange scene, so many of them below in that city dungeon, immured and possibly with a dreadful fate before them.

But the Veiled Captain did not occupy the few brief moments of light in looking at those around him.

He turned his eyes on the inclined plain of stone by which they had descended.

He was studying their exact position so that he

might know the direction to take.

He speedily perceived it, and ere the small match had burned out he had made his arrangements.

Taking Lucia's hand in his, he bade Hal grasp the other, and so on right through, so that they formed a long file of men linked together.

The match went out and they were in darkness again.

The slow march began.

In front the Veiled Captain groped his way with his eyes fixed ahead seeking to penetrate the gloom.

Ere long the promise of light began to be fulfilled.

The darkness softened, a faint whiteness appeared in the distance, and by degrees a soft twilight gladdened their hearts.

They could see around them and the mysteries of the underground city were before their eyes.

The marvellous sight we briefly described before, and there is little that is new to tell.

On every side was the impalpable dust, all that remained of a host dead and gone, it might be ere our present history of the world began.

What wonders there were to explore, but none of the band were disposed to linger.

The one great longing in their hearts was to get into the full daylight again.

The Veiled Captain noticed that the light was fainter than when he first saw this wonderful place and he judged it arose from the city above being in ruins.

He was right.

The upper city of the lake was a wreck.

With his keen instincts for locality he kept steadily on his way through the dull silent streets until he came to places he knew, and now, if all was well with the openings leading to the outer air, they were saved.

He came to the one near the inner part of the bridge by which he had first emerged from the underground city.

Bidding his friends wait a few minutes he

climbed up the incline plane and came to the huge stone flags above.

It worked by pulling the bolt down from the inside and it was still in order.

The room above, too, was intact, but the doorway was nearly blocked up with fallen masonry.

There was, however, an opening left wide enough for him to creep through.

He was soon outside and, standing erect, looked around him.

What a scene of ruin !

It was a chaos of marble. The vast city looked like a ground where giants had shot millions of cart-loads of huge stones.

Its beauty was destroyed for ever.

Then from the city he turned his eyes shoreward and saw what troubled him most.

The long bridge was gone.

It had vanished as totally as if it had never existed.

Not a stone peeped above the surface of the placid lake.

CHAPTER XXXV.

THE UTTER RUIN OF THE CITY—CAPTIVE WITHIN ITS RUINS—UNDER THE SILENT STARS.

NOT a vestige of it remained.

Even the great central arch had vanished as if it had never existed and nothing was to be seen of Smudge or the men left on duty there.

It was with a heavy heart that the Veiled Captain scanned the country round in the hopes of seeing some signs of them on shore.

But there was no vestige of them.

And the forest had suffered, too.

Many of the trees had fallen and others were half down and tangled together like a lot of sticks tossed carelessly together.

The face of the distant cliff was broken up. A great landslip had taken place, and part of the forest above had come with it, some of the trees being down and

RIGAULT MAKES A LAST APPEAL FOR MERCY.

others still erect as if unharmed by their being so violently shifted.

So far the changes on the earth were very great, but overhead the normal condition of things was restored.

The sky was without a cloud; the sun half-way towards the west had resumed its usual appearance.

In the distance were half-a-dozen birds quietly sailing in the air.

A peaceful scene.

The earthquake had ceased from its labours, and the world was at rest.

"In this way," said the Veiled Captain, "are wrought the great changes in the world."

Only one way out remained now, and that was through the passage under the lake to the temple on shore.

Was that way open to them?

If not, what was to be done?

Of all the men under him the Veiled Captain knew that not half-a-dozen could swim.

The rest would go like plummets to the bottom.

He stepped down into the room again and descended the incline plane.

They were all awaiting his coming with natural impatience.

In a few words he told them what he had seen, offering no surmise as to the fate of Smudge and the rest of the men.

He had no need to do so.

It seemed but too probable that they had perished.

"I will leave you here for awhile," said the Veiled Captain, "and see if the way out is clear. It will not take long."

After a few reassuring words whispered to Lucia, he went on and was soon lost in the gloom beyond.

For the most part the men remained silent until he returned. There was little or no disposition to talk.

Ere long the Veiled Captain reappeared.

"Friends," he said, "that way out is barred also. The

temple is down. Let us go into the open air and devise a means of getting ashore."

The task of getting out of their subterranean prison was soon performed, and the whole party gathered on the outside ruins

In the sweet pure air and brilliant daylight their spirits revived.

The sun was going down, and night would soon be here; but what of that—now?

They had escaped the mightiest peril of all, and surely they would not perish.

One thought was in the minds of many there — among them Rigault.

What had become of Larry Turrell?

Where was the once bold leader of the daring, blood-thirsty band of Red Robins?

Was that wrecked city his mighty tomb—a mausoleum fit for a monarch—could it be devoted to the covering of the bones of a merciless ruffian?

Some such thought passed through the Veiled Captain, and with it came a feeling of regret.

It was not for such an end to Larry Turrell that he had toiled.

The end of the leader, and his chief lieutenant, Rigault, had been otherwise devised.

"But if it is so let it be so," he said.

The position of his band of brave men was still bad, but not so desperate as before.

It is true that they had nothing but raw bird's flesh to eat, but there was no lack of water.

The lake was accessible, and they slaked their thirst.

By-and-by the sun went down, and the stars came out with wondrous brilliancy, as if desirous of doing their share towards making amends for the miseries of the past day.

In sheltered nooks among the ruins the men disposed themselves to rest.

For Lucia there was found a quiet corner, and Hal stretched himself on the bare ground not far away.

The Veiled Captain alone made no attempt to sleep.

The spirit of unrest that had troubled him so many times before kept him awake

He lay down at a distance to ease the minds of those who loved him so dearly, and when all was still he rose up and walked away among the ruins of the wrecked city.

Guided by the dim starlight, he clamoured over the piles of massive stones, pausing here and there to look around him, until he came to a spot which he judged must be near to what was once the entrance to the maze.

Here he remained awhile communing, dwelling on the events of the past twenty-four hours.

Was Larry Turrell dead?

Could he have been assured of that he would have rested that night.

But a feeling, amounting to a conviction, that the Red Robin chief had escaped, was upon him.

The records of nearly all great disasters show that marvellous escapes are not rare.

The escape of himself and his men from what seemed to be certain death was an instance of the possibility of Larry Turrell being yet alive.

There is an old saying that the worse a man is the harder he dies.

It is the good and true that suffer most, but not always.

Thus communing with himself the Veiled Captain stood awhile motionless as a statue.

His figure was in harmony with the scene, for it was spectral in the dim light of the stars.

He was like the "Last man," that Campbell wrote —the man whom the poet imagined to be the spectator of the death of all living things on earth.

> I saw a vision in my sleep,
> That gave my spirit strength to sweep
>   Adown the gulf of Time.
> I saw the last of human mould,

That shall creation's death behold
As Adam saw its prime.

So wrote the poet, and the pathetic figure of the Veiled Captain was fit to play the part he dreamt of.

"The end surely is near," said the Veiled Captain, half aloud.

It was little more than a whisper that left his lips, but it echoed softly around him, and died away into a sigh in the distance.

The weird spirit of the past seemed to cling around the city still.

A moment later and a slight sound on his right fell upon the ears of the Veiled Captain.

It was nothing more than what the slipping of a handful of chips of stone might have made.

A natural sound in that place so recently wrecked.

But the Veiled Captain's attention was turned in the direction of it.

Motionless he stood, eyes and ears keenly wakeful.

Another slip of masonry, and more noise than before, *and in the same spot.*

This fact sufficed to assure the Veiled Captain that something living was moving there.

Slowly and without the least sound he sank into a crouching position.

The spot on which he fixed his eyes, and from whence the sound came, was a sloping mass of broken stone, with great boulder-like pieces sticking out of it, huge slabs that had formed the heavier portion of a building.

In one part of the heap there was a dark spot, a hole showing that there was a hollow below.

In this the Veiled Captain directed his especial attention.

Something white, or nearly so, fluttered a moment at this hole and then disappeared.

With a slow movement, silent as a spirit, the Veiled Captain sank upon his hands and crept forward.

Inch by inch he moved on.

The white thing fluttered again and then rose slowly up.

It was the face of a bare-headed man—Larry Turrell.

By a miracle, as it may appear, he had escaped death in the great commotion.

He had got thus far on the road to freedom late on the previous day, and would have made good his escape by swimming ashore, but for the sudden appearance of his foe.

Turrell saw in the daylight the figure of the Veiled Captain standing aloft surveying the scene of ruin.

In terror he sought a hiding-place and found one in the hollow from which he was now emerging.

First his head and then his shoulders appeared.

Slowly as if he feared the very cracking of his joints would reveal his presence, he replaced the hat he held in his hand upon his head.

Nearer came the figure of the avenger.

Every projection to hide his form was utilised.

Larry Turrell looking about, with wild eyes—and quaking with fear—saw no living thing.

Up—up he rose until he was clear of his hiding-place and then he stood erect and looked about him.

Nothing in view to add to his terror.

"If I can only reach the water," he said.

He was a splendid swimmer, and the task of reaching the shore would have been a very light one to him.

And the faintly gleaming water was not far away.

Over a few heaps of ruins and across the great square, clear of obstacles in the middle, and then a quiet drop into the cool lake.

A hundred strokes with his strong arms, and he would be on shore.

There he could hide, and if need be, would live like a beast in the forest until all danger was past.

The tenacity with which men cling to life, when life

seems hardly worth the living, is wonderful.

The days and weeks of fear which had embittered his waking hours, still left Larry Turrell clinging to his wretched existence.

On, with now and then a slight slip, he went over the ruins.

Behind him came the shadow figure of the Veiled Avenger.

What hope there was in the Red Robin's heart?

His watchful eyes roamed on every side, but he saw nothing to trouble him.

All was still.

Once he turned to look behind him, but the Veiled Captain melted away behind some masonry and became a part of its shadow.

The square was crossed, and the spot where the bridge had once been was gained.

A short descent down the shattered stonework and the water would be reached.

Down, with redoubled care, went Larry Turrell.

Behind him, closing up, came the Veiled Captain, with that silent step that had helped to make him and his men so terrible to their foes.

The water was reached, it lapped over the soles of his boots, and he was cautiously stepping in, when a hand was laid upon his shoulder.

"Larry Turrell, yield yourself. Your hour has come!"

The voice of the Veiled Captain rang out loud and clear, echoing across the water and far away.

The Red Robin answered it with a despairing cry.

Then threw up his arms and sank in a senseless heap at the feet of the triumphant avenger.

CHAPTER XXXVI.

LARRY TURRELL—A VOICE FROM THE SHORE—THE WAY OF ESCAPE.

THE Veiled Captain stood for a few minutes looking at his fallen foe.

What was in his heart was not in any way expressed by word or action.

Exultant he may have been, and possibly was, for there lay the last of the long list of his foes within his reach.

Possibly he might have wished that he had shown more courage, but although the man was his foe he was ready to make allowance for the weakness that had laid him senseless on the ground.

Recent events had been sufficiently appalling to take the heart out of any man.

After awhile the Veiled Captain stooped and raised Larry Turrell into a sitting position.

Then he dragged him up a few feet and placed his back against a huge stone.

In that position he allowed him to remain, and taking the cord, which he, in common with his men, carried, the Veiled Captain bound his arms to his side.

Then he sat down facing his prisoner and awaited his return to consciousness.

He knew a man of Turrell's great natural strength would not long remain unconscious.

It was a strange scene.

There, immovable, sat the Veiled Captain, with his eyes resting on the last of the Red Robins brought within the mesh so deftly woven round them.

There sat Larry Turrell, blessed for a few brief minutes from unconsciousness, still also.

Above them both the quiet stars, around them the ruins of a city that had a right to be numbered among the wonders of the world.

By-and-bye he heaved a sigh and opened his eyes,

For a moment or two he sat quite still in a half dreamy state. Suddenly his eyes fell upon the form of the Veiled Captain and he uttered a short, agonised cry.

" Sit still," said his captor.

He would have risen, but on hearing this command he fell back again to the attitude in which he had been placed, staring with distended eyes at the veiled face.

" Who are you ?" he asked, after a silence.

His voice was so harsh that it sounded on the still night air like the croak of some bird of prey.

"That you will know anon," was the answer, given in a low, clear voice.

"Why have you so pursued me?" Larry Turrell asked, a moment later.

"I am the agent of Justice," was the answer. "The avenger of the wrongs of many. Let that suffice. You will know no more until your last hour comes."

"Is it not here?"

"No—not yet—and it may not be for many days. You will have to be taken to a Court of Justice."

"That will take some time," thought Larry Turrell, with a sigh of relief.

It seemed as if the Veiled Captain could read his very thoughts, for he immediately said:

"The court to which you will be taken is not one fashioned by the hand of man. There prisoners have been condemned but never tried. You will be both."

"Whatever I have done," said Turrell with dry lips. "I have bitterly paid for. Think of that, and have some pity for me."

"Pity!" said the Veiled Captain scornfully, "a strange word to come from your lips. When did you show it?"

"Never; I admit it," answered Larry Turrell, "but I ask it."

"Peace," said the Veiled Captain; "say no more. You ask in vain for pity, which in your mind means mercy. I cannot show it to you. It would be neither right nor just. For the sake of others you are lost, a man to whom none will be shown."

"And yet you talk of a trial."

"With the certain knowledge that you cannot escape condemnation."

"Ah, then it——"

"Silence."

Turrell closed his lips and fell into a mood of sullen despair.

He had made his appeal and had received his answer, What need to waste breath in asking for mercy?

So these two remained silent and still during the hours of darkness.

Occasionally Larry Turrell moved a little restlessly, but the Veiled Captain never stirred.

The terror of his prisoner was thus doubly and trebly increased, and gradually the Red Robin chief became as a man frozen with terror.

At last the night was over, and the first light of the morning came.

Barely was it reflected on the bosom of the lake when sounds of stirring of men were heard in the distance.

The Veiled Captain rose up and uttered a peculiar cry.

It was answered by a shout, and then there came hurrying towards him half a score of his men.

They uttered another shout when they saw Larry Turrell a prisoner.

"Ah! shout now," cried the Veiled Captain, "victory is on our side, our task is nearly done. The restraint so long put upon you is at an end."

Again they shouted and tossed their hats in the air.

They were answered in the distance, and in a few minutes Hal, with Rigault, and followed by Lucia and the rest of the gallant band, came over the ruins down to the lake.

Another hurrah.

It echoed far and wide ere it died away.

But hark! what is this? An echo far behind the rest, or a cry from the shore.

It came from the region of the wood, and created fresh echoes.

A light sprang into Hal's face.

"Friends ashore," he cried.

"Shout again," said the Veiled Captain.

The voices of his men rent the air and could have been heard a mile away.

Once more they were answered, and immediately after some men came rushing from the wood.

Smudge foremost.

It was not easy to mistake that familiar figure, and if any possible doubt existed his frantic caperings of joy would have dispelled it.

Such shouting and waving of hats followed as had never been indulged in during all their wanderings.

Even Lucia lifted up her musical voice and waved her handkerchief with joy.

The Veiled Captain and the two prisoners alone stood still and silent.

The latter had no share in this demonstration, and the former's time to remove his veil and toss his hat in the air had not yet come.

Rigault and Larry Turrell were placed side by side, and neither spoke at first.

It was Rigault who spoke at last.

"I am satisfied now," he said.

Larry Turrell turned his bloodshot eyes upon him as he replied huskily:

"And I too am satisfied. You were always a miserable dog."

"It is safe for you to say so now," returned Rigault. "Had we kept better together; had you shown a bolder front and been more of a man, we should not be here to-day."

"I had no faith in any of you," Turrell answered.

At that moment they were separated, and a guard of four men took possession of each.

The rest gathered about the Veiled Captain and Hal for instructions how to act.

Plans were being arranged to get ashore.

On the shore Smudge and the men with him were also engaged in discussing the important problem.

The Veiled Captain eventually solved it.

"All who can swim, stand out," he said.

Eight men advanced—two of them being part of the prisoner's guard.

Others were promptly put in their places.

"Go ashore," said the Veiled Captain, "and take with you the axes we carried with us during our journey; also every fragment of rope of which we are possessed, save those which tie the prisoners. It should be easy for you to make a raft that will carry at least three or four of us at a time."

The plan was good, and, as the Veiled Captain said, not difficult of execution.

With high hopes in their hearts his men proceeded to carry out his instructions.

The pieces of rope were gathered together, tied in two bundles, and fastened round the waists of the two best swimmers.

Half-a-dozen axes were also secured in a similar way —one to each of the other men.

Then they threw off their jackets and hats, took to the water, and struck out for the shore.

With keen anxiety they were watched as they made their way steadily along.

Burdened as they were, swift swimming was out of the question; but they were strong men, and one by one they finally reached land, where they were received with every demonstration of joy by Smudge and the men with him.

"We have nothing to do now but wait," said the Veiled Captain.

He sat down upon the ruins near him, Lucia taking a seat by his side.

Nobody asked him how he had captured Larry Turrell.

In his own good time he would tell them the story.

Meanwhile it was sufficient that he had captured the last of the robber band, and the task they had steadily performed, never swerving in their fidelity to their chief, seemed to be near its end.

CHAPTER XXXVII.

THE WAY ASHORE—GRACE TO THE MEN TO GROW RICH—RIGAULT'S LAST APPEAL.

"THE Raft."

It was Hal who cried out, and every eye was turned

towards the shore.

For three hours or more Smudge and the men ashore had laboured like giants, cutting the smaller trunks into suitable lengths with their axes, and afterwards binding them together with such means as they had at their command.

Only a small raft could be made under the circumstances, but it sufficed, and was indeed better than a larger one, as it could be the more easily propelled.

For the latter purpose, poles of young pine, about the thickness of a man's wrist at the smaller end, had been cut, and in addition two rude paddles were shaped by one of the men, a handy fellow who had been often found of use in an emergency.

The morning was getting on when the raft was taken from the edge of the wood down to the lake on rough rollers fashioned for the purpose.

It floated, and the water was shallow enough at first to enable Smudge and another man who had leaped upon it to punt it with the poles fifty yards from the shore.

Then in the ordinary course they came to deep water, and the poles were no longer of service.

For this emergency the paddles had been provided, but happily they were little needed.

The ingenuity of Smudge came to the rescue.

He guided the raft to where the bridge had been, and then found that the ruins of it were only a few feet under the water.

By following the straight course they could punt all the way

Rigault observing this, muttered to himself:

"Smudge has a head upon his shoulders, and we used to put him down as an arrant fool."

The process of getting the Veiled Captain and the rest was the work of time, but it was successfully accomplished without accident.

Four at a time, in addition to those who managed the raft, were all that could safely travel.

Hal and the Veiled Captain brought their prisoners ashore.

It was in the heart of both Rigault and Larry Turrell to jump off and make an end of their miserable existence.

But the old hesitation prevailed.

All was not over yet—all indeed might never be over —while there was life there was hope.

At last all were ashore, and the successful landing was celebrated with a feast and general rejoicing.

There was no lack of provisions, of a rough description, it is true, but with such appetites as they had the simplest fare was the sweetest of food.

Rigault and Turrell were treated in a very unceremonious fashion.

To prevent the necessity of employing half a dozen men to guard them, they were tethered to huge logs so that running away was simply impossible.

What a change there was in the Veiled Captain's men.

No longer grim and silent, they laughed and chatted. sang songs and exchanged jests.

The restraint so long upon them was taken off.

They were like sailors come ashore after a long voyage.

The Veiled Captain did not join in their merriment.

He sat a little apart with his face to the two tethered and humiliated prisoners.

Not even their slightest movement escaped him.

Smudge told the story of his escape with his men.

They stood several shocks of earthquake, until the great central archway began to break up.   Then fear took possession of them and they ran.

"I set the example," said Smudge, frankly; "my old self came back to me.   I don't think I ever ran so fast in my life."

"Nobody will blame you for it," said Hal; "that shifting of the earth is a horrible sensation.   I never felt anything like it."

"The bridge sank behind us as we ran," continued Smudge; "in fact, it was all under water before we reached the shore. Great fountains of water sprang up in the lake, playing with a fierce, hissing sound. The water went from the shore like a huge receding wave. Then it came back with a rush and swept us clean off our legs, landing us right up against the wood."

"There," continued Smudge, " the trees were being tumbled about like sticks. You see how they are. It was a fearful sight, and when we looked back and saw the city collapsing like a piled up pack of cards, we all thought the end of the world had come."

Then he told of their feeling certain that all the friends had been buried in the ruins, of their great grief and their final resolve to wait for two days, and if no signs of them appeared to go away and tell the women and children left behind of the loss they had sustained.

"But now all is well, and we can all go back together and tell a different story," Smudge said.

"We are not there yet," said Hal quietly; "it's a longish journey. It is always as well not to be too sure. At the same time, of course, we need not be funky."

Then arose the question in the minds of many, "Are we to go back as poor as we came?" but they only thought it, and no man uttered it aloud.

Under the ruins of the great city, and possibly in many places easily to be got at, there lay the wealth of kings. Some of it surely could be got at.

If so they would not only return triumphant but rich.

Before night fell they had another proof of the thoughtfulness of their leader.

The same idea had occurred to him.

A search party could easily go to and fro on the raft, and the reward of a few days' labour was pretty sure.

He called them together and said:

"Friends, you have done your duty nobly and an adequate reward from me is impossible. But yonder

lies that which will put you all above the cares of this world. We will rest here seven days. Do what you can in that time. On the morning of the eighth day, whether your search be fruitful or not, we depart from here."

The men cheered this announcement, and Hal at once divided the men into three parties.

One, composed of the men who could swim, were appointed to the work in the city.

This was done in case of any accident to the raft.

A second party had to provide food for all.

The third party, with Smudge for a captain, was to act as guard over the prisoners.

It was too late that day to do anything, so they spent the rest of the day in erecting two rude shelters, one for Lucia and the other for their leader, to be used at night.

The latter piece of work was somewhat superfluous, for their leader had no sleep.

While all but three men appointed to watch over the prisoners slept, he walked slowly up and down near them

Had there been any attempt on their part to escape he alone would have frustrated it.

But they did not think of it.

Both were worn out, and they slept until long after the men were up and busy.

The seekers of food had gone away on the trail of deer; the diamond and jewel seekers had returned to the ruins.

Part of the restrictions on Rigault had been removed, his legs were free, but Larry Turrell, as if he were the prisoner most valued, was still tethered.

Rigault, with a sudden impulse, rose up and walked towards the Veiled Captain, who stood quietly regarding his movements.

Close by was the guard, with their rifles awaiting the order to shoot him down or drive him back, as their Captain might desire.

But the order was not given.

"What is it, Rigault?" asked the Veiled Captain.

The Red Robin threw himself upon his knees.

"Put an end to my misery somehow," he cried, clasping his hands, "I have dreamt all night of *torture* such as I—I—have seen."

"Such torture as you have inflicted on others, you mean," replied the Veiled Captain, quietly.

Rigault moaned.

"I cannot deny it," he said; "it would be useless. It seems to me as if it were impossible to hide either the past or present from you."

"There are some things you cannot hide from me," was the answer; "but I am only mortal—like yourself."

"Tell me," said Rigault, with the dew of perspiration on his brow, "that I shall not be tortured."

"I will tell you NOTHING," replied the Veiled Captain sternly. "Back to your companion and beware how you take advantage of the little liberty given you. I tell you that *you cannot escape from me.* Go back."

Rigault rose up and returned to Larry Turrell, who met him with a sneering smile.

"I hardly recognised the bold Rigault," he said.

"I am breaking," was the answer; "I wish it was all over."

"It will come soon enough," said Larry Turrell, with a shudder. "Why don't you make a run for it and let them shoot you down?"

Rigault did not answer.

He sank down in a sitting position and buried his face in his hands.

Thus he remained until breakfast was brought and placed before the pair.

The day passed, and the Veiled Captain spent most of the time near them, and when he did leave them for awhile they felt that he was not far away.

His place was always taken by Smudge, who seemed proud of his position as jailor of the men who had formerly treated him as if he had been a mangy cur.

But he did not speak to them.

They reviled him in no measured terms, but with

indifferent scorn he stood at his post and uttered never a word.

Nor did anyone else speak to them that day.

The hunting party returned laden with the spoils of the chase, and the raft brought back the men who had been in the city with an ample reward for their day's labour.

Rigault and Larry Turrell saw a bag of jewels emptied out before the band, and listened to their estimation of the value of the find.

It was galling to be obliged to compare their lot of bondage, with prospective Death, to the light hearted freedom of their captors.

Both Rigault and Turrell suffered the torture of Tantalus.

It was the love of wealth, no matter in what form, that had made them what they were.

To be rich by a short route they had robbed and murdered in the old days—and though on the brink of a precipice, with the dark depths of Eternity below them, the old cupidity at the sight of those jewels was warmed up again.

"Oh! to be free and possessed of *that*," thought Rigault.

The bag, with its precious contents, was given to Lucia, who was to be their banker until the time came to divide the spoil.

In a covert way Rigault watched her every movement, and he saw her place the bag under the shelter where she slept. It was scarce a dozen yards from the spot where he sat captive.

Around him, in a slowly moving circle, paced the guard—four in number.

One was ever in front of him and one behind.

To make the least movement without being observed was impossible.

But when night came might he not risk it?

If it were very dark could he not creep across to that rude shelter and kill her?

Bound as he was he felt that he could do it.

CHAPTER XXXVIII.

PLAYING WITH THE MICE—RIGAULT HAS A CON-
GENIAL TASK SET HIM WHICH HE CARRIES
OUT WITH CREDIT.

IF no other way presented itself, Rigault could act like a wild beast. He had his teeth, sharp and strong, to use and he was ready to do so.

But while he was revolving certain things in his mind, Larry Turrell was watching him, and being a shrewd guesser at other men's thoughts he quickly hit upon what was revolving in his mind.

"It's no use, Rigault," he said, in a low tone, when evening had come and the pair sat in the line of a shaft of golden light putting a glory round and above them which was not at all in harmony with the darkness within them.

"What are you talking about?" asked Rigault, in a whisper.

"You can't get away without ME," said Turrell.

"You can't go," said Rigault; "they have shackled you like a beast."

"Yes; and you have some freedom—but I say that you shall not go without me. Try it."

"Well," said Rigault, "if you will tell me what I can do, I will do it."

"Can't you BITE through these cords?" asked Turrell.

It was a new thought and it only occurred to him at the moment.

They both marvelled that they had not thought of it before.

"Stoop your head," said Rigault; "look as if you were thinking. Yes, it is a good idea. We might do it for each other. Once free we can either run for it or try to get what they have given to the girl. If we could but get away——"

"Never mind what she's got," said Turrell; "if we can get away let us do so without stopping to run a risk of that sort."

"I won't go without the jewels," said Rigault. "What's life with poverty for a constant chum?"

"I suppose you will do as you please," said Turrell, with a stifled groan; "but I tell you the risk is too great."

To this Rigault made no reply.

He had set his heart on getting hold of the gems, and would not budge from his programme of action.

Everything seemed to play into their hands that night.

They heard one of the men say that the Veiled Captain had gone away on one of his excursions in search of solitude, and in all probability would not be back until dawn.

The men who had been out all day were tired, and before night had fairly set in many of them were asleep.

Lucia retired early too, and Hal, after changing the guard of the prisoners, also lay down, and seemed to sleep immediately.

As the night came on the darkness promised to be deep.

A thick mist hung in the air, obscuring the stars, and the moon would not rise until late.

Yes, everything seemed in their favour, and the two ruffians stretched themselves out, shamming sleep to throw the guards off from watching too closely.

Lying close together Rigault could easily get at the cords that bound his companion's arm, and, stealthily as a rat, he began operations.

The task was a heavy one, and could only have been performed under the pressure of circumstances, for the rope was strong, and the position Rigault was obliged to adopt very painful.

Slowly he worked his way on, pausing now and then to listen.

All around was still.

Even the tread of the sentries was not heard.

The latter fact caused Rigault some surprise, and set him thinking.

He sat up for a moment or two, and looked about him.

It was now so dark that he could not see very far,

but he was sure that nothing in the form of a man was near him.

"What can that mean?" he asked himself.

Then a thought that the men, wearied out, were neglecting their duty and skulking, asleep perhaps, flashed upon him.

It was a reasonable thought, and it made him exultant, for all things seemed to play into his hands.

"We shall get away," he thought, and, with renewed vigour, went to work again.

His sharp teeth bit through the rope, and it yielded. Larry Turrell, after a quiet struggle, got one arm free, and the rest was comparatively easy.

He then essayed to release his companion, but after a few bites gave up the job with a stifled curse.

"You must untie it," Rigault said, in the softest of whispers.

This was a stiff job, but Larry Turrel had some knowledge of knotting, and after feeling carefully all over the rope he got at the key to the way Rigault was bound.

A turn or two at the rope and he also was free.

Released, they could have shouted, but they were wary and sat still listening.

Not a sound.

Nobody apparently near them.

What did it mean?

"Let us go right away," whispered Turrell. "It's a chance and we shall not get another."

"I'll have that bag of diamonds," replied Rigault doggedly. "You stop here!"

On his hands and knees he started, crawling towards the rough shelter under which Lucia was supposed to be sleeping.

Every time he drew himself on a foot or so he stopped to listen.

The same strange silence as before.

"I'll have it," he muttered.

The shelter of boughs was before him. He could

see it faintly limned in the gloom.

And now he stopped again and listened for the sound of breathing within.

Not a sound.

Puzzled more and more, he crept nearer and listened again.

The same wonderful stillness prevailed.

"It's odd," he muttered.

And now he was near the shelter—then inch by inch crept under it, groping about.

What is this he touched.

A small bag—the prize!

It was his. He grasped it, and backed out of the shelter.

"There is no need to kill her *now*," he thought, "but shall I?"

It would be a sweet revenge upon the Veiled Captain, but the risk?

What of that?

Was it worth the while?

No.

He had the bag with its precious contents. Better for his own sake to get away.

Elated he crept back to where he had left Turrell and laid a hand gently upon his arm.

"I've got it," he whispered.

"And the girl?"

"I let her live."

"It was wise," muttered Turrell, "women and cats are both hard to kill."

Now if Rigault had dared to have done it he would have deserted his companion, but he knew that Turrell would at any cost raise an alarm.

So he kept to him, and the two men who hated each other with their whole hearts perforce joined issue in their efforts to escape from the Veiled Captain.

But already each was plotting in his heart against the other.

Still surrounded by foes and not by any means

assured of their escape, 'each arranged in his own mind a plan by which he was to become the sole survivor and possessor of that small bag of diamonds.

Murder to them was nothing, whether friend or foe were to be the victims.

It was simply a question of their own safety and profit that they considered.

"Caution," whispered Rigault, "the slightest sound may betray us."

He had kept in his mind the position they were in, and his plan was to make towards the wood through which they had passed on their journey thither.

Once within it he would feel tolerably safe.

True, there was the remembrance of those gibbering faces the Red Robins had seen, and the wild cries that rung in the forest that night were recalled by memory to his ears.

But even these horrors were as nothing to the fear inspired by the Veiled Captain.

To the forest he would go, and risk what came of it.

With a light step and slow he began the retreat, testing the ground each time before he put his feet down, in case some rotten twig should lie in the way.

Or perchance he might come upon one of his foes lying on the ground.

But no; they saw nothing, heard nothing.

The stillness of the tomb lay on all things around.

Puzzled, but still rejoicing at the prospect of escape, Rigault kept slowly on, halting when he came to a tree to rest a moment and listen.

On, on; no sound of foe about, and all around them terribly dark, Turrell close behind him

They had not far to go to reach the more open ground on the borders of the lake, and presently they came to it.

Here there was a little light to guide them, but not

much.

The stars were hidden by clouds.

Overhead, no dome of black marble could have been more opaque.

Everything favoured them.

"We shall get away," thought Rigault.

On, for a hundred yards or more, stopping to listen every two or three steps, they went groping their way and with watchful eyes looking out for the water.

At length Rigault paused, and Turrell pulled up close beside him.

The darkness seemed to be deepening, for now, though close, they could only faintly see each other.

"What does this mean?" asked Rigault.

"I don't know," replied Turrell.

"Did you ever see anything like it?"

"Never."

As the last word was spoken, the clouds above them seemed to be suddenly rent in twain, and a blinding light filled the air.

It was so fierce, so vivid, that they both sank upon their knees with the terror it inspired.

The next instant came a clap of thunder that was absolutely deafening.

Crouching on the ground they listened with quaking hearts until it rumbled and rolled away in the distance.

Then silence again.

Rigault was the first to recover himself and putting his hand to his face he found it was covered with perspiration that was cold and clammy.

"What's come to the world?" he asked, hoarsely. "Is this the end of it?"

"I don't know," replied Turrell, in cracked tones, "let us get on; can you see your way?"

"We must find it somehow," was the weary reply.

Once more they began their strange flight and could only crawl on their way.

Twice they walked into the waters of the lake and backed out with sodden feet.

The darkness was profound.

And now a new terror was upon them.

In addition to the fear of their foes there was the horror inspired by that blinding flash of lightning and prodigious clap of thunder.

Would there be another like it?

The fear of it induced them to walk with bowed heads, but as the moments passed and the stillness and darkness remainsd unbroken they began to hope there would be no more.

Vain hope.

Again the sky was rent.

This time the light seemed to be one vast sheet of flame and the thunder came simultaneously with it, with a tremendous crash that shook the earth.

Again the two Red Robins staggered, but they did not fall.

In a frenzy of fear they clung to each other, and with eyes closed awaited the dying away of the thunder.

But ere it ended another flash came.

Another and another.

Thunder and lightning—thunder and lightning—the dry air filled with the most appalling sounds—a chaos of the elements.

Nothing that they had ever experienced before could be said to approach it.

It was terrible, horrible.

And while the lightning flashed and the thunder roared, a hissing sound bearing down upon them was heard, even above the storm.

It was like the rushing of a river broken from its bed and then with the force of a thousand whips the rain fell upon them.

CHAPTER XXXIX.

AFTER THE STORM—A DISAPPOINTMENT AND ANOTHER HUMILIATION.

AND such rain.

It came down in huge drops and sheets.

It beat round about them and upon them with the

fury of something animate bent on pounding them to pieces.

They could barely stand up against its power, and only did so by clinging to each other.

In one moment, as they thought, they were drenched to the skin.

They could feel the water running down them as if from a waterspout, it gathered about their feet in a pool, it beat the lake into the semblance of a furious sea.

With this fearful downpour the vividness of the lightning sensibly diminished, but it still flashed and the thunder rolled unceasingly.

The two Red Robins were next door to being drowned.

Drenched to the skin they stood still until the fury of the rainfall began to abate.

Then by slow degrees they gathered back the power to walk, and guided by the frequent flashes of lightning staggered on by the shore of the lake, for now the worst of the storm, fit following to that terrible earthquake, was over.

The pall-like clouds lost their density, the rain sank to a drizzling mist, and the time elapsing between the flashes of lightning and the boom of the thunder showed that the centre of the atmospheric agitation was rolling away.

Then came breaks here and there in the sombre sky with a peep of the stars, never before so bright and beautiful to those two wretched men as they were that hour.

" I thought it was all over with us and everything else," said Larry Turrell. " Whoever saw the like ? "

" Well ! it is as good as over," muttered Rigault, " and as its left nothing but a wet skin I'm hanged if I care."

" Don't use that word."

" What word ? "

" Hanged."

" I won't if you don't like it," said Rigault. "Now what are we to do ? Can you keep on ? "

"Not very far," said Turrell, "I'm as stiff and sore as if I had been thrashed all over."

They were in as sore a plight as ever two wretched wanderers experienced in this world.

To rest on that rain-sodden ground was impossible, to go on far, weary as they were, was beyond their powers.

They passed along the length of the lake and came to the foot of the great landslip, and there fortune favoured them.

A hundred rills and minor cataracts were pouring down from the higher land above, but in one place some fallen trees had been knotted together with a huge clod of earth on the top, forming a roof.

Beneath it the ground was dry and into this shelter they crept with thankful hearts, and stretched their full length upon the ground.

"It is as good as a feather bed," said Rigault, "but hark you, Turrell, we must not sleep. It is only a rest we can take, and then on."

"I would give something for an hour's sleep," sighed Turrell.

But it was not to be, they dare not risk it.

The warmth of their shelter sorely tried them, and it required all their resolution to keep awake.

Perhaps the more powerful inducement to do so lay in the fact that they had each resolved to kill the other and naturally both had doubts about trusting his fellow.

So they rested an hour or so, and then went on.

The landslip, wet and slippery for the most part, had now to be scaled, and step by step they struggled to the summit.

It was exhausting work, and another long rest was imperative.

But now they were beginning to feel comparatively safe.

"We shall have a view of the country as soon as the light comes," said Rigault, "and we can see if they are pursuing us."

A cooling breeze fanned their heated brows, and despite the saturation of their clothes, they had need of it.

The night air was warm and sultry and below a dense mist was rising.

By-and-bye it enveloped them as in a vapour bath, and soon the sense of fatigue was no longer to be resisted.

They fell asleep.

Both seemed at the same moment to sink into repose, and, stretched at full length upon the sodden ground, they were lost in unconsciousness until the day returned.

Rigault was the first to awake, and he found himself in a luminous mist. The only object at all visible was something that looked like a log a few feet away.

Before he could clearly grasp his position, it stirred, and proved to be Larry Turrell, who sat up rubbing his eyes.

" Is that you, Rigault ?" he asked.

" Yes," was the reply.

" Where are we: in the clouds ? "

" No, this is a morning mist, but the sun will soon scatter it."

It did indeed in a few minutes grow lighter, and for a time they sat quiet.

Rigault took out the bag he had stolen and opened it carefully, turning part of its contents into his left hand.

An exclamation of a very bitter nature burst from his lips.

" What's the matter ?" hurriedly asked Turrell.

" Sold," gasped Rigault.

" What are you talking about ? " angrily demanded Turrell.

" This bag," said Rigault, " these stones—*cmmon pebbles*—the fiend must have guessed what we intended to do, and planted it for us."

His disappointment was so bitter that he clawed the air as he sat, then struck the earth with his fist as if

It had been the face of his foe.

"We are no match for him," said Turrell. "Come, let us get along. Hark! what's that?"

"I heard nothing" said Rigault, "but we shall see presently. Don't talk so loud—somebody may be near us."

"Somebody is near you," replied a voice behind him, and then out of the mist Turrell saw that dreaded form advancing.

A rope was dropped over Rigault's shoulders and drawn tight. A yell of dismay burst from his lips.

Turrell never stirred.

"Take care of him, Smudge," said the Veiled Captain, and a second figure came out of the mist.

In a few seconds Turrell was secured.

"Stand up both of you!" said the Veiled Captain sternly.

They stood up stiffly—obeying him like two well broken wild beasts.

Then a rope was put round Turrell's neck and carried on to Rigault, the end being passed on to Smudge.

"Take them BACK!" said the Veiled Captain, and Smudge, with a chuckle of joy, gave the rope a tug.

"Come along—you two," he said.

Neither had the heart to resist.

Utterly broken they obeyed and down the landslip they went with the mist fast rising.

Before they reached the bottom the air was clear, and Smudge, once their dog, their slave, led them like curs in the leash across the plain.

CHAPTER XL.

ONE MORE BID FOR LIBERTY, WHICH WILL PROVE
TO BE THE LAST—THE FIRING IN THE WOOD.

LIKE leashed curs they were led across the plain.

At first the two Red Robins followed Smudge meekly enough, both so cowed that they had not a word to say. Rigault was the first to find a tongue.

"Smudge," he said.

"What do you want of me?" asked Smudge, without looking back.

"You were always a kind-hearted fellow," said Rigault, "and never bore malice, even when we illtreated you."

"No, I did not bear malice, as you call it," said Smudge, "but I have not forgotten."

"I suppose not," returned Rigault, "but you can forgive."

Rigault had hastily looked back, and saw that the Veiled Captain was not in sight.

He had not followed them.

The two ruffians and Smudge were alone.

"All that you have done to me," said Smudge, "I readily forgive."

"Bravely, kindly spoken," answered Rigault. He made a sign to Turrell to watch him. "Forgiving us you can pity us."

Smudge did not immediately answer. After a silence he said,

"The wrong you have done to others you will have to pay dearly for, and it is just."

"We have paid dearly," muttered Turrell. "Was there ever such suffering as we have undergone?"

"*Yes,*" said Smudge, halting, and facing about with a face so stern that they could hardly recognise him as their old slave; "did you not once bind a lone man in his hut, nail up his door, and leave him to starve?"

They hung their heads and uttered not a word.

"For five days," said Smudge, "that man lay helpless, hungered and athirst, hoping for help, and at last praying for death to relieve him from his sufferings. He was released at last."

"How do you know we did it?" asked Rigault, hoarsely.

"Because he was saved," said Smudge, "rescued, with the hand of death ready to touch him. Spared at the last moment, John Gordon, the settler, lives."

"Well, if he lives," said Rigault, "we have not killed him, and we ought not to be hanged for that.'

"OUR FOES ARE LOST TO US." THE VEILED CAPTAIN SAID.

" You will not be hanged," said Smudge, curtly.

They looked at him with startled faces. What new terrors were there in store for them?

"What will be done to us?" asked Rigault.

"Better not to know," replied Smudge. "Indeed, I cannot tell you."

Rigault looked at Turrell again, and made a slight movement towards Smudge. Then he looked at the lonely wood which they were nearing.

Turrell seemed to understand him, and nodded slightly in reply.

"Do us one good turn if you will not do us another," said Rigault.

"What is that?" asked Smudge.

"Tell us who the Veiled Captain is."

Smudge laughed softly.

"Not yet," he said.

"You do not know," said Rigault, tauntingly.

"Well, believe so if you like. I will not tell you."

They were now quite close to the wood, and Smudge was walking with a quick step, lightly toying with the rope in his hand.

Another sign from Rigault.

A responsive one from Turrell.

Then with a jerk Rigault tore himself free, and he and Turrell leaped into the wood together.

"Keep close," said Rigault between his teeth, "and follow my lead."

Both were good runners, and they skimmed through the wood at a great rate.

Behind them came Smudge, shouting for help.

They did not look back, but Rigault judged by the sound of Smudge's voice that they were out-pacing him fast.

It grew fainter and fainter, and at length entirely ceased.

Then they paused a moment for breath, both leaning against the trunk of a tree—panting.

"Another bid for freedom," said Rigault presently.

"Yes," replied Turrell, gloomily, "but what can we

do ? They will be after us directly like sleuth hounds We cannot escape."

"You have not an atom of heart left, Larry Turrell," said Rigault; "it has all been shaken out of you."

"And how much have you got?" savagely demanded Turrell.

"Enough to make another effort to save my life. Listen a moment."

They stood quite still with ears stretched to catch the slightest sound. The wood was absolutely still.

"So far all is well," said Rigault, "now what would you do?"

"Let us get on," said Turrell.

"Ah, that shows your wisdom. Let us play fox and double back a bit."

"Double back?"

"Yes, and lie close somewhere among the undergrowth; they will think we have gone on and will scour the country ahead. In doing this lies our best chance of freedom."

"Rigault you ARE a fox!"

"With a bit of the wolf in me. Now back and walk as I do in places where your feet will make no mark."

Slowly and carefully they picked their way back, stopping now and then to listen.

All was silent.

By and by they came to a suitable spot for hiding, a thick clump of undergrowth offering a close hiding-place.

Selecting a spot where he could get in without much difficulty, Rigault crept and Turrell followed him.

Right in the thick of it they lay down side by side.

"The operation of last night must be repeated, said Rigault grimly. "I never knew before how valuable teeth may be. Now keep your ears on the listen while I work."

Turrell said he would and did so.

Ere Rigault had half accomplished his task, he whispered to him to stop.

Rigault paused and the distant tramp of feet fell upon his ears.

"They are coming," he said, between his teeth.

No two rats in a hole with dogs about were more still than they.

They scarcely breathed.

"Tramp, tramp."

The sound grew more palpable every moment, and by and by they heard voices.

Nearer and nearer came the sound, and at last Rigault could see the Veiled Captain and his band approaching.

Lucia was by the side of the leader, looking grave and sad.

Immediately behind was Smudge with his arms bound. He walked with his head upon his breast, the image of dejection.

Nearer and nearer they came, and *passed on.*

Rigault's breath came thick and fast. Larry Turrell breathed like a man who had been running.

"Quieter there," said Rigault angrily.

"I can't," replied Turrell, "I feel as if I shall faint."

"Faint then," muttered Rigault, "or die—anything to keep you quiet. Hark! what is that?"

A cry echoed through the wood.

Some words were spoken, but what they were could not be distinguished, but they sounded like an appeal for mercy.

Then followed a rattle of firearms.

"SMUDGE!" said Rigault. "The Veiled Captain thinks he has betrayed his trust—ha, ha."

"You be silent now," said Turrell.

"I can't, I can't," cried Rigault, "it is too good. Poor old Smudge—good Smudge—repentant Smudge. SHOT. It is the only joke I've met with since we had that accursed Veiled Captain on our trail."

He tried to stifle his laughter by biting the mossy earth, and in a measure succeeded, but he could not wholly check his laughter.

Larry Turrell was terrified.

"You will bring them back on us," he said.

"I can't help it," gasped Rigault, "and your beastly solemn face makes me worse than I would be. *Good* Smudge—who forgave us and pitied us--shot as a traitor when he was so true. Can't you see the joke of it, Turrell? Smile, if you can't laugh outright. Dear old Smudge. SHOT, and when he WAS so precious true to the fiend. I never met with such a joke in my life before."

CHAPTER XLI.

IN A LONE LAND—STILL ON THE TRAIL—UNDER THE MOONLIGHT.

IT was a week later, and the scene a rugged plain with low hills dotted about here and there.

In one of the hills was a low sand cave, rudely dug out by some men years before.

By the entrance sat Rigault and Larry Turrell, eating some small animal they had caught, RAW, as a wolf or tiger might have done.

For seven days they had wandered about a land that was strange to them, starving at first but afterwards subsisting on small animals they captured with a snare.

This snare was made out of the rope that a week before had bound them together.

Through woods by day and over plains at night they had wandered and never seen the face of man.

The country was strange to them, and they could only indefinitely guess whither they were going.

As far as they knew it might take months to reach a spot where civilized man could be found.

Back to the country of the cone, mountain they dare not go.

One consolation they had and that lay in the fact that there were of *two* them.

To have to wander alone in that desolate land would be torture—misery unbearable.

Once Rigault had given utterance to a fear.

"What a horrible thing," he said "if one of us

should DIE."

Larry Turrell shuddered, and his face paled with the sickening sensation created by the bare idea.

They did not refer to it again, but it never left their thoughts, and now they clung to each other and watched over their mutual safety as if they were their dearest friends.

On the morning of the seventh day they sat at the mouth of a cave, as we have said, eating raw flesh like wild beasts.

In that cave they had passed the night.

The morning was very fine, and the scene before them was, in an artistic sense, beautiful.

But they were more than weary of these vast solitudes of rugged plains and gloomy forest.

" Turrell, old man," said Rigault, " did you ever hear of wild men ? "

" Why, of course, I have," replied Turrell in suspense. " Didn't we see some of them one night over yonder ? "

" Yes," said Rigault thoughtfully, 'but I mean SOLITARY wild men. ? I used to read about them when a boy. Orson was one of them. Do you remember the book Valentine and Orson ? "

" Yes," Turrell sadly replied, " it was one of the few we had in the old home—Ah ! home—home— home. It seems *centuries* since I last saw the old place, and I shall never see it again."

" That's nothing," answered Rigault, " thousands of people leave old homes, and never go near them again. They don't want to."

" But I do," said Turrell, " Oh ! that I could turn back Old Time for twenty years, and go back to what I WAS."

" You can't do it," returned Rigault drily, " and it's no use hoping for it."

They were silent for awhile, and having finished their savage meal, rose up.

The movement was simultaneous. They never left each other for many moments, for fear that one might get lost.

When in the woods they walked like two children hand-in-hand, so great was their terror of being parted.

Surely they were paying heavily for the past.

That was what they said a hundred times a day, but the whole of their punishment had not yet been meted out.

"Stand," said Rigault suddenly, "stir not for your life. I hear footsteps. It is *him*."

They stood back within the shadow of the mouth of the cave, and listened.

Good cause for their blanched faces.

Tramp, tramp.

No need to look out to see who was approaching. Nor dare they do it.

Tramp, tramp.

A distinctive footstep surely had the Veiled Captain and his men. Once heard never to be mistaken.

Tramp, tramp.

Nearer and nearer, bearing down on the cave, and neither of the pallid wretches could stir.

If he were indeed coming for them, all was over.

Tramp, tramp.

The sound was so near that they momentarily expected to see the veiled form come round the jutting hill and sternly summon them to surrender.

But no. The sound of footsteps softened, grew faint, and in a little time died away.

And yet they stirred not for awhile.

As men turned to stone they stood with their eyes fixed ahead.

Then Rigault moved a little.

"*Gone!*" he said.

"*Hush!*" whispered Turrell, "let us make SURE."

They stood still for some minutes more, and then Rigault fell upon his hands and knees and crept round the hill.

The country before him was for a mile or more a rugged plain, and beyond that a long line of wood.

Into that the Veiled Captain and his men must have

gone.

Back to the cave went Rigault, and there the two skulked all day.

At night they crept out to continue their journey.

To avoid the line taken by the Veiled Captain they must bear north, and that was towards the Great Cone Mountain, which they judged was at least two hundred miles away.

But they were not sure of it.

Neither was capable of finding out by calculation their latitude.   It was all guess work.

There was a moon in the sky that night—a bright, full faced, cherry moon to glad people, but to them far from welcome.

"I want it dark to-night," said Rigault, "for who can tell what hawk's eyes there may be about."

"What could have brought him here?" asked Turrell.

He had put that question to Rigault a score of times at least, and always got the same answer.

"Chance."

In the old days the repetition of the question would have irritated Rigault, but not so now.

They had ceased to, quarrel being too dependent on each other.

Across the plain they went with watchful eyes about them.   The air was still, and the moon and stars looked quietly down upon them.

Oh ! the loneliness and desolation of that hour.

Not even the fact of their being *two* lessened the sense of solitude to either.

They had walked for an hour or more when Rigault suddenly clutched Turrell by the arm and pointed ahead.

Half a mile away was a broken dark line moving across the plain.

No need to go closer to see what it was. They *knew* it was their pursuers.

"Down," said Rigault in a terrible whisper of agony, "and lie still."

THE AVENGERS.

They sank down as silently as shadows, and stretching themselves out listened for the sound of footsteps to draw near.

But none were heard.

Rigault, who had the ears of a trapper, knew that he ought to hear something of his foes if, indeed, those forms were living men.

But he could hear nothing.

After a while he looked up and saw that they were gone.

It was not possible that they could have got clear of that moonlit plain, and yet the Veiled Captain and his followers had totally disappeared.

"Turrell," he said hoarsely, "let us get up and go on."

Turrell slowly rose to his feet, and once more they pursued their way.

It was a long time before they spoke at all, and then it was in whispers.

"I suppose it was HIM," said Rigault.

"Who else could it be?" asked Turrell wearily.

"It might be *nobody*," said Rigault.

"Nobody!"

"We are always thinking of him, Turrell, and I've got it into my head that we are coming to fancying we see him when we don't."

"Rigault," said Turrell, recoiling a step, "don't talk in that way."

"It may be so," said Rigault in grim despair, "such things have been. Men have been *haunted*. We are both of us in the strength of life, young men in a way, and if we live have a long time before us. Suppose we've come to having the fancy always with us?"

"Rigault."

"I can't help it. I must say what is in my mind. It will be a relief to me. I say that you and I may be doomed to wander like this for many years and I ask you is it worth while to endure it?"

"I know what you mean," said Turrell with a sneer, "but don't talk of that. Haunted or not haunted mean to live on while——. Look! they are here again."

He clung to Rigault, and with a hand that swayed to and fro as he pointed, indicated the spot where his terrified eyes had again singled out his foe.

It was true.

The Veiled Captain and some of his men were advancing.

Rigault even in his terror recognised the fact that there were not more than half the band there, for they were spread out and approaching in a semi-circle.

In the centre and a few paces in advance was the Veiled Captain.

In his hand he held a sword that gleamed ominously in the moonlight and as he drew near he slowly raised it aloft.

When within a few paces of the terrified men he stood still holding the gleaming weapon in the air.

Then the semi-circle closed in upon the two Red Robins, moving with the old silent step that only the keenest ears could detect the sound of.

They closed in and neither Rigault nor Larry Turrell offered resistance by word or movement.

Once more their arms were bound and the Veiled Captain, sheathing his sword, waved his hand northward and captors and captives set out in that direction.

"It's all over NOW," thought Rigault; "we have had our last run for life and liberty."

And he was right

CHAPTER XLIII.

THE SILENT MARCH—BACK TO THE OLD PLACE— A LAST LOOK UPON THE PLAIN.

THE party did not tramp far that night.

To Rigault's and Turrell's astonishment they went straight back to the cave where the Red Robins had been skulking all day.

Not a word was spoken until it was reached, and then the Veiled Captain, by signs, gave some directions te his men.

"Put them into their lair," his actions seemed to say.

To the two prisoners he said not a word, nor did he apparently so much as look at them.

Having given instructions to his men he departed, and that night neither of the Red Robins saw him again.

They found themselves left with a guard of about a dozen men, a part only of the usual following of the Veiled Captain.

It was clear, therefore, that he had parted with some of them, and the reason for this Rigault could not understand.

Larry Turrell was too wretched to speculate or even think of such a matter at all, but Rigault's restless mind led him to do so.

The pair were placed with bound arms within the cave, two men accompanying them and taking up a position one on either side.

Two men paraded up and down outside the cave and the others lay down on the ground to rest.

"All of you are not here," said Rigault to the man nearest to him.

No answer.

"What's come of the rest?" asked Rigault after a silence.

Not a word in reply.

"Are you dumb?"

Not a movement betrayed that he was heard, and the Red Robin got into a passion.

"Is it too much to speak a word to a poor devil like me?" he said.

The man stood as silent as before.

"Did you ever come near such a curmudgeon lot?" Rigault asked Larry Turrell.

"Oh! let them be and me too," was the testy response.

Rigault, foiled on both sides, stretched himself upon the ground, and for a time scarce a sound was heard.

The men inside the cave stood as still as statues.

The men outside walked with their cat like footsteps, and the sound they made was scarcely perceptible.

Rigault was irritated.

He felt that he could not endure this silent treatment for long. It was torture almost unbearable.

"I am hungry," he said, after a time, "what can you give me to eat?"

The men as guard inside the cave never stirred, but the men outside brought in some meat and a coarse kind of bread, which they placed before Rigault.

Sitting in the gloom it was difficult to see it, so one of the men struck a match and lighted a pine torch, which he fixed in a crevice of the wall.

"What is this?" asked Rigault, holding up the food as well as he could.

No answer.

Both men stood immovable.

"Can't you speak, or won't you?" hissed Rigault.

If he had been speaking to a sphinx, his remarks would not have been received with more indifference.

To speak mildly, it was very trying.

"Larry Turrell," said Rigault, turning to his companion, "you ask them something. Perhaps they have a bit of tongue for you."

"Why don't you keep quiet?" wearily asked the Red Robin chief.

"Speak to them, then."

"I won't."

Rigault leant over and picking up the meat with his confined hands, stooped over it and fell upon it like some savage beast.

Not that he was particularly hungry, but he wanted something to do to stem the current of the fury within him.

Many times that night he tried to get a word from his captors, but in all his attempts he signally failed.

Every trick that he could think of to induce or lead them into breaking silence he resorted to—but in vain.

At last he lay at full length, and while brooding over,

and cursing his fate, fell asleep.

The morning came, and he awoke to find that the Veiled Captain had returned, and the men were preparing breakfast.

As on the previous night they were silent.

Rigault took stock of these men, and saw that they were, for the most part, past the prime of life, and there were faces among them which were familiar, although he could not call to mind exactly where he had seen them before.

They were good-looking, well set up men, inured to hardship, and evidently fully conscious of being upon very serious business.

Not a smile was on any of their lips, not even a jesting look, not a word uttered.

Breakfast was given to the prisoners, and they both ate, Rigault because he belonged to the class of men whose carnal appetites never flagged.

He would, if need be, have eaten his breakfast on the scaffold with the rope around his neck.

Larry Turrell ate because he felt the need of keeping up his strength, if only to meet his fate, whatever it might be, with some show of bravery.

The morning meal over, the men stood up, and the prisoners were motioned to take their places.

They did so with the feeling that it was better for them to do so, and any resistance would only bring upon them additional punishment.

A signal from the captain, and they moved on, bearing in a northerly direction,

"We are going back to the Cone," thought Rigault; "but WHY?"

Vague fancies were flitting through his brain, but they did not take sufficiently tangible form to ease the agony of curiosity he suffered from.

Turrell walked with his head down and his eyes fixed on the ground, dejected, hopeless, and broken.

All that day they marched, halting twice for food, and not one word was addressed to the prisoners.

When would that dreadful silence be broken?

"Can't you talk?" Rigault asked Turrell, and the only answer was a low moan.

Night came again, and they halted by a river.

Here, Rigault thought, would be a fitting place to end his misery, and he was planning a sudden rush so as to throw himself into the water, when the Veiled Captain beckoned to one of his men, and pointed at the prisoners.

Immediately a rope was put round their arms, and knotted so that they were linked together.

Then they were drawn aside, and, with another rope, secured to a tree.

"Can you read my thoughts, fiend?" demanded Rigault.

No answer was vouchsafed him, and the Veiled Captain turned away, leaving him gnashing his teeth.

The two Red Robins were so secured that they could lie down, an advantage they availed themselves of.

A portion of the evening's meal of deer's meat was served out to them, and after they had partaken of it one of the men came up to Rigault, and, quick as thought, slipped a gag into his mouth, and tied it fast round his head.

Larry Turrell was not so honoured, and once more had Rigault an evidence of the watchful knowledge of his relentless foe.

Their first day was so like the four which followed that we need only briefly dwell upon them.

The road taken was, in a sense, no road, for there were no indications of its having ever before been trodden by man.

It was a wild country of hill, wood, and plain.

Here and there the river had to be forded, and when that was the case the two Red Robins were led across with ropes like restive horses.

Not even the doubtful favour of being allowed to commit suicide was granted them.

Many herds of deer and other wild animals they met

with, but not a single human being crossed their path.

It was a country that had lain fallow for many, many centuries.

If man had ever inhabited it, his race and habits were alike buried and forgotten.

By the end of the fifth day Rigault as well as Turrell, were reduced to a state of abject misery.

His many unavailing efforts to extract the sound of a voice from those mystic beings, who stalked so grimly by his side, had worn him out.

Now, like Turrell, he walked with his head upon his breast, forlorn, dumb, and despairing.

It was on the morning of the sixth day that the long silence was broken.

They had risen early, and were travelling across the plain, the prisoners with hanging heads.

Suddenly the voice of the Veiled Captain was heard:

"Halt!"

Every man stopped, and Rigault and Turrell hurriedly looked up.

Had the end come at last.

That was the thought that sprang simultaneously into their minds.

No—not yet—but the end was not far off.

"Look to the front," said the Veiled Captain, extending his arm and pointing ahead.

The two Red Robins turned their weary eyes in the direction indicated, and simultaneously uttered a cry of terror.

In the horizon proudly rearing his head was the mountain that had the appearance of having been cleft in twain:

The Great Cone.

Their old haunt and hiding place, the scene of many a dark tragedy and coarse carouse, the place from which the Veiled Captain had driven them.

For what?

Only to bring them back again apparently.

"You know it," he said, in his clear voice.

"Why do you bring us here?" demanded Rigault. Who

are you? I have had my thoughts that you might be
_____."

"Forward," cried the Veiled Captain.

Now they moved with a quick step as if to hasten the
end, and Rigault and Turrell fain would have held
back.

But there was no halting now.

On, as straw in a rushing stream, they were borne
across the plain.

Ah! well they knew it.

They passed the spot where Espardo had been
captured by his veiled foe, and taken back to judgment under the shadow of the Great Cone.

And there before them was the mountain towering
up and their eyes could almost make out the path they
had taken on that night when they vainly attempted to
flee.

To the right was a great rent in the mountain. Were
they going through that, once the hiding place of their
enemy?

No.

Their way lay over the mountain up by almost the
same route they had taken—ah! how long was it
ago?

Not so many months, and yet it seemed years and
years.

Up by the winding way they toiled, resting here and
there until noon came, and the summit was reached.

"Halt!" cried the Veiled Captain again.

Then turning to the two Red Robins, he went on,
speaking slowly and clearly:

"Look down on yonder plain for the last time—your
last day has come, and your last hour is at hand."

CHAPTER XLIII.

BACK TO THEIR OLD HAUNTS—THE LAST HOUR OF
THE RED ROBINS—JUSTICE SHEATHS HER SWORD.

THERE was very little change in the scene around the
Great Cone.

Below, on the other side, the small gold-field still

remained deserted, just as it had been left when the Red Robin band of ruffians fled for their lives.

The only difference was that the old haunt of the robbers was now occupied by the other portion of the Veiled Captain's men.

The two prisoners were taken down the mountain side, passing the hut which Larry Turrell used to call his own.

He turned his eyes towards it with a curious longing look, although it could have very few pleasant memories to him, save that when he occupied it he was a free man.

About fifty yards beyond it the Veiled Captain again ordered a halt, and the prisoners were faced about.

Looking up they saw that the hut had been fired and one of the Veiled Captain's men were coming from it.

"Ere the sun sets," said the mysterious leader, "every vestige of your occupation here shall be scattered to the winds."

They did not answer him.

Even Rigault, who had a certain amount of audacity when in trouble, had no longer anything to say.

He was beginning to understand now.

Out from the past dim shadows were coming, intensifying and forming themselves into solid reality.

Forward down the mountain leaving the burning hut behind them.

The lower limbs of the prisoners seemed now to have a volition of their own, carrying the doomed men forward whether they would or no.

Larry Turrell was the more especially conscious of this feeling.

He felt that even if he tried to cast himself down he could not. Whether he would or no he had to go on—on to his doom.

Down to the old line of huts which had been their last herding place upon the mountain where now the rest of the Veiled Captain's band had assembled

A few minutes before they had been moving to and fro. Now they were drawn up in two lines on the slope that led down to the precipice.

And standing in command of the men, a little in advance of the rest, was one man, at the sight of whom a yell of furious disappointment burst from Rigault.

Smudge.

Yes, there he was, and both the prisoners knew that they had been fooled by a little bit of farce introduced into the tragedy of their flight.

The Veiled Captain held up his hand, and the cavalcade stopped.

"Place them there," he cried, pointing to one particular spot, just where the slope took an extra incline, and shot down at an acute angle to the precipice.

"Bind their limbs,"

In a trice they were both bound, and stood helpless before their triumphant avenger.

Not that he bore himself as one who triumphed.

On him was the air of a stern judge who holds in his hand the power to punish offenders and does not shirk his duty.

"Rigault and Turrell," he said, "you have been brought here to meet your just doom, because it was in this spot that some of your grossest cruelties were perpetrated. I need not enumerate them. They are known to yourselves, as well as to all here ; but even as in civilised lands the vilest criminals are allowed to say a word in their own defence, I call upon you to speak and point out, if you can, a reason why mercy should be extended towards you."

"Why not to us as well as to Smudge ? " asked Rigault, the words coming hot and dry from his lips, "he was one of the Red Robin band, he shared in what we did and he has been to you what we never were—a traitor."

"It is a lie," said the Veiled Captain, sternly, " do not add to your infamy by dying with a falsehood on your lips. *You were allowed to escape.* The binding of Smudge was done to blind you, to give you a sense of false freedom, but know this fool, as well as knave, that never once were you lost sight of, in all your lone wanderings, your long nights of apprehension and days of terror, we were near you."

"Fenced round and about," the Veiled Captain continued, "by men who had sworn to avenge their own wrongs and those of others, men who obeyed the cries that came from the dead to punish such monsters as you have been, you had no chance of escape. The world was not big enough to hide you from them. You were taken when and where we pleased, and you are brought here to expiate your crimes on the one spot above all others where the full measure of your iniquity may possibly be brought home to you. Gordon, stand forth!"

Then out of the ranks stepped a man who looked at least sixty years of age, but well set up—strong and hardy.

"You know this man?" said the Veiled Captain.

"I do not, except by name," replied Rigault.

"Look at him," said the Veiled Captain; "he is forty years of age, and it was your monstrous cruelty that brought old age upon him. You left him bound to die of hunger and thirst. Why? Because he defended his poor wife and children from your dastardly cruelty. He could not save them, and the penalty of acting as a husband and father is shown in his white locks. They can never be restored to the dark colour of his prime, but he has regained his strength and lives to see the monsters who wrecked his happiness, die the death they have justly earned."

He waved his hand, and Gordon stepped back into the ranks. Then the Veiled Captain, speaking in a lower tone, resumed his address to the prisoners.

"On the spot where now you stand, there stood one morn at early dawn, two brothers, bound as you are. Their crime was that they had resisted you, or one at least had done so, in your nefarious work. Here, from this spot, you launched them over yonder precipice with shouts of laughter. Do you remember the time?"

They did not answer, their faces were blanched to the livid hue of death.

All was clear to them now, save by what miracle either had escaped destruction.

"One brother," pursued the Veiled Captain, "the younger and delicate one, shot clean off the precipice and fell to the ground two thousand feet below. Life was gone from the poor lad long ere he touched the earth, and he died without a cry, brave even in those dark moments of death, with a heart stronger than yours although his strength was that of a girl.

"The other brother," said the Veiled Captain, advancing a pace, "did not go sheer down. Fifty feet below there was a small stunted tree, with its roots fixed strongly in the rocks. Into this he fell, the force of his fall breaking the bonds of his arms asunder. Instinctively, as the drowning seaman clutches a straw in the ocean in the dark, he grasped a branch of the tree and was saved.

"Still he had much to do and much to bear, which I will say little upon. It is enough that by-and-by his lacerated hands removed the bonds from his feet, and then, being a fair mountaineer, he found a path to the ravine below. There, beside the mangled form of his fair-haired younger brother, he vowed that he would never rest until you and your band of ruffians had been destroyed in such a manner as should strike terror into every ruffian who heard the story."

The Veiled Captain paused, and no sound but the breathing of those around him was heard, but the strained attention of all showed how keenly they felt the excitement of the hour.

"I vowed I would hide my face from all," the Veiled Captain continued, "and eat and drink with no man, until my work was done. I buried my poor brother under a heap of stones, the only grave I could make for him, and at night stole back to my old home where I fashioned the veil I have worn since. In secret I went round to the men of Sweet Water plain, and roused them into action. Overnight they stole away, and hid their wives and children from you by the Eagle's Craig. Then they went forth and gathered others who had suffered at your hands. A clipped beard here, a grown one there, a change in attire, sufficed to disguise them so that your dull eyes knew them not. Then we begun our work. By the way I went down from here I have returned many a time, day and night, to strike terror into your hearts by the written calls to death. You know me now. You called me boy, laughed at me, and the triumph for the time was yours; but who is victor in the end?"

Another silence, broken by a hoarse whisper from Rigault to Turrell.

"To think it is a mere lad who has brought us to this!"

"It is no lad," muttered Turrell, "the story is told in jest. He is some fiend mocking us."

Rigault turned his pallid face towards the Veiled Captain.

"You have as good as told us that you are Harry Forster, but we can't believe it. Let us see your face?"

"No," was the answer.

"Why not?"

"Because I will do nothing to satisfy you, even now."

"You are not a man, but a spirit," shrieked Turrell.

"I have no more to say," returned the Veiled Captain. "Here, from the very spot where you launched, you believed, two helpless brothers to death, will you now be hurled. If fortune favours one or both of you, as it did the elder brother, then your lives are your own. Away with you."

The men suddenly closed in upon them, and both shrieked aloud for mercy, their cries echoing far away over the Eagle's Craig.

For a few minutes there was a trampling of feet, and then, suddenly, the Veiled Captain's men drew back.

Two shrieking men were rolling down the slope gathering momentum at every turn, and then shot over the precipice.

A dead silence fell upon all.

One cry only was heard after they bounded over, and after the lapse of a few moments, the dull thud-thud of their falling on the rocks below fell on the ears of the listening men.

* * * *

"All is over; everything is avenged," cried Hal, advancing out of the throng. "Captain—dear captain—let us see your face."

"Not yet," he answered; "I must know that the end has come. I must make sure. Follow me!"

Quickly, with his drawn sword in his hand, he descended the mountain with his men behind him.

There was no unseemly rejoicing over the death of the Red Robins, no exuberant display of satisfaction.

The men talked in whispers, and conducted themselves as officials after the execution of ordinary malefactors.

The base of the mountain was reached and Smudge, who was immediately behind his leader, called to mind the day when he fled from the Red Robins for his life.

All the incidents of that day so memorable to him were recalled as they hurried over the rocky ground.

There was the narrow mouth of the ravine where the Veiled Captain had stood so defiant, so indifferent to the presence of his foes.

Smudge could see all again in his mind's eye almost as plainly as if it were being enacted again.

They entered the ravine and now all, following their leader in that respect also, walked with the quiet step adopted in the march of vengeance.

Scarce an echo was made in the narrow rift of the mountain.

It widened out, showing the old rough characteristics with here and there a short stretch of smooth sand, until they came in sight of a rude cross erected close to the cliff-side.

Involuntarily all looked up, although there was no need to do so.

That cross had been erected immediately under the spot where the recent scene had been enacted.

From aloft the eyes of the men came back to the ground and rested on two dark forms lying at the very foot of what they knew to be poor little Dick Forster's grave.

In silence the Veiled Captain strode up to the spot, and stood there a few minutes, looking down upon the two Red Robin leaders.

They were, strange to say, not much disfigured by the fall, but the velocity of their descent had burst their bonds asunder.

Of their being dead no doubt could exist. The dreadful STILLNESS of their forms bore witness to it.

Some moments elapsed ere the Veiled Captain faced about.

He sheathed his sword, and took off his cap as he did so.

Then, in a low voice, he said, " Justice is satisfied at last ! " and removed his veil

CHAPTER XLIV.
AFTER THE DAY OF VENGEANCE.

No longer a Veiled Captain, but simply Harry Forster, the hero of so many startling adventures, stood before his friends.

The sadness of the past, a long course of stern thinking, and the lapse of time had combined to stamp full manhood on his face.

And it was a handsome striking manhood that they looked upon.

Smudge, who barely remembered him, although he had witnessed the scene, when the Red Robins rolled him over the cliff, rightly thought that there were few such faces in this world.

It had the commanding look of a Napoleon, softened by the natural kindness of his heart.

" First remove these," he said, pointing to the two dead Red Robins, " give them decent burial, and put a cairn of stones over their grave. When that is done, go on to the old camp, and there await my coming."

They did as he bade them, bearing the dead men away up the ravine until they came to a sandy spot, and there they dug a broad shallow grave.

Side by side they placed the men, companions in many a dark crime in life, companions in the stillness of death.

They covered them, and over all raised a great heap of stones. Then left them.

Their course lay up the ravine to the old camping ground, where their women and children awaited their coming.

It was a joyous throng that hailed their arrival, and many were the gladsome words exchanged.

A little distance apart stood Hal and Lucia, the latter pale, but with the stamp of a beauty that was rare, upon her face.

"Shall I go and meet him?" she said.

"If you desire it," replied Hal. "Perhaps it will be as well if you first meet alone."

She stole softly away some distance down the ravine and then sat down to wait.

By-and-bye he came along with a light springing step.

All his sorrows, all his anxieties were over.

He was reconciled to the past as far as the loss of his dear ones was concerned ; he had performed the task he had set himself to do and a joyous future was before him.

Lucia rose up and raised her face to his. He imprinted on it a long warm kiss.

"The first," he said. "Oh! my darling, my darling, how I have longed for this hour."

"And I—oh! how I hoped for it, yet feared," she answered.

"Darling," he said softly. "from this hour we will not speak of the past but live for the future. Happy in each other and joyful in the knowledge that Sweet Water Plain is for ever rid of its remorseless foes. Come, let us go to OUR people and spend a quiet day.

To-morrow, a time of rejoicing shall begin.

＊　　＊　　＊　　＊　　＊　　＊　　＊

On Sweet Water Plain, where once there was so much trouble, now stands a young, prosperous, and rising town.

It is filled with inhabitants to the number of two thousand, and dotted away over the plain are other towns which look up to the other as the mother of them all.

There Harry Forster is virtually king, and the friends of his many wanderings might be called the nobles, so rich and successful are they.

Hal has married, and has little ones that run about and play with Lucia's children, who have not as yet heard the story of their father's life.

But by-and-bye they will know it, and then, how proud will they be that they are the offspring of a man who, by his coolness and daring, destroyed a tyrannical horde of ruffians, established justice in a new land and freed a people.